The Laura Black Scottsdale Mysteries

Scottsdale Squeeze

Scottsdale Squeeze

B A TRIMMER

Saguaro Sky
Media

Editors: Stacey VandeKoppel, 'Andi' Anderson, and Kimberly Mathews

Composite cover art and cover design by Janet Holmes using images under license from Shutterstock.com and Depositphotos.com.

ISBN-13: 978-1-951052-03-4
Saguaro Sky Media Co.
070124pb

E-mail the author at LauraBlackScottsdale@gmail.com
Follow at www.facebook.com/ScottsdaleSeries/

For Alison, Chris, Ronnie, and Jim.
In my heart and in my thoughts, always.

*Special thanks to Tammy, Alison,
and my little sisters Linda and Stacey
for their ideas, help, and encouragement.*

Scottsdale Squeeze

Introduction

If you've never read a Laura Black Scottsdale mystery, you may want to start with *Scottsdale Heat*, the first book in the series. If you'd instead start with this book, here are a few of the people you'll need to know:

Laura Black – Laura grew up in Arizona and currently works as an investigator in a successful Scottsdale law firm. She'd love to make the world a better place. She'd love to have a full-time boyfriend, but she also has bills to pay.

Jackson Reno – Reno is a detective for the Scottsdale Police Department and Laura's former boyfriend. Although he's attracted to her, he's not sure if he'd like to become involved with Laura again, at least not on a full-time basis.

Sophia Rodriguez – Laura's best friend who works in the law office as the receptionist and paralegal. She sometimes gets to help Laura in her investigations. Sophie's a former California surfer chick and a free spirit who enjoys dating multiple men at the same time.

Gina Rondinelli – Laura's other best friend. She's a former Scottsdale police detective and the law firm's senior investigator. She has a strict moral code and likes playing by the rules.

Leonard Shapiro – Lenny is the head of the law firm. He

has no people skills, but with the help of Laura, Sophie, and Gina, he usually wins his cases.

Anthony "Tough Tony" DiCenzo -- Head of the local crime family. After the events in the last story, he now owes Laura a favor.

Maximilien – The number-two man in the local crime family. He's attracted to Laura, and she feels the same way about him.

Gabriella – A former government operative from somewhere in Eastern Europe. She currently works as a bodyguard for Tough Tony. She takes pleasure in hurting men.

Grandma Peckham – Laura's longtime neighbor who has recently decided it's time to start dating men again.

Chapter One

When I was a little girl, my grandmother described me as high-spirited. When I was a teenager, my mother labeled me as rebellious.

When I started dating, my boyfriend said I was a sexy kitten. And, when I was married, my husband called me a pain-in-the-ass.

Now that I'm on my own, I've learned to embrace all of those sides of my personality. I've found that my high-spirited side keeps me going with a happy and positive outlook.

My rebellious and pain-in-the-ass sides keep me from being a pushover. And my sexy kitten side seems to keep my life in a constant state of turmoil.

Because of this, I've always seemed to have a problem with men. Lately, I've been having trouble with a man named Jackson Reno. He's a plainclothes cop for the city of Scottsdale, and my problem is that I want him to be my full-time boyfriend.

Unfortunately, I'm not sure if Reno feels the same way. We've indeed shared some romantic nights over the past couple of months. Still, it's not blossoming into the kind of passionate relationship I've been looking for.

He blames scheduling conflicts, but I think it may go

deeper.

~~~~

Tonight, I was having a problem with a naked man named Paul Marston. For the past hour, he'd been in his house with two women, who were also bare. My problem was that I couldn't get a picture of all of them together.

It was nine-thirty on a Monday night in late March. I was sitting cross-legged on the top of Marston's plastic picnic table in the backyard of his house in north Scottsdale, trying to obtain evidence of his infidelity. This was evidence Mrs. Marston needed so Lenny Shapiro, her lawyer, my boss, could get her top dollar during a future divorce trial.

Being on a stakeout and getting pictures of cheating spouses is something I seem to do way too often. The work is brainless and dull. But it pays the same as doing actual work, and I almost never get shot at while I'm doing it.

When doing this sort of thing, it's normal for me to install a few tiny spy cameras in the house's bedrooms and simply record a few weeks of activity. But for this assignment, Mrs. Marston had wanted to use spy cameras in the bedroom only as a last resort. She lived in fear of naked pictures of herself showing up on the internet.

I couldn't say I blamed her. I've had a few pictures of me taken over the years, and I also worry someday I'll show up naked on some website.

Mrs. Marston had arranged with Lenny to be out of town for a week, knowing her husband couldn't resist the chance to throw a private party or two while she was gone. I had until Friday to gather the evidence on Mr. Marston, and I was determined not to let Mrs. Marston down.

I'd been sitting on the picnic table for a little over an hour, and my leg had already fallen asleep. I perked up when

I saw that Marston and the two women had finally made it into the master bedroom. I'd chosen my perch on the table because it had a clear view of most of the bed through an opening in the curtains.

First, I saw a naked woman sitting on the bed. She got up and, a minute later, was replaced by a naked Mr. Marston. Next, Marston got up. Two minutes later, the other naked woman was on the bed.

True, it was all extremely suspicious, but for it to hold up in court, I needed a picture of Marston and at least one of the women together, along with a proper chain of custody.

I looked through the camera viewfinder, waiting for the perfect shot, when I heard a noise to my left. I turned and was suddenly nose-to-nose with a dog. A very big dog.

Crap.

We looked at each other for a few heartbeats before he started to growl. It was a low rumbling growl, like somebody starting up a diesel truck. As he snarled, a big glob of slobber dripped from the side of his vast toothy mouth and splatted on the ground.

Gross.

They say dogs can smell fear. If that's the case, this one was getting a nose-full. I stood up and carefully walked backward until I was at the gate to the street. I slowly opened the gate and let myself out.

Backyards in Scottsdale are usually enclosed by a high cinderblock wall. Wooden fences are seldom used. They dry out in the Arizona heat, then snap off during the summer monsoons.

I walked over to the side of the wall nearest the bedroom, then lifted myself up and peered over. The dog was sitting on the lawn, looking up at me. He was still drooling, and he didn't look happy.

I eased myself back down and walked back to my car, which I had parked on the street, half a block away. I drove to an open Bashas' grocery store and bought a thick sirloin steak. Twenty minutes later, I was back at the house.

I cracked the gate open and looked in. The dog trotted over and sat down ten feet in front of me. He closely watched as I pulled the butcher paper off the steak. The dog cocked his head to one side and licked his slobbery lips.

I waved the steak back and forth like a red surrender flag. He trotted over and took it with a quick snap of his massive jaws. He then walked to the corner of the yard to gnaw on it.

I made my way back to the picnic table and looked into the house. The lights in the bedroom were off.

Angling myself around to the far side of the house, I saw that all of them were now in the living room, drinking champagne and smoking cigarettes. Everyone had their clothes on.

Damn.

~~~~

My name is Laura Black. I'm five foot seven, thin to the point of being skinny, with shoulder-length medium brunette hair parted down the middle.

I'd love to be a famous Hollywood actress. Instead, I'm an investigator for the Scottsdale, Arizona, law firm of Halftown, Oeding, Shapiro, and Hopkins.

Jeff Halftown started the firm, but he retired to Florida years ago. Paul Oeding and Mark Hopkins both passed beyond this world to wherever lawyers end up in the great beyond. Probably some sort of dark purgatory where the judge always rules against them and their clients never pay.

The remaining partner, Leonard Shapiro, took the firm and made it into one of the most successful boutique law offices in Scottsdale. He did this by being somewhat shady, occasionally underhanded, and by having questionable ethics.

In other words, by acting like a typical lawyer. The fact that Lenny isn't burdened with either empathy or a conscience seems to help him sleep at night.

Over the past few years, Lenny's successfully positioned the firm as the go-to legal office for all high-profile criminal, civil, and divorce cases in Scottsdale. Charging outrageous fees seemed to bring in more and wealthier clients. Once he figured that out, Lenny made sure to charge more than any other law firm in Scottsdale.

~~~~~

I returned to my apartment at about eleven-thirty. It's on the third floor of a five-story apartment building originally built as a small hotel back in the seventies.

The building is starting to look somewhat shabby due to a lack of maintenance. The elevator is slow and sometimes stops entirely.

The residents are mainly the type who gravitate toward a low-end apartment house, primarily the elderly, college students, and young couples just starting out. But it's safe, the rent is relatively cheap, and it's close to the office. What more could a girl want?

I unlocked the door and walked into my apartment. It's a one-bedroom with a big living room and a small kitchen. I tossed my clothes in a basket on the floor in my bedroom and put on an oversized Arizona Diamondbacks T-shirt.

As I brushed my teeth in front of the bathroom mirror,

Marlowe, my grey and white tabby came in through his cat door from the balcony outside my bedroom. He walked over to the pile of clothes and sniffed at them.

He let out a pathetic little squeak, which is his version of a meow. He then turned and walked back out through the cat door and onto the balcony.

I collapsed on the bed and was out within seconds.

~~~~

Jackson Reno and I had been back to dating for about two months. So far, it hadn't entirely gone as I'd envisioned it.

But tonight is going to be different.

Tonight, we were in a beautiful suite at the Scottsdale Blue Palms Resort. The windows on the balcony were open, allowing the warm Arizona air to drift in.

From our place on the king-size bed, we sipped champagne and watched the lights of Scottsdale twinkling in the distance. It was gorgeous.

He'd been acting distant the past few weeks, but tonight I could tell his hesitations were gone. I leaned over and snuggled against his broad chest while he put an arm around me.

The scent of his cologne was driving me mad, and the champagne was making me a little giddy. Needless to say, my lust meter was running in the red.

I was feeling more than a little naughty, and I was going to make sure tonight would be memorable. The phone started ringing, but it was in the next room, so I ignored it.

Using only the tips of my fingers, I started at his chest and slowly traced a line downward. Reno felt what I was doing and let out a low moan.

The phone rang again, only this time it was the phone in our room. Puzzled, I looked up at Reno.

"It's probably for you," he said. "Sophie never calls me."

What?

This time when the phone rang, I recognized Sophie's ringtone.

Crap.

I opened my eyes and saw my bedroom drenched in full daylight. I looked around and noticed Marlowe asleep on the bed near my feet.

Another great dream completely wasted.

I'd left my phone on the nightstand, and Sophie's ringtone, Rihanna's *S&M*, was jingling through the room. I hit the answer button and mumbled what I hoped was a friendly hello into the phone.

"Damn, girlfriend," Sophie said. "You sound terrible. Weren't you up already?"

"Sophie, why are you calling me? What time is it?"

"It's almost nine o'clock. Happy Tuesday! You know, you shouldn't sleep in so late. I read in Cosmo last month that too much sleep makes you gain weight. You don't want to sleep yourself fat. After you get up, swing by the office. Lenny has a new assignment for you."

"I'm already working on one."

"Well, I guess now you're working on two."

~~~~

I climbed out of bed and dragged myself into the shower, after which I went into the kitchen and put on a pot of coffee. I then plopped a spoonful of Ocean Delight into Marlowe's bowl.

Fortunately, he'd already left the apartment, so I didn't have to see him go through his usual process of eating and then throwing up. I poured the entire pot of coffee into *The Big Pig*, my oversized travel mug; then I was out the door.

I took the stairs and headed out the back door. In the corner of the parking lot sat my poor car.

The paint was scraped and gouged along the driver's side, and the side mirror was held on by silver duct tape. The bullet hole in the rear fender was like the point on an exclamation mark.

Oh well, it still runs great, and it's paid for. That's good enough for me.

~~~~

The law office is located in the Old Town Arts and Antiques District, the oldest and still one of Scottsdale's most fashionable shopping areas. Crowds of winter visitors, or "Snowbirds," as the locals call them, gather here in the winter months.

They stroll through the souvenir shops, eat at the fashionable restaurants, and browse the high-end art galleries, which primarily specialize in southwestern art and artists. The law office is located between two of these art galleries and always looks a little out of place.

I pulled into my covered parking space behind the law office. Lenny's red Porsche and Sophie's yellow Volkswagen Beetle convertible were both already there.

I used my key and went through the heavy back-security door. This leads into a short hallway with a bathroom, copier, and a small kitchenette-lunchroom on one side. There is a larger open space on the other that contains four cubicles.

One cube is mine. My fellow investigator, Gina Rondinelli, has the second. The other two are currently vacant. Lenny always promises us more help, but so far, it hasn't happened.

As I walked into the front reception area, I spotted Sophia Rodriguez at her desk, reading the Southern California Surf Report on her tablet. Sophie handles the paralegal and administrative assistant duties for Lenny. In addition, she's my part-time partner and full-time best friend.

Sophie grew up in Southern California and had a free-spirited youth. This included being a full-time surfer chick, skating in the Roller Derby, and being the lead singer for the L.A. punk rock band *The Black Plague*.

About five years ago, she followed her husband from California to Arizona when he got a transfer. The husband was soon history, but Sophie became a permanent Scottsdale resident.

When I needed a better job after my divorce, she suggested I apply for the open investigator position at the law firm where she worked as a paralegal. To my surprise, I got the job. Even more of a surprise, I liked the job and was actually good at it.

Well, maybe good is too strong a word. More like I hacked my way through the job without managing to get shot, stabbed, or blown up.

I once broke my leg but otherwise hadn't been seriously injured. The money could be better, but it's a lot more than I made bartending at Greasewood Flat.

I even received a bonus for an assignment I completed a couple of months ago. The money went to paying down some credit cards, but it provided enough motivation to keep me going.

~~~~

"Hey, Sophie," I said.

"Hey, Laura, how's it going with the Paul Marston assignment? You get the money shot yet? Lenny's already bugged me about it twice this morning."

"No, I ended up watching naked butts running around in front of windows for an hour but didn't get anything usable. I think tonight I'll change to video."

"Good idea. Hey, cool necklace, is it new?"

"Thanks, I picked it up from the jeweler yesterday. What's the new assignment? Hopefully, it's something good. I'm beyond broke."

"Don't know. Lenny dropped a folder on my desk when he first got in. He said to give it to you whenever you showed up."

Sophie shuffled through a pile of folders on her desk. Suddenly, her head shot up. Her eyes were fixed on the necklace.

"Holy crap!" she said. "Is that what I think it is?"

"What?"

"Don't give me that *what* shit. That's one of those big sparkly diamonds, isn't it?"

"Yup," I said, fingering the necklace.

What caused Sophie's excitement was the diamond dangling from the gold chain around my neck. It was given to me for helping out some people during an assignment a couple of months back.

Unfortunately, the diamond hadn't strictly come into the country legally. There was even a strong possibility the police might think it was evidence in a case they were currently working on.

"You know," Sophie said. "You could sell it and buy a damn fine car, maybe even a house down in Tempe or Mesa."

"I can't sell it, and I shouldn't even be wearing it. According to Reno, the police have information that a shipment of large-high-quality diamonds has come into the country. Their informant told them the diamonds are headed to Scottsdale, so they'll be on the lookout for anyone selling one, probably for the next year or two."

When not starring in my dreams, Jackson Reno works as an undercover cop for the city of Scottsdale. He's been in and out of my life for almost a year and a half.

Currently, he's back to being in. Reno doesn't seem to fully realize this yet, but I'm sure he'll come around sometime soon.

"The cops just heard about the diamonds?" Sophie asked. "Guess they need to hire better informants. So now you're jewelry-rich and cash-poor, huh? It's a damn shame you can't sell it, but it does make a nice necklace. Does Reno know anything about your shiny new bobble?"

"Yeah, I told him it was a fake diamond Gina got for me the last time she was in Las Vegas."

"Did he buy your story?"

"It's sometimes sort of hard to read Reno. But I think he knows me well enough not to ask too many questions."

"Damn good trait in a man. So, what's up with him? It's been like two months since you supposedly got back together. For him being your new boyfriend, you two don't seem to see a lot of each other. Is he still kinda spooked about the idea of being with you again?"

"I'm not sure. We seem to be stuck at seeing each other once or maybe twice a week. Sometimes it's just for dinner."

"That doesn't seem like he's actually back to being your boyfriend then. What's the problem?"

"Our schedules never seem to match up. He works days, and I keep working nights on the cheating spouse patrol. Plus, he's been working a lot of undercover and surveillance assignments, which always seem to chew up our weekends."

From the look on her face, I could see Sophie was unimpressed with my explanation. The truth was, I was unimpressed with it as well.

Even after we spent a fantastic night together, about two months ago, Reno still hadn't warmed up to me in the way I'd been hoping for. We still see each other, but I can constantly feel the distance between us.

"How are you in bed?" Sophie asked a look of concern suddenly on her face. "A lot of guys judge a woman by that, you know. Are you good enough to keep his interest up? Does he view your sexual style as both adventurous and playful?"

"What are you talking about?"

"I read an article on Yahoo saying a woman's sexual style should be both adventurous and playful to make her man happy. For most guys, playful usually means first thing in the morning, and adventurous means sex in parking lots. For me, being playful is more about him taking me shopping two or three times before anything good happens."

"Oh, that's so not true," I said. "You've gone to bed with plenty of guys on the second date or even the first date."

"Well, sometimes. But only if it feels like true love. If it's true love, I sorta can't help myself."

"True love? More like if he's bought you a couple of drinks."

"It's not my fault drinking arouses me. I like men. What can I say?"

"Folder?" I said, holding out my hand.

"Actually, I'm surprised you've even gotten this far with Reno. I didn't think he'd ever want to see you again after what you did to him the first time."

"Hey, you know most of that wasn't my fault. Do you have the folder or not?"

"Well, what about that mafia guy, Maximilian?" I know he has the hots for you. Milo says he talks about you all the time. I bet a few dates with him could make waiting for Reno to come around a little less painful."

"Milo? I thought you dropped him."

"Well, I did. But I've sort of picked him up again. His underworld ranking is only henchman, not lieutenant, like yours, but he'll do for the moment. Do you know what I'm thinking? You and Max could double date with Milo and me. We're going to the Rhythm Room on Friday. It'd be fun to all go together."

"Aren't you forgetting, I'm already dating a cop, and Max is an underworld crime figure?"

"Well, yes, but no man's perfect. Besides, you're only kind of dating a cop. The way I see it, Max may only be a crime-lord-in-training, but he has a great smile and the nicest butt. Looking at it reminds me a little of Ashton Kutcher's butt."

"Ashton Kutcher? What happened to Jon Bon Jovi?" I asked. "I thought he had your ideal butt."

"Well, sure. Bon Jovi has the best *classic ass.* But the other night, I was watching an old *Two-and-a-Half Men* episode. You know, it's the first time I got a peek at Ashton Kutcher's butt. It was network, so I didn't get a good peek. But now I'm thinking about watching some of his old movies. Tonight, I'll look on Netflix and see if he's in any that are rated R. Maybe I'll get a better look at it then."

"Folder?" I said and again held out my hand.

Sophie found the folder and handed it to me.

I took the file back to my desk, flipping through it as I walked. I looked it over for about five minutes, then walked back up to Sophie's desk.

"Are you sure this is a real assignment? This looks like a missing person. Shouldn't this go to the police or at least a private investigator, like a real one? Besides, if we really are doing this, Gina usually gets them. She has actual police training on missing persons."

Gina Rondinelli works as the firm's senior investigator and has been my mentor since I started here. As an investigator, she's a combination of Sherlock Holmes and Wonder Woman.

Before working for Lenny, Gina worked with Reno as a detective for the Scottsdale police. One of Lenny's former partners once implied he would make it worth her while if she would change her testimony in an embezzlement case.

When she turned the bribe down and threatened to arrest the guy, Lenny was amazed. He'd never seen anyone so honest.

After the case was over, he hired her for twice what she made with the police department. Gina knows Lenny is slime, of course, but she says this way, she still gets to be an investigator and can keep a close eye on Lenny.

16

"I don't know," Sophie said. "Lenny dropped the folder off and said to give it to you. You should ask him. Maybe he thinks you're getting better at missing persons. You did the Alexander Sternwood one, and that worked out okay."

I looked over and saw the door to Lenny's office was closed.

"Client?" I asked.

"He's interviewing a candidate," Sophie said. "Lenny had me put an ad on the internet. He's been getting resumes in for a week. He said with the workload, he'd need me full-time on the paralegal side. He's getting someone new in to handle the admin. He has this interview now and another one scheduled for this afternoon."

"Well, he's right. You do need someone to help. Work's been nuts lately. Does she seem nice?"

"Didn't get much of a chance to talk to her. She seems a bit timid. Dresses okay, but a little on the boney side. She's also kind of pale for someone who lives in Arizona, if you ask me, but she does have a degree in criminal justice."

"A degree? Lenny wants a degree for an admin?" I asked. "You do that part in your sleep."

"Lenny had me put in a bunch of qualifications. I think it's just his way of getting somebody good on the cheap."

"How long's she been in there?"

Sophie looked at her watch. "About twenty minutes. She must be made of some pretty strong stuff. Lenny always has a way of showing his worst side when he's interviewing."

"You mean the Darth-Vader-crossed-with-Lord-Voldemort side?"

"That's the one."

The door to Lenny's office was flung open, and a nicely dressed woman in her mid-twenties stepped out. She had on a red pants-suit, a cream blouse, and matching red flats.

Unfortunately, her face was also red, and she didn't look happy. She marched to the door, wrenched it open, and stomped out.

"Huh, guess I was wrong," Sophie said.

I walked into Lenny's office. He was sitting behind his desk, writing on a yellow legal pad. He looked up as I came in.

Physically, Lenny is short and looks sort of like the actor Danny DeVito, back when he played the Penguin in *Batman Returns*. His hairline has started to recede, and he's starting to get a little chubby.

He has poor interpersonal skills, and he's usually in a bad mood. The only time I've seen him smile is when he gets a wealthy new client or when he gets a big settlement check.

He was married once, but the divorce was several years ago. Lenny doesn't seem to have much of an outward interest in women.

He doesn't date, and, except for always trying to look down Sophie's top, he's never shown the slightest interest in any of us. Gina says, unless it's in a business setting, Lenny is painfully shy around women.

"Interviewing for a new admin?" I asked.

"Yeah, but she wasn't qualified."

"Don't you think you'll get in trouble upsetting people like that?"

"Hey, I know employment law. I never ask anything out of bounds. If they infer something, that's not my problem. I want someone good who won't get pissed off every time I try to talk with them. I've been told I have a difficult personality, so it's probably best they get a sense of my style before they start to work here."

"Don't you think you'll get a reputation as being a little, um, aggressive?"

Lenny just looked at me with a vacant and slightly confused expression on his face. I could see him working the concept around in his mind, but nothing was registering.

"I need to talk to you about this," I said as I dropped the folder on his desk. Lenny's eyes came back into focus as he opened the folder.

"Yeah, this one. What's the problem? I thought you'd like this. It's your chance to do a good deed. I know how much you like to save the world, and this one should be straightforward. Besides, it'll be a nice break before doing the next cheating spouse stake-out."

"It's a missing person," I said. "We don't do missing persons. Shouldn't we hand this over to the police or at least a real private investigator, like Magnum, P.I., or somebody?"

"The client is Terry Lennox. He can afford what I'm going to charge him. He sings in a local band, but his father is a wealthy Scottsdale developer and an old friend of mine. His dad set him up with a trust fund the size of Camelback Mountain about five years ago."

"That must be nice."

"Yeah, Howard and I worked together a few times over the years, and I owe him one. This will help me clean the slate. Go on over to Terry's house, and he'll fill you in on the details. Did you get the pictures of Paul Marston yet?"

"I'm working on it. I've run into a dog problem."

"So, you've met Buddy?"

"Buddy? He looked more like a Cujo. Why didn't you tell me he had a dog? He's huge, and he drools. I could have been eaten."

"According to Mrs. Marston, he usually keeps the dog in the house. He must have had to poop or something."

"I'm putting the steaks on the expense report. The way he ate the first one, I might need to buy four or five more."

"I could care less about a few steaks. Get him a side of beef if you think it'll help. Just hurry up and get me a million-dollar shot. I'll need you full-time on this new one."

~~~~

I went back to my desk and flipped through the folder. Terry Lennox, the client, had a fight with his girlfriend, Jacquelyn Wade, and she'd run out on him.

According to the file, he hadn't seen her in over a week. He wanted us to find her, supposedly so he could try to patch things up. He hadn't contacted the police because he didn't think there was foul play involved.

Jacquelyn apparently had money and didn't need to work. She had no family in the state except for an ex-husband named Roger. She had a couple of grown children living in southern California.

Her cell phone was either turned off or was out of range. Either way, she wasn't answering his calls. Terry's occupation was listed as a singer, and his address was listed in a lovely part of Scottsdale.

In the file was a picture of Jacquelyn on a tropical beach somewhere. The background was a white sand beach, a blue ocean, and a grove of bright green palm trees.

She looked somewhere in her late forties and was pretty. Her long auburn hair was wet as if she'd just gotten out of the ocean. She had on a periwinkle two-piece swimming suit and brown sandals.

When I saw her, I thought she looked familiar, but I couldn't place her. This feeling isn't unusual for me. In the course of my work, I meet a dozen new people every day.

I went up and asked Sophie to run the standard checks on her: DMV, employment, and criminal background. I also asked her to check for recent bank and credit card activity.

I went back to my cubicle and called our contact at Jacquelyn's cell phone carrier. I asked her to see if Jacquelyn's cell phone was turned on and if we could locate her through that.

~~~~

I went out the back security door and walked to my car. Since it was the end of March, temperatures had been climbing back into the nineties a couple of times a week. The winter had been beautiful and mild, as it usually was in Scottsdale. Still, I loved the feeling of sunshine and being warm again.

With the warm weather, the Snowbirds had started to drive their Cadillacs, Buicks, and RV's back to Canada, North Dakota, or wherever they go in the summer. The Scottsdale roads were already feeling less congested. It was now possible to again get into most of the restaurants without a reservation.

Just thinking about it made me feel warm and happy all over. I rolled down the window and shoved Green Day into the CD player.

Chapter Two

I drove up Scottsdale Road to Jackrabbit, then west to Monte Vista Drive. Terry Lennox lived in a large house in the prestigious Stoneview subdivision, to the east of Camelback Mountain.

The houses here have desert landscaping with jumping cholla, ocotillo, mesquite trees, and at least one colossal saguaro cactus per block. I've always liked this part of Scottsdale. It's a nice change from the tropical oasis theme in the rest of the city.

I pulled into the large circular driveway and then stopped to make sure I had the correct address. In stark contrast to the rest of the pristine houses on the block, this house was trailer-trash gone wild.

There was a pile of garbage and beer cans piled against the side of the house. The landscaping looked like it had been neglected for months, if not years. It was a mix of both dead and overgrown vegetation, along with a pile of tumbleweeds stuck against a row of dying rosemary bushes.

I got out of my car and walked to the front door. On the porch, next to the front door, sat a toilet that had apparently been there for some time. Someone had set a plastic flowerpot in the cracked toilet bowl.

The flowers had died long ago, but the flowerpot was still there. It added to the whole shabby feeling of the property. It goes to show, money can't buy class, even in Scottsdale.

I rang the doorbell, and a man I presumed to be Terry Lennox came to the door. He was somewhere in his late twenties. He wore leopard-spotted gym pants, a tight black tank-top, and was barefoot.

His long blond hair hung in loose curls, and he sported a three-day-old beard. I'll admit he was cute and had a nice body. Unfortunately, the illusion was shattered as soon as he started to talk.

"Yo, must be my lucky day," he said, looking me up and down. His voice had a New York ghetto rapper accent, sounding more MTV than the actual ghetto. "What can I do for you, beautiful lady?"

I handed him a business card. "I'm Laura Black. I work for the law firm of Halftown, Oeding, Shapiro, and Hopkins. I'm looking into the disappearance of Jacquelyn Wade. Are you Terry Lennox?"

He took the card, then turned and walked back inside, leaving the door open. I took this as an invitation to follow. His sparsely furnished living room was as much a disaster as the outside of the house.

There were overflowing ashtrays, empty pizza boxes, and beer bottles everywhere. Dirty laundry was draped haphazardly over most of the furniture and on the floor. The room reeked of cigarettes and unwashed socks.

"Yeah, Jackie-D," Terry said as he collapsed onto a black leather couch.

He picked up a half-empty beer bottle sitting on the coffee table and drained it. "I hope you can find her. We had a fight last week, and she took off. No one's seen her since. I just want to talk to her and see if we can patch things up. We weren't together very long, but I could tell Jackie and me had a real connection."

"I've read the file, so I know what you've already told Lenny. However, I'd like to get some more background information. How'd you two get together?"

"See, it's like this. I've known Jackie-D for a couple of years. Everyone knows Jackie-D. She's sort of a groupie for the band. First time I saw her was when we were playing Barcelona. That was a few weeks before they closed it down, which was a damn shame, by the way. It was a great club."

"When did you start dating?"

"Jackie and me didn't actually get together until last month. She came down to hear the band when we played the Roxy, and we got to talking after the show. You might have heard, I'm the talent of the band Dog Farts."

"You're the talent?"

"Yeah, all great bands are based around a talent. Some, like the Stones, or U2, are built around two talents. But in Dog Farts, I'm the one."

"You know that's a terrible name for a band, don't you?"

"Yeah, I get that all the time. But it only sucks when you first hear it. It actually promotes ridiculous name recognition. How many times have you gone to a club and then can't remember the name of the band a week later? Everyone remembers Dog Farts."

I handed him the picture of Jacquelyn from the file. "Do you know how old this picture is?"

"She texted this to me right after we got together, so about a month, maybe?"

"Any idea where this is or who took the picture?"

"She just said she was at the beach with friends. She didn't say where or with who. Jackie gets around, you know?"

"Any idea where she could be now?"

"She usually hangs out at the clubs, but no one has seen her all week. I've gone over to her house a couple of times since she took off, but it looks like no one's been over there either. The newspapers and mail are piling up."

"Do you have information on her friends? Can I get some names and addresses?"

"Names are easy, addresses are tougher. There's Shannon, Elle, Annie, Sonia, Pammy, and Cindy. I don't know any of their last names, but they're an easy group to find. They're older but still hot. Annie is the only young one in the group."

"Perfect. Any idea where I can locate them?"

"Sure. If you want to find Jackie's friends, just go to the Roxy, Maya, Casablanca, or even the Living Room lounge. It's only Tuesday, but some of them will probably be out trolling."

I told him to give me a call if he heard anything. He said he would.

~~~~~

Golf is to Scottsdale as skiing is to Aspen, or gambling is to Las Vegas. Golf drives the economy and directly or indirectly employs most of the people living in the city.

Most of the best courses are part of large golf resorts. These golf clubs are surrounded by some of the most desired real estate and housing in Arizona. Jackie's house was located along a fairway at one of these upscale resorts.

I drove up Scottsdale Road to Greyhawk Drive. I then went east until I found Jackie's house and parked in the driveway.

Like most of the houses along the golf course, it was beautifully landscaped and well-maintained. As Terry had said, a small pile of newspapers was in the driveway, and the mailbox was full.

I rang the doorbell, and when no one came to the door, I tested the lock. Having no luck, I went around to the side of the house, where there was a gate in the wall leading to the backyard. It was unlocked, so I let myself in.

I couldn't see in any of the windows since all of them had inside shutters. The back door was locked, but I could see the deadbolt was covered with fresh scratches.

It appeared that someone who didn't know what they were doing tried to pick the lock. Unfortunately, I couldn't tell if they had succeeded or not.

I spent another ten minutes walking around the house, trying to look in windows and testing door locks without success. Finally, I convinced myself the house was indeed empty.

~~~~

As I drove back down Scottsdale Road, I called Sophie at the office.

"Hey, anything on my missing person yet?" I asked.

"I'm still gathering," she said, "but nothing exciting so far. I'll have the report put together in the morning."

"You interested in dinner before the schedule goes to hell again? I need a burrito."

"Oh, dinner sounds great. It's been a long day, and I could use a margarita or maybe even a Top Dropper. Gina should be here in about a half-hour. I'll see if she wants to come too."

"Perfect, I'm stopping by my place to change, then I'll swing by the office. See you in about an hour."

~~~~

I took the elevator to the third floor and walked down the hall to my apartment. As I got closer to my place, Grandma Peckham opened her door and stuck her head out.

I'd met Grandma when I first moved into the apartment, just after my divorce. She came over the first day and had offered me a Diet Pepsi as a housewarming present.

Diet Pepsi is all I've ever seen Grandma drink, and she now has me hooked on the stuff as well. Sometimes she slips in a little Appleton Rum with her Diet Pepsi. She calls these drinks Jamaican Jerks. I know from experience it only takes two of these to make Grandma loopy.

"Well, Laura, come on in," Grandma said. "It's been a week since we've talked."

I went in and saw Marlowe asleep on his afghan on his chair. Grandma also has a cat door in her bedroom door to the balcony.

Marlowe thinks he lives in both apartments, which he sort of does. About two years ago, Grandma had crocheted a cat-sized afghan for Marlowe and designated a chair just for him to sleep on.

Grandma went to the fridge, pulled out two Diet Pepsis, and handed one to me.

"It's so good to talk to you," she said, lightly touching my arm. "I was wondering if you were doing okay. Did you break up with that policeman boyfriend of yours again?"

"I'm not sure he's really my boyfriend again. We get along okay for a couple of days, then nothing for a week. I don't know what to think."

"Well, that explains it," Grandma said. "I knew you two had started dating again. Oh, if I could ask a favor from you?"

"Um, sure."

"Let me know ahead of time if you're going to start dating someone like that again. The first time you brought him back over was about two months ago. I was asleep when you started moaning and screaming. It startled me awake. I had to listen for about five minutes before I figured out you were with the policeman again and not being chased around the apartment by an axe murderer."

Oh God, how embarrassing.

"Of course, the thing clinching it for me was the little high-pitched whimper you always get towards the end. Only the policeman ever made you do that."

Really? I do?

"I'm not sure what to do with him," I said. "Our schedules are so messed up. We hardly ever see each other for dinner. Getting together for the night almost takes a miracle."

"Well, I'd tell you about my sex life, except I don't have one. I told you about the time when I tried to have sex with Walter from the drugstore and what a disaster it was when his penis wouldn't work. Lately, I've been thinking the best way to get some action might be to put an ad on one of those internet dating sites."

"That's an idea."

"I've been looking at one called NaughtyMatureBabes.com. Land sakes, the site is crawling with men looking for some no-strings-attached sex."

"Is that what you're looking for?" I asked.

"I think so. To be honest, I'm not sure I want a full-time boyfriend. I'm kind of settled, and I don't think I want to go through the problems of learning to be with someone new. But it would be nice to have a gentleman caller from time to time. It's been so long, even once would be a nice change."

"Sounds good to me. Can I do anything to help?"

"Well, now that you mention it, I've noticed most of the women who put ads on the website put in a couple of naked pictures of themselves. I guess the pictures drive the men wild with thoughts of having dirty sex with them."

"Really?"

"Of course, back in my day, a man would need to marry a woman before he got to see those things, but I guess times change. I'm going to need some naked pictures to put in my ad. Maybe you could come over and take some of me?"

Oh, God.

The thought of taking naked pictures of Grandma Peckham sent a cold shiver down my back.

"Um, you should probably stick with selfies, or maybe you could try taking some in front of the bathroom mirror. I've heard guys really like those."

"That's a good idea. I'll let you know how it works out."

~~~~~

I pulled into my space behind the office and went in through the security door. Lenny was out, apparently for the night.

Gina was there and said she had time for dinner, so we all went out the front. Sophie stopped to lock the door and set the alarm.

The three of us walked across the street and down Craftsman Court to our favorite Baja place, Dos Gringos. It's a great place to day-drink, the food is good, and the atmosphere on the patio is always lively.

We walked in from the street and grabbed one of our favorite tables, up front, near the sidewalk. Our waitress came over, and I ordered a margarita, Gina had a Corona, and Sophie requested a Top Dropper with an extra shot in it. Within five minutes, our drinks arrived, and we ordered dinner.

"How's it going with Paul Marston?" Gina asked.

"Slow. I need to get the money shot before Mrs. Marston comes back into town on Friday."

"If you can't get a good photo by then," Gina said, "I don't think we'll have any choice but to install cameras in the house. I know Mrs. Marston doesn't like the idea of cameras in her bedroom, but it may be the only way. What about your new one, the missing person? At least it's a break from cheating spouses."

"Too soon to tell," I said. "The woman in the photograph looks vaguely familiar, and her boyfriend doesn't think there was foul play. Sophie's running the standard checks, so we should know more in a day or two. What about your assignments? Aren't you working on three of them?"

"Actually, I'm working on four of them. Three are cheating spouses, but one's an old friend of Lenny's who's trying to put together an alibi for a crime that happened a few months ago. It seems the police are sniffing around, and he's getting nervous."

"You mean he's rich," Sophie said. "Every time Lenny has an 'old friend,' it means he's a rich guy Lenny happens to know."

"You're right. I've noticed the same thing," Gina said with a laugh. "The police suspect this 'old friend' may be involved in a string of drug-related crimes that have happened over the past two years."

"Well," I asked. "Is he?"

"I don't know yet. The police seem to think he's some sort of broker or middleman in some massive volumes of cocaine and heroin that have come up from Mexico. They have evidence he was directly involved in receiving a heroin shipment coming into the country about three months ago. I'm trying to show our client was elsewhere when the drug deal took place."

"How's it going?" I asked.

"So far, I'm getting nowhere. His story isn't checking out, and the people he was supposed to be with at the time can't be found."

"That's never a good sign."

"Nope."

"What about the one where the wife's supposed to be cheating with the pool boy?" Sophie asked.

I cocked my head to the side. This was a new one for me.

Gina saw my look and started laughing. "We were hired by the husband to gather evidence that the wife's cheating. She's the one with the money, and she made him sign an ironclad prenup. The only way to break the contract is for him to prove infidelity. The husband suspects the wife's been cheating with the pool boy, possibly for quite some time."

31

"Well?" Sophie asked.

"I don't know about the wife, but Raphael, the pool boy, is having an ongoing affair with the daughter. She comes home from high school at about three o'clock and seems to have a standing appointment with him every Monday, Wednesday, and Friday."

"Seriously?" I asked.

"The house is empty then because mom is always at one of her charity or social events until five or six. I got permission to record in all the bedrooms, not only the master, so I got some amazing material. She's incredibly flexible, as in feet crossed behind her head."

"She's a gymnast," Sophie said.

We both looked at her.

"What?" she said, looking back at both of us. "I read it in the file. She's been on a gymnastics team since she was a little kid."

"Well," Gina said, "it would explain how she could get into some of those positions. I'm not kidding. It was like watching a circus act."

"Are you giving the information to the dad?" I asked.

"Nope. Lenny's only contracted to obtain evidence of the wife being unfaithful for use in the upcoming divorce," Gina said. "The daughter's eighteen, and it's outside the scope of the investigation. Per the contract, after I viewed the video to make sure it wasn't material evidence, I erased the file."

Sophie held up her glass. "Here's to pool boys and the women who love them."

We all clinked our glasses. Living in Scottsdale, almost every woman has a happy pool boy memory or two.

~~~~

I got to Paul Marston's house about eight-thirty, but the place looked dark and empty. I opened the gate to the backyard and went in. I saw the bedroom was dark, but the opening in the curtains was still there.

I was walking to the living room side of the house when Buddy trotted around the corner. He walked over to me and sat down. He licked his drooling doggy lips and slowly wagged his tail.

I reached into my bag and pulled out a thick sirloin. I'd bought it at the same Bashas' as the night before. Buddy's tail wagged a bit faster as I held the steak out for him.

He took it with a fast snap of his massive jaws, but he didn't eat it. Instead, he held it in his mouth like a baby with a pacifier.

I walked to the living room window and peered into the darkened room. I couldn't see anything inside other than a few dark shapes.

When I looked down, I saw Buddy had followed me, tail still wagging. I walked to a window with a view into a side hallway, and again the dog followed.

I then went back to the bedroom to see if anything was visible in the darkened room through the opening in the curtains. Once again, Buddy followed along beside me.

I looked down at the dog, who was wagging his tail harder. He looked so cute. I couldn't help myself. I reached down and scratched behind his big ears.

With the steak still in his mouth, he flopped on the ground and rolled over so I could rub his tummy. After a few seconds of rubbing and scratching, he started kicking his back leg and began making happy doggy noises.

"You aren't much of a watchdog, you know?"

I sat on the picnic table and waited. Buddy sat on the grass and chewed on the steak.

It appeared the house would be empty for the night, but you never know. I was hoping Paul Marston would still show up, and he'd have the women with him again.

By ten o'clock, the house was still dark, so I decided to call it a night. I got up and stretched, then started walking back to the gate.

Buddy hadn't left my side as he gnawed on his dinner. He got up and trotted next to me as I walked through the yard.

When I got to the gate, Buddy let out a mournful whine. I looked down at him and scratched behind his ear again.

"Don't be sad," I said. "I'll be back tomorrow."

~~~~

I drove back down into Old Town and parked in my space behind the law office. One convenient thing about my place of employment is the proximity to twenty of the best bars, restaurants, and nightclubs in Scottsdale.

First on my list in the hunt for Jacquelyn Wade was the Casablanca Lounge. Terry had mentioned Jackie and her friends often went there. It seemed like as good of a place as any to start.

The Casablanca is on Stetson Drive, a couple of blocks from the office. It's a cocktail lounge on the third floor of a building where most tourists don't think to look.

There's a patio with great views of both Old Town and Camelback Mountain, plus there are several fire pits, which are perfect in the winter. The menus have tiny lights in them to show you what new drinks they've concocted.

I went in and looked around to see if I knew anyone. In my line of work, I tend to meet a lot of people, and I seem to keep running into them. The way I look at it, Scottsdale isn't such a big city.

Unfortunately, there wasn't anyone I knew, either in the lounge or out on the patio. I went to the bar and asked both guys who were working if they knew the woman in the picture. The first guy looked but didn't recognize her. The second immediately knew who she was.

"That's Jackie-D," he said. "She's usually here with a girlfriend or two, but I haven't seen any of them for a while."

I asked him if he knew the names of Jackie's friends. He said he only knew them as Elle, Pam, Sonia, and the young one, Annie.

~~~~~

Next on my list was the Rock Bar. It was only a short walk on Craftsman Court, down the street from Dos Gringos.

I hadn't been here since it was called the Acme Bar. I went in and really liked the changes. It's always been a great place to watch a band, and the drinks won't make you go broke.

Looking around, I didn't spot anyone I knew. I went up to the bar and showed the picture to the woman tending the bar.

"Sure, I know her. That's Jackie-D. I haven't seen her in a while, but a couple of her friends just left, maybe a half-hour ago. There was the brunette named Pammy and the younger blonde. I'm not sure what her name is. I think they were headed over to Nexxus."

~~~~~

Nexxus is only about a quarter-mile east of the Rock Bar, but it's a pain to get across Scottsdale Road on foot. I decided to go back to my car and drive over. When I did, I surprised myself by finding parking on the street only two blocks away.

As far as nightclubs in Scottsdale go, Nexxus is one of the nicest and is also one of the most expensive. It's really two clubs in one. One side is an ultra-modern dance and live music club, and on the other side is a more comfortable cocktail lounge.

I'd been there a few times over the years, usually with a guy who wanted to impress me to the point that I'd go to bed with him. Couldn't blame them for trying, and sometimes it even worked.

I went in and looked around. This time, I got lucky. Sitting at a table in the lounge was a blonde woman who looked familiar. It only took a few seconds for me to place her.

I realized this was Annie and that I'd met her a couple of months before while working on an assignment. Seated next to Annie was an older brunette woman I didn't recognize.

Annie was in her mid-twenties, medium height, with a medium build. Her short blonde hair was cut in a style that nicely framed her face. As soon as I recognized Annie, the woman in the picture also started to make more sense.

I walked up to Annie and said hello. She looked at me quizzically for a few heartbeats then recognition flooded her face.

"Laura?" she asked, jumping up to hug me. "Wow, it's so great seeing you. It's been months since Jeannie's."

Annie turned to the brunette.

"Pammy, this is Laura. Laura, this is Pam.

Pam was in her forties, tall, and athletic. She had short brunette hair and bright blue-green eyes. She had on a ton of gold jewelry and wore some type of expensive perfume I couldn't place.

My first impression was that she was one of the wealthy single women I occasionally see shopping in the Scottsdale Fashion Plaza. One of the ones who always seem to have four or five bags from the high-end stores swinging from their arms.

I held out my hand, and Pam shook it.

"I'm glad I caught up with you," I said to Annie. "We need to talk. The last time we met, we didn't get around to discussing what I do for a living. I'm an investigator for a law firm here in Scottsdale."

Pam and Annie both turned to look at each other, shock and surprise on their faces, then they both turned back to me.

"You're looking for Jackie!" they both said at once.

They saw the surprise on my face.

"Wow," I said. "Yes, I am. What do you know about it?"

"We haven't seen or heard from Jackie in a week," Pam said. "At first, we thought she'd hooked up with someone, and we'd hear from her in a day or two."

"Yeah," Annie said, talking over Pam. "When she's with someone, we usually don't see her for a couple of days. But even then, she'll still send out some texts or tweets. But there hasn't been anything since last Monday."

"When's the last time you saw her?"

"We all went to the Roxy last Saturday night," Pam said. "There was a band Jackie wanted to catch."

"Dog Farts?" I asked.

Annie wrinkled her nose. "Isn't that the grossest name for

a band?"

"She'd planned on hooking up with the singer after the show, so we all went," Pam said. "Even Elle and Shannon went, and they both hate Terry Lennox. Elle was with him a couple of times last year, but now she says his singing voice reminds her of cats having sex. Jackie and Terry took off together after the show, and it's the last time we saw her. She sent out a couple of texts, and she was on Twitter Monday, but nothing since."

I pulled out the picture of Jackie that Terry Lennox had given me. I showed it to Annie and Pam.

"Annie, is this the woman I met with you at Jeannie's a couple of months ago? When I met her, she was made up and had big hair. This picture is from a distance, and her hair is wet, but it looks like her."

"Sure," Annie said. "That's Jackie. I took the picture the last time we all went down to Rocky Point, maybe a month ago. Jackie leases a house in Las Conchas, and we'd been there at the beach all afternoon."

"Do you think she could be there now?"

"I doubt it," Pam said. "Mexico is safe enough when you go down in a group, but I can't see Jackie going down there by herself."

"I've already talked to Terry Lennox," I said. "He's claiming Jackie is his girlfriend."

At that, both Pam and Annie burst out laughing. Annie laughed so hard she couldn't breathe, and tears began to roll down her face. She finally stopped and looked at Pam, and then they both started laughing again.

"Boyfriend?" Pam said, still laughing. "Terry isn't exactly the kind of guy you would want to be with long-term."

"Yeah," Annie said. "And with Terry, long-term would be anything more than about an hour. You said you've talked with him? Then you'll know the man is as stupid as a rock."

"So true," Pam said with a smile. "Terry is clueless, but Jackie said he was good enough for what she wanted him for."

"Sooo, you wouldn't say they were dating?" I asked.

"Terry was only a hook-up," Annie said. "They'd been together four or five times in the past month. He's cute and can sing, but he gets annoying fast. I can't stand Terry, but Jackie said he was okay, as long as he didn't talk too much."

"I'm about out of leads on Jackie," I said. "I know you don't think she would go down to Mexico by herself, but something's starting to feel wrong about this. I'm thinking tomorrow I'll drive down to Rocky Point and look for her there. Do you have the address of the house she's leasing?"

"I'm not sure it has an address, at least not one I've ever seen," Pam said.

"I'm free tomorrow," Annie said. "I go to college part-time, but I don't have a class tomorrow. I'll go down and show you where the house is. I'm worried about Jackie, and I'd like to help."

"Perfect," I said and then gave her my card. "Meet me at the office at nine o'clock, and don't forget your passport."

~~~~

Walking back to my car, it started to bug me that I knew both Jackie and Annie from a previous assignment. It almost seemed like too much of a coincidence.

I'd met them both at a strip club in south Scottsdale

called Jeannie's Cabaret while I was trailing a guy named Alexander Sternwood. Since the club was only about ten minutes away, I jumped in my car and headed down to Jeannie's to see if I could find out anything.

~~~~

As I pulled into Jeannie's parking lot, I saw it was almost full. Pretty impressive for a Tuesday night. When I drove around to the back of the club, I saw a familiar blue Porsche 911 parked near the stage entrance.

I drove around until I found a space and parked. Standing on either side of the entrance was a huge bouncer. Each was dressed in a black coat and tie. They looked me up and down, then let me in.

It took a minute for my eyes to adjust to the low lighting as I entered the cavernous club. I always noticed the music first in these places. It's always classic rock and always played loud. As I walked in, Warrant's song, *Cherry Pie*, pounded throughout the club.

I looked around and saw that my friend Danica Taylor was working as a cocktail waitress. Tonight, she wore a scant red, white, and blue leather cowboy outfit, complete with long fringe. She was walking back to the bar with an empty drink tray in her hand.

I was about ten feet from her when she noticed me walking toward her. She broke out in a smile that lit up her face. She squealed and ran over to hug me.

I'd met Danica a couple of months before when her boyfriend had turned up missing. I helped find him and eventually got him back where he belonged.

"Danica," I said. "It's so great to see you. How's everything going with you and Alex? Everything still okay?"

40

"Better than okay," she said as she held up her left hand. On the third finger was a massive sparkly diamond engagement ring.

"Oh my God!" I said, and I hugged her again.

"I know I shouldn't wear it in here, it cuts down on tips, but I can't help it. Alex gave it to me last week, and I don't want to take it off."

"How's he doing?" I asked.

"It's so amazing. He's going to be a manager at the new resort his grandmother's building in North Scottsdale. He moved in with me last month, and that's working out great. His grandmother even released his trust fund. I'm not sure what all happened, but after Alex was kidnapped, he finally seems to have found himself. Thank you again for everything you, Gina, and Sophie did. Things could have really turned out differently."

"I'm just glad things worked out," I said. "Actually, I was wondering if you could help me out with a new assignment I'm working on? I'm looking for someone named Jackie Wade." I pulled out the picture of Jackie on the beach. "Do you know her?"

"Sure, that's Jackie-D. She likes to hit the dance clubs, usually with her group of cougars."

When Danica referred to Jackie and her friends as cougars, the light came on in my head, and that part suddenly made sense. Scottsdale is famous for its cougars, wealthy and attractive middle-aged women who hit the clubs and bars to pick up guys half their age.

Cougars typically use a guy for a night, or maybe even a weekend, toss him, and start the hunt for the next one. I wasn't sure what Annie was doing in that group since she was only in her mid-twenties.

"Why Jackie-D? Her last name is Wade."

"It stands for Jackie Delicious. It's what the bouncers and the guys in the clubs call her. I never knew what her last name was. Cougars usually just go by their first names."

"Have you seen her lately?"

"I saw the group of them about two weeks ago in one of the clubs, Maya, I think. Is Jackie okay?"

"As far as I know, she's okay. She's dropped out of sight for a few days, and her friends are a little worried."

"Well, good luck finding her. Jackie-D's always been nice to me. I'd hate to think she could be in trouble. Let me know if I can do anything."

"Thanks, Danica," I said. "This is a huge help. Congratulations on the engagement."

"Tell Sophie and Gina hello. The wedding's in June. I'll be sending everyone a wedding invitation in a few weeks. I hope they can both make it; you too. Come back sometime when it's slower here. I'd love to catch up."

~~~~

I talked to both huge bouncers at the front door and the two women tending the bar. They all knew Jackie by her picture, but none of them had seen her in the past week.

I went out to my car and drove back to my apartment. I dug around in my nightstand drawer until I found my passport.

I tossed it in my bag, along with a bottle of sunblock. I set the alarm, put on an old T-shirt, brushed my teeth, and collapsed onto the bed.

Chapter Three

I woke up to the alarm and rolled over. I'd set it for six, and for some reason, that now seemed way too early. I hit the snooze three times and then had to rush into the shower as a result.

Since I was going into Mexico, I wanted to wear something comfortable which would help me blend in. Of course, I also wanted something that would work in a fun beach town. I settled on white capris and a maroon and gold Arizona State University Sun Devils T-shirt.

I poured a fresh pot of coffee into *The Big Pig,* fed Marlowe, and headed out the door. I'd purposefully timed Marlowe's feeding so I wouldn't have to deal with his morning eating ritual. Just the thought of it made me a little queasy.

~~~~

When I got to the office, it was about eight forty-five. Gina was already there, talking with Sophie at her desk.

"Good morning, ladies," I said.

"What's happening?" Sophie asked.

"I saw Danica Taylor last night. She's engaged to Alex."

"Oh my God, that's great!" Sophie squealed. "When's the wedding?"

"Sometime in June. We'll all get invites. It should be an amazing party. I bet Muffy knows how to put together a celebration. Danica wanted me to thank both of you again for rescuing her and Alex."

"I'm glad no one on our side was seriously hurt," Gina said. "We were lucky on that one. How's your missing person hunt coming along?"

"Slow. Jackie's been nowhere for a week. Have there been any hits on her credit cards?" I asked Sophie.

"Nothing on any of the cards, although she did take a butt-load of cash out of three different ATMs in Scottsdale last Monday afternoon. If you ask me, she knew she had to disappear for a while."

"There's a chance she's down in Rocky Point," I said. "One of her friends will be here in a few minutes. We're going down there to look for her. If either of you would like to come along, the company would be great."

"Wish I could," Gina said. "But I've got a full day ahead."

"Actually, that might work for me," Sophie said. "We had two depositions scheduled for today, but I got a call that opposing counsel has the flu, and they postponed. My calendar is clear until tomorrow morning at eleven. As long as you don't mind that I'll be answering e-mails all day on my tablet, I'll be glad to go. I've been aching for a Rocky Point shrimp cocktail for weeks."

"Perfect. I'm glad you're coming. Some things are starting to seem weird about this. Apparently, Terry Lennox and Jackie Wade aren't as close as he let on. Seems odd that Terry would go through so much trouble to find her when

Jackie was just using him for occasional sex."

"Maybe it was only sex to Jackie but love to Terry?" Gina asked.

"Terry Lennox," Sophie said. "Why does that name sound familiar?"

"He's the lead singer for Dog Farts," I said.

"Of course!" Sophie said. "I knew that name sounded familiar. I love Dog Farts. I've seen them a bunch of times around town. I've had their first CD, *Silent Surprise*, on my phone for a couple of years now. I even got their new CD, *Smell of Success*, a couple of months ago when they played at my cousin's wedding. They signed it and everything. Terry Lennox is a total panty dropper. You could have come with us too, but you were busy being kidnaped by gangsters that night or something."

I looked over and saw the door to Lenny's office was closed.

"What's up?" I asked. "Client?"

"Nope," Sophie said. "He's doing another admin interview. He did the two yesterday, but I guess he wasn't impressed. The one yesterday afternoon had a business degree, and she'd worked in a law office before."

"A business degree? So why was she interviewing for an admin job?"

"I guess times are tough."

"What about this one?"

"Don't know much about her. Lenny brought her in a few minutes ago. I haven't seen her résumé. He said her name is Amber."

"What's she like?"

"Dresses trashy. Looks slutty. Stinks like a farm animal. Nice shoes, though."

"I guess she doesn't know sexy women scare Lenny," Gina said. "I can't even remember the last time Lenny had a date."

I'd been smelling something nasty since I walked up to Sophie's desk. The odor now made more sense.

"Amber's perfume? Is that what the stink is? Seriously? It smells more like an old cat box," I said.

"I had a friend who had a ferret, and his whole house smelled like Amber's perfume," Sophie said. "It got to be so gross that people stopped going over there. Smelling it for more than a few minutes made me want to vomit."

The front door opened, and Annie came in. A pair of red plastic sunglasses rested on the top of her head, and a big purple beach bag hung over her shoulder. I made introductions with Sophie and Gina.

Annie looked around the office and made a strange face.

"Don't worry about the nasty stench," Sophie said. "I expect the woman wearing it will be leaving the office soon." She looked over at Gina and me. "She's been in there for almost twenty minutes. It shouldn't be long now."

We heard a strange noise coming from Lenny's office. It was sort of a cross between a pig grunting and a dog whining.

"What was that?" Sophie asked. "It sounded sorta like Lenny."

The noise sounded again, but this time it was louder.

"Yup," I said. "Definitely Lenny."

We stopped talking. Everyone strained to hear more noises. When it happened again, it sounded kind of like an angry gorilla making *whooo-whooo-whooo* noises.

"That'd better not be what I think it is," Gina said, sounding a little aggravated.

As a group, the four of us slowly shuffled over to Lenny's office. We got to within about three feet of the door, then stopped. Everyone held their breath. All of us craned our heads, straining to hear what was going on in the office.

At first, there was nothing, but then the *whooo-whooo-whooo* noise came again, only it was louder and more desperate this time. What followed was a loud *aaaahhhhhh* sound. After that, the office went totally quiet for almost a minute.

We looked at each other, and Annie let out a giggle. At the sounds of furniture scraping on the floor, then of footsteps moving towards the door, we all took two steps back, trying to look like we weren't eavesdropping.

The door to Lenny's office opened, and he stuck his head out. His face was red, and he was breathing hard.

"I hired the new girl," he gasped. "Sophie, get the paperwork together."

He disappeared back into the office, and the door slammed shut. We all looked at each other, no one saying anything.

"Interesting place you work at," Annie said to no one in particular.

"Oh, that's nothing. It's been a lot worse," Sophie said.

"Remember the way the Simpson divorce case ended?" Gina asked.

Sophie started laughing. "Oh my God, I almost forgot about that one. It happened about a year before you got here," she said, looking at me.

"We'd been trying to split up the marital assets for about two hours," Gina said. "We were all in the main conference room – Lenny, opposing counsel, Sophie, Mr. and Mrs. Simpson, and me. After a while, we were getting nowhere, and everyone was just getting pissy with each other. Finally, Mrs. Simpson asked if she could spend a few minutes alone with her husband without the lawyers being present. There was never a history of violence, so the counsels agreed."

"What happened?" Annie asked.

"We were all in the back breakroom having coffee when we heard a noise up front," Sophie said. "It kinda sounded like a woman screaming. So, of course, we all ran up to the conference room. When we got there, Mr. Simpson was laid out bare-ass on the conference table, his pants down around his ankles and his legs hanging over the side. Mrs. Simpson was on top, riding him like a cowgirl trying to break a wild horse. Her navy blue skirt was bunched up around her waist. I remember she still had her heels on. I was sorta worried they'd scratch the conference table."

"You have to understand," Gina said, now laughing. "That's the main conference room." She pointed to the room with a vast table, clearly visible through a floor-to-ceiling glass wall. "After two or three minutes, Mrs. Simpson looked over and saw us all watching, but by then, she'd passed the point of caring. We all stood there and took in the show."

"Seriously?" I asked.

"Nobody knew what to do," Gina said. "I swear, it's like what they say about watching a car crash. We didn't want to watch, but it was like we couldn't help ourselves."

"I think it was because of all the moaning and screaming," Sophie said. "Mrs. Simpson was really loud, and her moans had a weird vibrating sound. It was sort of like watching bad porn."

"So, after another minute or two, we were finally able to tear ourselves away and went back to the break room," Gina said. "Opposing counsel was the last to leave. He stood there, watching and sipping his coffee while she moaned and screamed and rode his client like a woman possessed."

"As far as I know, the Simpsons are still together," Sophie said. "Go figure."

Lenny's door opened. We all turned and watched as a woman walked out. She looked to be in her early twenties and was bone thin. Her limp dishwater-blonde hair hung down over her face. She wore no makeup except around her eyes, where she'd used way too much and bore a striking resemblance to a raccoon.

Even as I looked at this train-wreck of a girl, the thing that immediately hit me was her perfume. Smelling it quickly made my eyes water and my stomach tighten. It was a cross between burning garbage and stale dog pee. I knew it would have some name like *Summer Musk,* and it would cost about twelve dollars a bottle.

We all stood there looking at each other. Finally, Gina held out her hand, and Amber shook it limply.

"Hi, Amber, I'm Gina, one of the investigators here. This is Laura and Sophie. They also work here. And, this is Annie. She's helping us with an assignment."

Annie smiled, then held up her hand and finger waved to her.

"Great, my coworkers," Amber said with an uninterested tone to her voice.

"What's your degree in?" Gina asked.

"I don't have one. Actually, I dropped out of college a couple of months ago. Going to school was such a hassle, and my professors were all idiots. I couldn't see the point of doing all that homework. It's not like I don't have a life, you know?"

"Do you have any legal experience?" Gina asked.

"I've gotten a butt load of parking tickets, you know," she said, laughing like a donkey while she elbowed me in the arm.

"Do you know how to use a computer?" Sophie asked hopefully.

"Sure, I have an X-Box. I'm excellent at *Skyrim*."

"Know how to use any of the Office software?"

"No, but I'll probably pick it up pretty quick. Look at all the morons who use that stuff. It can't be too hard, you know?"

She laughed her donkey laugh and elbowed me again. I had a pleasant vision of grabbing her stringy blonde hair and slamming her face against the top of Sophie's desk. I thought one slam probably wouldn't be enough. I'd probably need two or three really good face slams to shut her up.

"Did Lenny tell you what your duties would be?" Sophie asked.

"Oh, I know what my duties will be. And, from what happened during our interview, it looks like it'll take me about thirty seconds, two or three times a week, for me to do my job, you know?"

"Um, there's an empty cubicle you can use in the back offices," Sophie said. "If you want to get started, I'll be glad to show you the computer and filing systems."

Amber started to laugh her donkey laugh again. I half expected her to begin braying and kicking.

"Filing? You've gotta be shitting me. I'm Lenny's new executive personal assistant. All I'm supposed to do is hang around the office and wait for him to call me."

"What?" Gina asked. I could tell she was frustrated.

"Sure. When Lenny goes to court, I'll carry his briefcase. When he travels, I'll go along and see to his personal needs. I don't do filing. Sorry, but I have a nail appointment in half an hour, so I'm outta here. I told Lenny I also need a personal day off tomorrow. He said it was fine with him."

She turned and walked out the front door. If it hadn't been for the lingering stench of her perfume, I'd have sworn she'd been a mirage. I looked over at Gina, and I saw she was getting angry.

"Where's my gun?" Gina asked. "I'm gonna shoot Lenny."

I told Annie to wait while the three of us went into Lenny's office. He was sitting behind his desk with a dazed and slightly confused look on his face. The nasty odor of Amber's perfume hung in the air.

"What happened in here?" Gina asked, now sounding a little pissed.

Gina's the only one I know who can talk to Lenny like that. Part of it is she was a Scottsdale police detective, plus she thinks Lenny needs a mother.

"I don't know what happened," Lenny said in a confused voice. "I met Amber at Martini Ranch last night. She said she was looking for a job, so I told her to come over today for an interview. She comes in, and the next thing I know, she's on her knees working on me. It was like I couldn't stop her."

Lenny looked up to see all three of us looking at him. He must have seen the looks on our faces.

"Hey," he said. "I wanted to stop her, but it was like I couldn't. It's not my fault. Seriously."

"You know you can't have her working here," Gina said in a stern motherly tone. "You know it will disrupt things. You know you don't want the clients to see her. And most of all, you know how much trouble this could bring."

"Yeah, I know," Lenny said. "You're right. I'll get rid of her."

"Right away?"

"Right away."

~~~~~

We walked back out to reception, and Sophie started closing down her desk for the day. Before we left, I called my contact from the phone company.

As I suspected, Jackie's phone was either not turned on or had gone out of range. The reason I suspected her phone would be turned off was that it would have made my job way too easy. I don't seem to get those kinds of breaks very often.

I also called Grandma Peckham. I told her I would be traveling for the day and might not make it back in time to feed Marlowe. She said not to worry since Marlow had already had a second breakfast at her place.

~~~~~

Sophie, Annie, and I climbed into my car, and we headed south. At Casa Grande, we found a truck stop where we loaded up with drinks and snacks.

We then headed west to the desert town of Gila Bend. After that, we turned south and headed into the deep deserts of southern Arizona.

I know some people can't see the beauty of the Sonoran Desert. All they see is dirt, rocks, and half-dead plants. For me, the drive down to Rocky Point is breathtaking.

I love the feeling of cresting a hill and seeing fifty miles of colorful desert stretched out before me. There's no haze or pollution in the dry desert air, so details don't seem to blur with distance.

It's gorgeous after one of the rare winter rains. Two weeks after a rain, the desert becomes a bright green carpet, with every cactus, tree, and bush flowering at once.

We stopped in Ajo, a small copper mining town with a lovely town square, to get money from the last ATM before Mexico. We then made a quick bathroom stop at the tourist-trap gas station called The Why Not Travel Store.

We were briefly stopped at a roadblock checkpoint by the border patrol, a mile north of the Organ Pipe Cactus National Monument. Finally, we were at the truck-stop-sized town of Lukeville, which marks the border with Mexico.

As always, I felt a little intimidated when crossing over into Mexico. And, as always, I was a little sad as I drove through the poverty-stricken border town of Sonoyta. Needless to say, I kept well under the speed limit.

With the last of the border town in my rearview mirror, the final stretch of desert opened up before us. This part of the Sonoran Desert is especially severe, consisting entirely of sand and dirt with almost nothing growing, save for an occasional creosote bush or clump of desert grass.

~~~~~

At about one o'clock, our destination came into view in the distance. Although the name on the map is Puerto

Peñasco, everyone from Arizona just calls the town Rocky Point. I've always assumed it's named after the mountain-sized rock located at the end of the three-mile-long peninsula on the Choya Bay side of town.

Rocky Point is a beautiful semi-tropical fishing village sitting on the northern end of the Gulf of California, which the locals call the Sea of Cortez. The beaches here are bright white, and the sea is a brilliant blue. The music is festive, the food is excellent, and the prices are reasonable.

In college, we'd drive down to Rocky Point a couple of times a year. We'd lay out on the beaches during the day and hit the clubs at night. It was well known the bars would serve anyone old enough to walk up and ask for a beer.

Spring Break in Rocky Point was almost mandatory for all Arizona State University students. Everyone would have a crazy good time. If you didn't get laid, it was only because you weren't really trying.

Annie had said Jackie was leasing a house at Las Conchas, a loose community of beach houses about a mile east of town. I'd been there a couple of times before when a group of us would rent a place for the weekend. It's a lot quieter than the hotels by the port, and the beaches aren't nearly as crowded.

After several minutes of driving through the narrow and winding streets, Annie directed us to Jackie's house. It was located on a small hill about a hundred yards up from the beach.

The house was small but well maintained, painted the traditional yellow with orange accents. Several fan palms and bright green and red bougainvillea were planted around a large front deck that looked out over the sea.

As we climbed out of my car, I felt the warm, humid air

and heard the pounding waves coming up from the beach. Seagulls circled and cawed in the distance.

There was a slightly salty scent to the air that I've come to associate with being down at Rocky Point. It all brought back a flood of memories from the previous times I've been here.

Jackie's car, a maroon Jaguar convertible, wasn't visible anywhere near the house. We went up to the door but knocking produced no results.

A quick peek in the front window showed someone was living there since some breakfast dishes were still on the table. We spent five minutes looking in windows before we convinced ourselves Jackie wasn't in the house.

"Jackie usually goes into town for lunch," Annie said. "Her favorite place is Señor Amigo. Then she stops by the fish market to grab things for dinner. We can probably catch her there."

~~~~~

The heart of Rocky Point consists of the harbor, where thirty or so shrimp boats dock. Next to the port sits the central shopping district, featuring a large fish market with maybe twenty concrete stalls, each set up as an independent business. Here you can buy freshly caught shrimp, scallops, and fish at ridiculously low prices.

Surrounding the fish market are a dozen restaurants specializing in fresh seafood and traditional Mexican dishes. Scattered among the restaurants, the tourist curio shops sell the ceramics, T-shirts, and souvenirs that help make Mexico such a colorful place.

Jackie's car was parked in one of the spaces overlooking the sea, down the street from the fish market. We decided to split up. I took one side of the road while Sophie and Annie took the other. In less than five minutes, Annie found her, looking through one of the stalls in the fish market.

Annie ran up to Jackie, and they gave each other a long hug. As I remembered from the last time I'd seen her, Jackie looked to be in her late forties and was pretty. Like most wealthy Scottsdale women, she looked like she regularly went to a gym, was fashionably thin, and had some curves that looked doctor-assisted.

She had sparkly diamond rings on her fingers, a thick diamond and ruby bracelet on her wrist, and several strands of gold draped around her neck. Her long auburn hair was softly curled and nicely styled. Her skin and makeup were flawless.

Jackie saw Sophie and me walking towards her. A look of panic washed over her face, and I could see she was deciding whether to run or not.

Her body froze as she stared at me, trying to remember where she'd seen me before. She quickly looked at Annie and then back to me, trying to make the connection.

"I'm Laura Black," I said as I walked up and held out my hand. "We met a couple of months ago in Jeannie's."

"Oh, right, I remember now." I saw her body relax. "You were in there looking for someone. Did you ever find her?"

"That one worked out great, but right now, I'm looking for you. Terry Lennox contacted Leonard Shapiro, my boss. He said you two had a fight, and he wanted me to find you so he could try and patch things up."

Jackie looked stunned. Like that was the last thing she expected me to say.

"Terry and I didn't have a fight. I used him for sex a few times, then I dropped him. Terry's an idiot, and I could care less if I ever see him again."

Now it was my turn to look stunned.

"Look," Jackie said. "I really don't want to talk about this on the street. Let's head back to my place, and we can talk. Besides, I think I need a drink."

I told her I agreed. Her place seemed like a good idea. Sophie and I drove back in my car. Annie caught a ride with Jackie.

~~~~

In less than thirty minutes, we were sitting on Jackie's deck, overlooking the Sea of Cortez. The humid air was warm, and the light breeze coming in from the water was cool.

Jackie made a pitcher of sangria, and soon we were all sipping from a glass. The view of the sea was peaceful and beautiful.

I watched as a couple of shrimp boats slowly moved across the horizon and saw a pod of dolphins popping out of the water close to shore. I could see why Jackie liked this place so much.

After twenty minutes, we'd finished the first round, and Jackie was pouring the second. Sophie and Annie were on the other side of the deck, chatting like old friends. I thought maybe this would be an excellent time to talk with Jackie about why I was here.

The deck had a round table with four chairs. I sat in one and motioned Jackie to another. As soon as we started talking, Annie and Sophie quietly came over and sat in the other two.

"I'm here because Terry hired our law office to find you," I said. "He said you were his girlfriend, and you two had a fight. He also said he wanted to talk to you to try and patch things up."

"You have to understand," Jackie said, "I was only with Terry because I thought it would be fun to hook up with the singer from one of my favorite bands. He also has a pretty face and a great body. He started asking me out about two months ago, so I figured, why not? But the guy is an idiot and has the personality of a tuna sandwich."

"Do you know why he would claim to be your boyfriend?"

"No idea at all, but the past couple of times we've been together, I've been getting the feeling something's not right with him."

"What makes you say that? I've met him, and you're right about his personality. But, other than that, he's just your typical twenty-something guy."

"Well, it was only a feeling, but being with him was starting to give me the creeps."

"What happened?"

"Well, as I said, initially, he was the one who asked me out. It was great the first couple of times. But whenever we were together, he always insisted we go to my place. I live in the resorts in north Scottsdale, and Terry lives off Jackrabbit. Still, he always wanted to drive up to my place anyway."

"That's sort of a long drive," I said. "Any idea why he always wanted to go to your house?"

"He said he really got a good vibe from my bedroom. Actually, I was starting to think he liked my bedroom more than he liked me. When I was in the shower the time before last, I think he went through my room. I couldn't be sure, but the things in my drawers looked out of place. When we were together a week ago Saturday night, I told him it was going to be the last time."

"How'd Terry take the news?" I asked.

"Like a guy. He pouted and got a hurt look on his face. He started in with how much he needed me, how we were soul mates, and how he was starting to fall in love with me. You know how it goes, *blah, blah, blah*. To get him to leave, I finally had to tell him that maybe we could see each other again, eventually. That finally seemed to cheer him up enough for him to go away."

"Would it be okay if I tell Terry where you are?" I asked.

"You can tell Terry I'm okay, but also tell him I don't want to see him anymore. At least, not like that. I'll still go to his shows, but I can't stand listening to him talk anymore. I'm going back to Scottsdale tomorrow, but I think I'll stay with Pammy for a few days. I'll give her a call first, but I'm sure it's okay. I don't want to stay in my house."

"Okay," Annie said. "That explains Terry. But why are you hiding in Rocky Point?"

"And what's wrong with your house?" Sophie asked.

The color leached from Jackie's face, and she looked like she had remembered something terrible.

"Because two days after we all went to the Roxy," she said slowly, "I got a call from a man saying he was going to kill me."

Annie sucked in air, and Sophie's eyes got big, but neither of them said anything. They both wanted to hear what Jackie said next.

"What happened?" I asked. "Tell me everything you remember."

"There isn't a lot to tell. I got a phone call on the house

land-line," Jackie said. "It was Monday about noon. When I answered, there was a man on the phone. He said I was a stupid useless bitch, and he was going to come over to the house and kill me."

"You didn't go to the police?" Sophie asked.

"Sure, I thought about calling the police, but what would I tell them? That I got a crank phone call? What do you think their response would have been? I Googled the phone number, but it was only a payphone in Phoenix. But to be honest, the death threat was only half of it."

Sophie and Annie looked at each other and then back to Jackie.

"Well?" I said.

"I think I recognized the voice on the phone. I've only met him once, and it's nothing I can prove, but I think it was one of the people my husband worked with. I think he's serious about killing me."

Jackie paused, visibly shaken. Annie had silently started to cry. By mutual agreement, we all got up and took a break.

After a few minutes, Sophie led Annie to the other side of the deck to give Jackie and me some privacy. Sophie knows how I work, and she knew a one-on-one conversation with Jackie would probably get more results.

Jackie and I sat back at the table. I topped up her drink, and we started talking.

"A lot of things aren't adding up," I said. "I really need to understand what's going on. Would you talk to me about your marriage?"

"There isn't much to tell," Jackie said. "I was working and getting my master's at ASU when I first met Roger. He'd moved to Arizona from California with his wife to join his family's real estate business. When their marriage ended, we got together."

"How long ago was that?" I asked.

"Jeez, probably twenty years ago. I was married to Roger for over fifteen years. I have two wonderful kids from a previous marriage but, fortunately, none with him. It was great at first, but over the last few years, Roger started to change. The serious trouble started when real estate values crashed a couple of years ago."

"What happened?"

"Roger's entire family buys and sells land. They've been doing it in Arizona since Roger's grandfather moved out from California back in the 1950s. We didn't ever discuss business, but I know he took some big losses."

"What happened with Roger? How did he change?"

"At first, he started to drink, a lot. That was bad enough, but then he started to have mood swings. He'd be on top of the world for a week or two, and then he'd spend the next week crying and telling me how his life had gone to shit."

"That must have been terrible," I said.

"That's not the worst of it. After a year of this, he stopped even trying to hide the fact he had girlfriends on the side. I'd known about them, of course, but the fact that he didn't care if I knew really hurt me."

I didn't know what to say, so I reached over and held her hand.

"Towards the end, he started to become abusive. Nothing physical, fortunately, but he would love to get drunk and call me horrible names. He'd then yell at me about whatever he thought I'd done wrong during the day. He also started to get involved with some pretty shady people in his investments.

Finally, I'd had enough and moved out."

"What kind of shady people?" I asked.

"I've only met them a couple of times, but these weren't your normal business people. You see, Roger would often bring in outside partners to develop a property before he sold it. In the past, he'd always been open about who he was working with. We'd often get together socially with his partners, and I'd get to know both them and their wives."

"I take it you didn't get to know these people?"

"With the last few deals, Roger hardly said a word about his partners. As I said, I only met this particular associate of Roger's once, but I'm pretty sure it was his voice on the phone. He was a nasty type of person who made an instant impression."

"Tell me about him."

"He seemed to be the leader of some kind of investment group. He was big, arrogant, and always seemed on the verge of anger. In the ten minutes I was in the room with him, he became livid twice, yelling at Roger and one of the other investors."

"Jeeze, the guy sounds horrible."

"When he was yelling at the other guy, it was in Spanish. I didn't understand all of it, but I really didn't need to understand the words to get the meaning. He struck me as the kind of guy who would offend easily, then go after whoever had pissed him off."

"About how old is he?"

"Maybe late thirties or early forties."

"Do you remember his name?"

"No, I'd need to ask Roger."

"Would you be able to recognize him from a picture?"

"Sure, you don't forget that kind of face. He has short black hair, dark bloodshot eyes, and a full black mustache. He also has a big scar on the left side of his face, as if he'd been in a knife fight or something."

"You got divorced about a year ago?"

"Well, legally, I'm still married. After I moved out, Roger begged me not to divorce him. He said too many things were in my name, and it would take the lawyers forever to get things straight."

"Why did he put so many things in your name?"

"I've never kept track of Roger's business things, but I think he had me down as some kind of partner in his company. He always had me signing papers."

"What about now?"

"Ever since I moved out, I told him I wouldn't sign anything else unless he sends them to my lawyer to review first. I don't think Roger would try to screw me out of anything, but I think a girl can't be too careful."

"I can understand that."

"Roger sends me a check every month, which is more than enough to live on. He's gone his way, and I've gone mine. I don't plan on getting married again, so it's never seemed like a big deal."

"You tell everyone you're divorced. Doesn't that cause some confusion?"

"Well, my friends know what's going on. And honestly, it's easier to say I'm divorced than to recite the entire story."

"Works for me," I said. I held up my glass, and Jackie clinked hers against it.

Chapter Four

We spent another two or three hours on the deck, drinking and talking. The topics switched to men, then to music, the clubs in Scottsdale, and then back to men.

Gradually the mood lifted. Jackie and Annie began to smile and laugh again, undoubtedly helped by both the sangria and the beautiful view. By late afternoon, it began to seem like a girl's weekend.

"I'm starving," Jackie said. "Anyone up for dinner?"

"Yeah," Sophie said. "All this talk of being threatened and creepy men really builds up an appetite."

"La Casa del Capitan? Jackie asked.

"Isn't that where we went the last time to watch the sunset?" Annie asked.

"The Captain's House? I love it up there," Sophie said. "That would be perfect."

~~~~

I'd switched to Diet Pepsi after my second sangria, so everyone stuffed themselves in my car, and I drove us into town. Casa del Capitan is one of the best restaurants in Rocky Point and certainly has the most beautiful view.

The restaurant sits on a small hill overlooking the downtown shopping district, the fish market, and the harbor. The view extends down the five miles of white sand beach to the mountain-sized rock at the end of the peninsula. The food is the delicious Rocky Point blend of freshly-caught seafood and traditional Mexican.

We drove up the hill, parked in the small lot, and then walked over to the restaurant. The place was packed, but we somehow got an outside table with a great view of both the town and the sea.

The restaurant was alive with the noise of over two hundred people, everyone talking, laughing, and eating. The air was warm, but there was still a light sea breeze coming in.

We could see three fishing boats in the distance, slowly making their way back to the city harbor. The sun was about half an hour from setting. People were already taking pictures of the changing colors on the horizon.

We ordered a pitcher of margaritas and the chilled seafood appetizer for four. There is something unique about eating seafood that has been freshly caught and well prepared.

After we spent some time on the appetizer, we ordered dinner. We all laughed and clapped when Sophie placed her dinner order in rapid-fire Spanish.

A three-piece Mariachi band wandered through the restaurant as we ate, playing songs table-side for a few dollars each. When they stopped at our table, Jackie asked them to play something cheerful. I'm not sure what the name of the song they played was, but it was energetic and bouncy.

By the end of the song, most of the people on our side of the restaurant were clapping and singing along with the band. The lively music just added to the festive feeling.

Five minutes later, a buzz started in the crowd. We

looked out and saw the sun was about to set. It was positioned on the sea, slightly to the left of the enormous rock mountain at the end of the peninsula. The few clouds out in the gulf were starting to light up with iridescent reds, yellows, and oranges. As we watched, the sun touched the sea then slowly sank below it.

We heard the clicking of cameras as everyone got in at least one shot. I saw both Sophie and Annie had their phones out and were taking pictures of the beautiful sunset.

As the last sliver of sun disappeared below the horizon, there was cheering and applause from everyone in the restaurant. The four of us held up our glasses and clinked them together.

A few minutes later, a waiter brought out our dinners, and we dug in.

"Jackie," I said between bites. "I know how you and Annie got together."

Annie blushed a bright red, and we all laughed. Everyone knew the story of how Annie had gone to the strip club to hunt for a man for sex.

"But I was more wondering about you. How did you end up joining a group of cougars?"

"I didn't start out that way," Jackie said, waving her fork as she talked. "I've known Elle and Pammy for years. After their divorces, they just started seeing younger guys. Not actually dating as much as hooking up for a night or maybe a weekend."

"But why younger?" I asked.

"I don't think they originally planned on younger guys. Still, they'd both come from bad marriages, and neither one was looking for a long-term relationship. They both occasionally tried to go out on actual dates with guys their own age, but it never worked out. Fifty-year-old divorced guys are sorta clingy, and the younger guys are just easier to deal with."

"And they have those firm little butts that need to be spanked," Sophie said.

"Damn right," Annie said. At that, we held up our glasses and clinked them together.

"Yeah, young guys don't think so much about long-term commitment," Jackie said. "With them, it's all about the sex. And I'm talking passion all night. There's no blue-pill problem with these boys."

It was such a lovely image, we couldn't help it, we held up our glasses and clinked them together one more time.

"When my marriage started to fall apart," Jackie continued, "I started hanging out with Elle and Pam. At first, I only wanted to get out of the house, but we eventually became a regular threesome. We'd go to the clubs three or four nights a week. After I moved out and had a place of my own, I'd sometimes go home with a guy and sometimes not. But the three of us always had such a good time together. Everyone at the clubs knows us and is really nice to us."

"That seems reasonable," I said.

"Shannon became a regular with our group about a year ago," Jackie said. "Cindy and Sonia hang out with us too, whenever they have free time. After I met Annie, we took her on as a puma."

"What's a puma?" Sophie asked.

"Oh," Jackie said. "It's a cougar in training."

"We all like men in their twenties," Annie said. "So, we have that in common. I'm just a poor college student by day.

But at night, I get to share in the glamorous life."

"That sounds like a lot of fun," Sophie said.

"Well, everyone in the group thinks they're my big sister, and they're all very protective," Annie said. "They give me advice and steer me to guys when they think I might find a connection. Only in my case, I'm looking for something a little more long-term. I wouldn't even mind getting married."

We all moaned, and I saw Sophie roll her eyes. But we understood her feelings. A girl should get married, at least once, to help get it out of her system.

~~~~

After dinner, we drove to Jackie's house and ended up back on her deck. The moon was a little past full, and it was casting a beautiful glow over the sea. In the distance, we could see boats slowly moving back and forth over the water.

A hundred yards further down the beach, a group of teenagers had gathered around a bonfire, laughing and shooting off fireworks. We could hear the sparklers and rockets making popping sounds and occasionally sending a shower of sparks into the air.

Jackie made a pot of coffee for Sophie and Annie. They both had to get back to Scottsdale, and we decided Sophie would take my car.

Jackie was also driving back to Scottsdale in the morning, and she said it was no problem if I spent the night at her place. This was fine with me. Now that I'd found her, I didn't want Jackie to disappear again.

I went out to my car and grabbed the small overnight bag I keep in the trunk for such occasions. We made up a bed in one of the guest bedrooms. I then opened the window and fell asleep to the sound of the ocean.

~~~~

I woke to the sound of seagulls fighting over some scrap of food they had found on the deck. I was a little stiff from sleeping on the unnecessarily hard bed, but overall, I felt good.

The sun hadn't come up yet, although there was a soft red glow on the horizon. I got dressed and left a note on the door informing Jackie I was on the beach.

I love taking an early morning walk along the shore and was not about to waste this opportunity. The sky in the east slowly turned bright orange as I strolled down the beach.

The smell of the ocean and the feel of the wet sand was wonderfully soothing. An occasional jogger ran past as I enjoyed the solitude of the sea and the gentle pounding of the waves.

Before I got back to Jackie's house, I found a beautiful pink and white spiral shell. It made a nice souvenir of our trip to Mexico.

Jackie made us a quick breakfast while I showered, then she got ready while I did the dishes. The drive up through Mexico was uneventful, and the wait at the border was mercifully short.

As we were driving back, I talked with Jackie and learned more about her life. She was one of those women who had done everything and been everywhere.

It's meeting people like her that keeps my job interesting. It's also one reason I usually can't walk into a bar in Scottsdale without running into someone I know.

As we drove through the desert toward Gila Bend, I questioned her further about the phone call. I hated to upset her, but I needed to find out what was going on.

"The phone call doesn't make sense," I said. "Why would anyone want to kill you? Do you have any enemies? Even if it was the man you think it was on the phone, did you ever do anything to piss him off?"

"That's what I've been asking myself all week. Truthfully, I've been expecting to get a call someday from an angry mother who's upset I deflowered her twenty-one-year-old son. Still, I have no idea where this came from. It was so sudden, and he sounded so angry. I just don't know what to make of it."

"I agree, staying with your friend will help, but it's only a short-term fix. You can't hide forever."

"I know, but I'm not sure what else to do."

"I work at a law firm run by a guy who has a lot of connections within the Scottsdale bureaucracy," I said. "If you wanted to have him look into it, maybe he could get the police involved at a higher level. Then they won't think you're just a hysterical woman calling in a crank phone call. He's kinda expensive, but it could be an option."

"Money isn't a problem. Roger sends me three times what I need to live on. Most of the money he sends me just goes straight to the bank. Maybe I'll take you up on it. I'm not really sure what else to do."

~~~~

We got into Scottsdale around noon. The temperature was in the mid-eighties, there was only the faintest hint of a breeze, and there wasn't a cloud in the sky. You gotta love living in Arizona.

"I need to grab a couple of things from the house before I head to Pammy's," Jackie said. "Would you mind coming with me? I really don't want to be alone until we figure out what's going on. I'll drop you off wherever you want after that."

~~~~

As we pulled into Jackie's driveway, she hit the button for the garage door. As it slid upward, we could see the garage floor was littered with open boxes. Piles of smashed and broken stuff were everywhere.

Jackie let out a loud gasp, bolted from the car, and ran into the house through the garage entrance. I was right behind her and almost ran into her when she came to a sudden stop, three steps into her living room.

We both stood there, mouths open, our eyes refusing to accept what we were seeing. Jackie then made a strange high-pitched noise. I couldn't tell if it was a scream or the start of choked hysterical laughter.

Crap.

The house had been trashed. The living room was in shambles, and from what we could see, the kitchen was as well. Everything from the bookshelves had been tossed on the floor.

The cushions from the couches were shredded, the lamps were broken, and everything was overturned. There were even a couple of large holes bashed into the walls.

Shit.

Unfortunately, I've had experience with this. I told Jackie to go outside while I looked through the house. Odds were that whoever had done this was long gone, but there was always the possibility they were still waiting for us upstairs.

Since we'd just come up from Mexico, I wasn't carrying my pistol. Instead, I went out to the garage and grabbed a five-iron from a set of clubs emptied out onto the garage floor.

I first went into the kitchen and noted that everything in the cabinets had been pulled out and thrown on the floor. The contents of the refrigerator and freezer had been tossed around, and everything was ripped open. The putrid stench of rotting meat wafted through the kitchen while dozens of tiny fruit flies circled the pile of rancid food.

I looked through the rest of the first floor but didn't find anything other than destruction. I then went back into the living room and slowly climbed the stairs.

The upper floor consisted of an open game room with a sewing table and an overturned big-screen TV. From there, bedrooms and bathrooms branched off in all directions.

Whoever made the mess downstairs was just as destructive on the second floor. Everything that could be removed from the bookshelves had been pulled off and ripped apart.

Every piece of furniture was turned over and gutted. As with the rooms downstairs, it looked like someone had taken a crowbar to the walls.

As I walked through the house, holding my five-iron like a baseball bat, I quickly became convinced the people who had done this were not just kids or vandals. This had the appearance of someone looking for something specific.

Every time they found a wall that sounded too hollow or some furniture that could hold whatever they were looking for, it was bashed, ripped open, and shredded.

I checked two of the bedrooms. One was set up as a guest room and the other as a storage room, but I found nothing in either. I then walked down the hall to the master.

The door to the bedroom was closed. I cautiously pushed it open and looked in.

The destruction here had been taken up a notch from the other rooms. Several chunks of the wall had been pulled off and were lying in pieces on the floor. Splintered furniture, clothes, and books littered the floor.

But what my eyes were drawn to was not the mess but to the man sprawled over what was left of the shredded mattress. From what I could see, he had been shot several times and looked very, very dead.

Shit.

Then the smell of the body hit me. Apparently, he'd been lying there for several days, and once the putrid smell registered, I couldn't focus on anything else.

Tiny black spots danced in front of my eyes as I staggered from the room. I made it back to the game room and dropped down to one knee while I made a determined effort not to throw up.

~~~~

I'm not sure how long I was in the game room before eventually making my way back downstairs and stumbling out onto the driveway. I sat for a minute on a plastic chair next to the garage.

Jackie walked over to me. She looked shaken and confused, tears silently sliding down her face.

"I need to call the police," I said. "There's been a murder."

~~~~

I made the call on my cell phone, then went over to Jackie. She'd moved to a chair on the front porch and stared vacantly down the street.

From the rapid and shallow way she was breathing, I

suspected she might be on her way to a panic attack.

"I know this is terrible," I said, "but we'll still need to go through the formal process. The police will be here soon, and this will take all afternoon. There'll be four or five people who will talk to us when they get here, and they'll all ask the same questions. Try not to get too frustrated with them."

Jackie nodded her head to show she understood.

"At this stage, everything we say is only background information to help them figure out what to do next. Don't worry if something you say sounds bad or puts you in a bad light. It's always best to get it out now rather than in the middle of the investigation."

Jackie again nodded her head, but I could tell she wasn't listening. I took both of her hands in mine. This seemed to stir her enough to focus on me.

"If anything they ask makes you uncomfortable, let them know you'd like to discuss the question with counsel before you answer," I said. "We'll get through this together, I promise."

~~~~~

About five minutes later, a Scottsdale patrol car pulled up. Chugger McIntyre climbed out, followed by his partner Arny Montoya.

"Hey, Laura," Chugger said. "When dispatch said a woman had called in a dead body, we volunteered to take the call. Somehow, I knew you'd be here. It's been a couple of months, and you've been overdue."

"Hey, Chugger," I said. "He's upstairs in the master bedroom. I didn't touch anything, and I don't think there's anyone else in the house."

"You didn't happen to put an extra slug into this one, did

you?" Chugger asked, a broad grin on his face.

"Jerk. I was startled last time, and the gun just went off. It's not like I enjoy shooting dead bodies."

Chugger looked over at Jackie. She was now openly crying and had a confused and helpless look on her face.

"Jackie Wade," I said quietly, "the homeowner."

"Thanks," Chugger said, "I'll secure the scene, then I expect homicide, forensics, and the M.E. to show up. Looks like there'll be a lot of paperwork on this one."

Chugger went into the house while Arny started the formal paperwork process by getting our IDs. He handed us each a clipboard along with the standard forms to write out our initial statements. He then started typing our information into his patrol computer.

After about five minutes, Chugger came out of the house. His smile was gone, replaced by the stone-faced look all cops seem to develop. He motioned me over to where he was standing in the garage.

"I pulled the ID from the victim," he said. "His name is Roger Wade. Is he related to her?"

Oh no.

"Damn," I said. "That's Jackie's husband."

~~~~

Within an hour, Jackie's house was swarmed by uniformed police, two homicide detectives, the medical examiner, a forensics team, and every neighbor on the block. After five minutes of hysterical sobbing, Jackie had settled down to sniffles and a vacant stare.

Fortunately, the detective in charge decided to transport us to the district station before the news vans started to set up their live feeds. Enough had gone wrong today, and I was glad Jackie's tear-stained face wasn't going to be the lead story on the local news.

On the way to the station, I called Sophie and downloaded her on what happened. She said she'd tell Lenny and see how he wanted to handle it.

I've tried to contact Lenny directly for things like this before. But with his constant questions and bad attitude, it takes forever to give him the information.

"Thanks," I said. "This really sucks for Jackie, and I want to do whatever I can."

~~~~

Jackie and I were each questioned by a separate detective for almost two hours. Finally, we were given the okay to go home. I called Sophie to collect us, and she showed up twenty-five minutes later.

Rather than going back over to Jackie's to pick up her car, I asked Sophie to drive us directly to Pam's house. I didn't want to see the crime scene again today, and I didn't think Jackie did either.

On the way, Jackie asked about Lenny. "From the questions the detective kept asking me, I may eventually need a lawyer. Is Lenny as good as everyone thinks he is?"

"Lenny has a terrible personality," I said. "But he's connected with everyone important in Scottsdale, and he goes all out for his clients. You could go in and talk to him and then see if you want to take it any further."

"Lenny comes in about eight-thirty and doesn't have an appointment tomorrow until eleven o'clock," Sophie said. "I could pencil you in at nine."

Jackie agreed this would be okay with her.

When we dropped Jackie off at Pam's house, Pam met us at the door and invited Sophie and me in for a glass of wine. It sounded terrific, but we passed. Sophie was already late for a date, and I still had a lot of work to do.

"Try to get some sleep tonight," I said to Jackie. "I'll pick you up tomorrow about eight o'clock, and we'll head over to the office. You can talk with Lenny, and then we'll figure out what to do next."

~~~~~

Sophie dropped me off at the office, then took off for her date. She'd left my car there, and I needed to talk to Lenny.

After I called Sophie and told her about the murder, she'd spent the afternoon researching both Jackie and Roger Wade. So far, she hadn't found anything helpful. She said Lenny had been on the phone all afternoon trying to piece together what the police had on Jackie.

Lenny was still in his office when I got there. As I walked in, he was sitting at his desk, drinking a Jim Beam on ice. When he saw me, he got up, went to his office bar, dropped an ice cube in a glass, and poured two fingers of his sixteen-year-old Glenlivet scotch.

He handed over the drink and smiled at me. Seeing him smile was kind of creepy, but sipping the fantastic scotch helped me get over it quickly.

"Laura," Lenny said, still smiling. "I gotta tell you. You're getting good at this. When you first started working here, Gina said you could be a great investigator, and I'm starting to believe her. I send you out to find Jackie Wade, and you find her, just like that. I'll be able to collect the full fee from Terry Lennox. Now Jackie's husband Roger is dead, and things don't look so good for her."

"But Jackie didn't have anything to do with his death," I

said.

Lenny only shook his head and counted off on his fingers.

"Roger Wade was killed in Jackie's house. She'll gain financially from Roger's death. She can't verify her location when Roger was killed, and a lot of people are looking at her running to Mexico as suspicious, to say the least."

"Well, sure. When you say it like that, it doesn't sound so good."

"Plus, if my sources are correct, Roger was killed by a thirty-eight, which is the same caliber as a pistol registered in the name of Jackie Wade. I'd say it's pretty obvious she's currently the chief suspect in Roger's murder."

"I was there when she walked into her house. She was as surprised as I was."

"Well, if she's innocent, it will make our job somewhat easier. But in any case, your friend Jackie's going to need a good lawyer to get herself out of this. And, I just happen to be a good lawyer," he said smugly.

"You want to represent her? Sophie made an appointment for nine o'clock tomorrow, but I wasn't sure you'd even want to talk with her."

He saw the puzzled look on my face and registered disappointment I hadn't put it together for myself.

"What Jackie probably doesn't realize yet, but I've spent the afternoon verifying, is she will soon become an exceedingly wealthy woman."

"How does that happen?" I asked.

"The actual ownership and finances are rather tangled. Still, it appears Roger Wade was either the part-owner or full owner of half a dozen Scottsdale resorts, along with several prime parcels of undeveloped land. Not as many resorts as Tough Tony DiCenzo, but he wasn't doing too badly for himself. Upon his death, the properties will presumably all go to Jackie. Well, that's assuming they don't sentence her to lethal injection for his murder."

Jackie will own half a dozen resorts? Wow.

"Here's what I need you to do," Lenny said. "Tomorrow morning, when you drive her over here, let Jackie know that it's likely she's going to be charged with the death of her husband. But, also let her know I'm already working on it. It will put her in an extremely receptive mood when we have our initial consultation."

"I guess it will," I said.

"I'm glad you've hidden her away at her friend's house. Otherwise, she'd already be getting phone calls from the other vultures in town. When you bring her in, we can get this started. You'll be the lead on this. Gina is booked solid for at least another week, but consult with her and have her help out if she does get any free time. You can even use Sophie if you need her."

Lenny's smile was back. Getting a wealthy client who has a hopeless case is what he lives for.

~~~~~

I went back to my cubicle and took a seat. I felt exhausted. This was coming too fast for me to take in all at once. I pulled out my phone and called Reno.

I was glad when he picked up. I always hate talking to his voicemail.

"I need to see you," I said. "I'm having a really crappy day."

"I heard you were the one who found the body at the

Wade murder. Why is it always you?"

"I didn't look for it."

"You never do," Reno said. "Actually, I was expecting you to call ever since I heard about it. I need to be back on shift at ten o'clock tonight, but you can have me until then."

"Which part of town?"

"I'll be down by you."

"Great, meet me at Zipps? I'm starving, and a burger would be perfect. Mind if I eat while we talk?"

~~~~~

Zipps Sports Grill is a friendly neighborhood bar on Camelback, about a mile from the office. It's where I go for burgers when I don't feel like driving down to the Chuckbox in Tempe. I got there first and ordered a green-chili burger, fries, and a Diet Pepsi.

Reno arrived ten minutes after I did. He was dressed in jeans and a faded Aloha shirt, his typical outfit for blending in with the Scottsdale tourists.

As usual, when I saw him come through the door, my heart stepped up a few notches, and my tummy started feeling a little fluttery. I really like those feelings.

Reno has the kind of body you usually see on the cover of a fitness magazine. As a rebellious youth, he spent his free time boxing and working out in the gyms of south Scottsdale.

Now that he's gotten older, he's stopped boxing, and he's not as steadfast about going to the gym. Fortunately, he's lost the lumpy bodybuilder look he had as a youth and instead has filled out into a beautiful hard-bodied man.

Reno walks with confidence and is always in control. Part of it is his police training, part of it is his great smile, but most of it is simply the way he is as a person.

He's one of those people with charisma and natural leadership abilities. It's always drawn me to him. He's the one people turn to in a crisis, and he doesn't take crap from anyone. Well, anyone except me.

He walked over to the table and gave me a quick kiss. Nice, yes, but not exactly what I'd been hoping for. Okay, so maybe my fantasy about him dragging me into the back room and bending me over a pool table was a little over the top.

But a girl can always dream.

"So, un, you heard about my day?" I asked.

"It's hard not to. I think homicide was running an office pool on when you'd find the next dead body. How long has it been? Two months?"

"Jerk, you know exactly how long it's been."

And that dead body had his hands hacked off. Yuck.

"It's not like I enjoy it," I said. "Finding these dead bodies always creeps me out."

"Have you considered a different line of work? Maybe your old job? You could go back to working with your friend Mary behind the bar at Greasewood Flat. Bartenders almost never find dead bodies."

"Yeah, but bartenders almost never pay their rent on time either."

"From what I hear, Roger Wade had been there a while. I imagine it was pretty nasty."

"The grossest part was the smell. As I walked through the house, I assumed I was smelling rotting hamburger from the mess in the kitchen. Turns out I was smelling rotting Roger. It's a good thing Jackie left on the air conditioning.

Otherwise, he would have been both dead and runny."

"From the office scuttlebutt, it doesn't look so good for Jackie Wade. How well do you know her?"

"I've only really gotten to know her yesterday and today. She seems like a nice person. I think Lenny's going to represent her."

"Well, if anyone can help her, it'll be Lenny. He's slime, but he does seem to always win his cases."

"If you were going to prove someone was innocent of a murder, how would you do it?"

"Well, the easiest way would be to show she was somewhere else when it happened. If she has a solid alibi, then she's home-free. From what I hear, the ME had the time of death sometime between a week ago Monday and a week ago Tuesday."

"That won't help. Border patrol will show Jackie crossed over into Mexico Monday night at about six. If they could say for sure he was murdered on Tuesday, then she'd be in the clear."

"Maybe they'll narrow it down, but the victim had been there for over a week. I doubt it'll get a lot better than what they already have."

"Jackie said she'd been called and threatened, which made her run to Mexico. What can I do with that?"

"There'll be a record of any calls she received. Does she know where the call originated?"

"Only that it was made from a payphone in Phoenix."

"Does she know who made the call?"

"She thinks it was an associate of her husband. She doesn't know his name, but she could probably recognize his picture. There must be records of who Roger Wade did business with."

"Probably. I assume you told the detective all of this?"

"Three times. I don't think he believed Jackie had been threatened."

"Most everyone who flees a murder has some story about why they fled. It usually involves being threatened, or they were somehow fearful for their safety." He stopped and looked at me.

"You really think she's innocent?" he asked. His voice held a lot of doubt in it.

"I'm sure she didn't do it, but I'll need to prove it."

"Well, you were always the queen of lost causes," he said. "Okay, assuming someone did call and threaten her, if you could find out who made the call, it would go a long way toward explaining things."

"I was thinking the same thing."

"The other obvious path is to find out who tossed the house. The detectives are probably going to conclude Roger was alone and in the process of ransacking the house when Jackie came home. They'll say she shot him in her bedroom, then panicked and fled. If you can discover there was someone else ransacking the house with Roger, it will give you another path. I'd also talk to Gina. She has more training than I do in this sort of thing. She may have some better ideas."

I looked down at my watch. "I need to stop by the grocery store before it closes."

"Shopping at nine-thirty at night?"

"I need to buy a dog a steak," I said. "Long story."

Reno walked me out to my car and kissed me. Again, it was nice, but not exactly the kind of kiss a lover should give his passion-starved girlfriend.

Plus, I was sort of hoping he would at least offer to give me a quickie in the back seat. I really needed to talk to Reno about his attitude.

Chapter Five

I arrived back at Paul Marston's house at about ten. I desperately wanted to be home in bed, but Mrs. Marston was due to be home in the morning, and I didn't want to lose my last chance at collecting evidence.

There were two cars in the driveway, and I could see lights were on in the house. I opened the back gate and looked around, but Buddy was nowhere to be found.

I quietly went to the bedroom window and was glad to see there was still an opening in the curtains. Unfortunately, the bedroom lights were off.

I went around to the living room side of the house, where the lights were on, but the curtains were tightly closed. Feeling a little frustrated, I went back to my perch on the picnic table to wait until Mr. Marston and his guests returned to the bedroom.

I sat on the table for about an hour and a half without anything happening. I was thinking about calling it a night when there was a noise from the living room side of the house.

I heard the patio door slide open, and then close. Buddy came trotting over to the table and looked up at me, head cocked to the side, tail wagging slowly.

I pulled the steak out of my bag. Buddy's tail wagged harder, and he licked his slobbery dog lips. I unwrapped the steak and handed it down to him.

He took it eagerly enough but again didn't wolf it down. Instead, he laid it gingerly on the bench of the picnic table.

He then started walking back to the living room side of the house. After about ten paces, he stopped and looked back at me.

When I didn't follow, he walked back to the picnic table and gave a little *woof*. Curious, I got up and followed.

The dog led me back around to the living room side. They must have opened the curtains to let him out because there was now a beautiful view of the entire living room.

With a feeling of triumph, I saw that all three of them, Paul Marston and the two women, were naked on the couch. They were naked and very, um, *active* on the couch.

I looked down at Buddy, who was wagging his tail. I could swear he was smiling.

I watched for almost a minute and tried to process what I was seeing in the living room. Again, it was the same two women from the other night.

All three of them were on the couch in a wiggling tangle of arms and legs. There were butts and boobs everywhere, but it was sort of hard to tell what belonged to whom.

I shook it off, grabbed a plastic chair from the patio, sat down, and pulled out the camera. I had the lens set to full zoom and the camera set to high-definition video.

I spent almost twenty minutes recording as they went through some remarkable feats of flexibility and sexual stamina. I got Paul Marston from every angle, including a few that were extremely unflattering.

When everyone in the living room was finished, and the champagne and cigarettes were being passed around, I got up and walked back to the gate. As always, Buddy trotted next to me.

When I reached the gate, he sat down and stared up at me. He had a pitiful look on his big doggy face.

When I reached my hand out to open the gate, he let out a little whine. Feeling a little melancholy, I sat down next to him, rubbed his head, and scratched behind his big floppy ears.

"That's okay, boy," I said. "You're a good dog. I'll come back and visit. Sometime soon."

Buddy started wagging his tail again. He walked over to the picnic table and picked up his steak. He then trotted to the corner of the yard to gnaw on it.

I got up, opened the gate, and walked down the street to my car. I was exhausted and couldn't wait to get to bed.

~~~~

I woke up the next day at six-thirty with the alarm happily chirping away. I hopped out of bed and quickly got ready. I felt terrible about what was happening with Jackie, and I wanted to get on it right away.

I put on a pot of coffee and plopped a spoonful of Tuna Delight into Marlowe's bowl. As always, my cat ran to his bowl and sucked up the food as if he was starving.

I did a quick job on the makeup and hair. It wasn't great, but it was passable. I felt ready for whatever was going to come my way today.

I went into the kitchen, poured myself a coffee, and sat down at the table. I needed to get myself organized, and I hated the feeling of not knowing what to do next.

After staring into space for about ten minutes, I still didn't have a game plan. Maybe I'd get a better idea of how to attack this problem after Jackie and Lenny had a chance to talk it over.

From the corner of the kitchen, by the refrigerator, I heard a disturbingly familiar sound: *Aaaaaaaaaak!*

I didn't need to look. Marlowe was throwing up his breakfast. At least he only did it in the corner of the kitchen on the tile. Sometimes, I seriously think about trading him in for a hamster.

~~~~

The drive up to Pam's house was quiet, and traffic was relatively light. I was starting to feel better about the day.

Pam lived in an upscale neighborhood near the Pinnacle Peak Golf Club, not too far from Jackie's house. This part of Scottsdale is a nice blend of desert landscaping mixed in with a lush tropical oasis wherever there's a swimming pool.

I knocked on the front door of Pam's house, and Jackie opened it right away. As I looked closer, I saw that her eyes were bloodshot, and there were dark circles her makeup couldn't completely hide. I doubted she had gotten a lot of sleep.

When Sophie and I had dropped Jackie off the night before, we hadn't gone any further into the house than the front entrance. But even from my brief glance into the house, I'd seen the high vaulted ceilings and the extensive woodwork.

I always wondered what people did to make enough money to afford one of these houses. It certainly wasn't what I did.

Jackie led me into Pam's kitchen, which was as beautiful

as the rest of the house. The countertops were polished marble, and the cabinets were dark cherry. There was a fresh pot of coffee, and Jackie poured each of us a cup.

"How are you doing?" I asked.

"It was a long shitty night," she said. "I was holding it together and doing okay until I watched the ten o'clock news. Apparently, I'm officially a person of interest in the death of my husband. I'm afraid I kept Pam up most of the night with my talking and crying. She only got to bed about two hours ago. I knew you were coming over soon, so I decided to stay up."

"I've talked to Lenny, and he's eager to get started," I said. "I'll be working full-time with him to get this cleared up as quickly as possible."

"From the questions the detective asked yesterday, they think I did it. At first, I thought they were only fishing for something wrong in my story, but now I'm not so sure."

"Right now, they only have a lot of crazy coincidences."

"I hope you're right."

"I hate to ask, but do you keep a gun in your house?"

"I have a Smith & Wesson Model 10, thirty-eight special. I keep it in the nightstand, and I keep it loaded. I'm a woman living alone, and I've always known how to shoot. Is that bad?"

"Lenny heard a rumor that a thirty-eight was the cause of death. Nothing's official at this point, but I thought you should know."

"This is really starting to suck."

I looked at her and saw there were tears in her eyes.

She dug in her purse, which was sitting on the counter,

and pulled out a card in a tiny pink envelope.

"This is for Terry," she said, handing it to me. "I know you'll have to see him when you tell him you found me. It says he's a nice guy, but I never want to date him again. I thought it would help you finish up things with him."

"Thanks," I said. "Come on, let's go see Lenny."

~~~~

The drive down to the office was uneventful, and if it hadn't been for the current situation, I would have said it was a beautiful day in Scottsdale. I pulled into my space behind the office, then we went in through the rear door.

Sophie and Gina were talking in reception when we walked in. Sophie went to Jackie and gave her a long hug.

I introduced Gina, who expressed her sorrow to Jackie for her loss. I then walked Jackie into the inner office and introduced her to Lenny.

I left Jackie alone to talk to Lenny. He sometimes prefers a one-on-one meeting for the initial consultation.

He says it gives him a chance to size up the client. Whether he means their personality, their truthfulness, or their bank account, he's never really said.

I went out to where Sophie and Gina were talking. Gina put her arm around me, knowing I was taking this one harder than most.

"Thanks," I said, trying to sound normal. I took a sniff and noticed there was a faint odor of microwaved cats in the office.

"Was Amber here today?" I asked.

"Yup," Sophie said. "She got here about a half-hour ago. Last time she looked like a slut. This time, I swear she was in her jammies. Lenny told her to wait in the conference room, and he'd come in to talk with her."

"What happened?"

"She waited about fifteen minutes. Then she came out and said she had the start of a migraine and needed to go home."

"So, she's still working here?" I asked.

"For now," Gina said.

"How's your drug dealer alibi assignment coming along?" I asked. "I might need your help with this one."

"It's slowly coming together, although so far it looks like it may be coming together in the police's favor. The deeper I dig into our client's activities, the more it looks like he's involved in some big-time drug trafficking."

"That's not good," I said.

"From what I can gather, there's going to be some sort of exchange next week on Tuesday or Wednesday, somewhere in south Scottsdale. Our client has been overly generous with the information and letting me know he'll be nowhere near the deal when it goes down. His actions seem rather transparent. He couldn't possibly have this type of information unless he was deeply involved, but I guess we'll see."

"Can I do anything?"

"Actually, if you're free by Tuesday, I may need your help. If his information on the drug exchange seems authentic, we'll need to let the authorities know. I'll then hang around the area and see if the exchange actually takes place. If it does, I'll recommend to Lenny that the client turn himself in, and we go for a plea deal."

"If I'm free by then, I'll be glad to help," I said. "How's your pool boy assignment coming along?"

"That one's getting interesting," Gina said. "I was telling Sophie that it turns out Raphael's having sex with the other daughter as well. This one's twenty-two years old and goes to school up in Flagstaff."

"Oh, my God. Seriously?"

"From what I've found out, she comes down into Scottsdale once or twice a month. She meets up with Raphael in her old bedroom on Sunday mornings, when she knows everyone will be out of the house at church. Apparently, it's been going on for some time. I don't think the older sister knows about the younger sister."

"Is she as flexible as the younger sister?" Sophie asked.

"Not by a long shot," Gina laughed. "Older sister is more into being tied to the bedposts, blindfolded, and then being spanked with a long leather paddle."

"Leather paddle?" Sophie asked. "You know, I've been thinking I could really use one of those. Spanking these bare butts always makes my hand hurt, especially when the guy works out a lot and has a really firm tush. I'd need a quality one, not one that would fall apart after I'd used it four or five times. Maybe you could ask Raphael where he got his, if you ever talk to him."

"Why don't you go on the internet," I said. "Isn't that where you've gotten all of your other S&M toys?"

"Yeah, but when I spank a guy, I like to put some effort behind my swing. You can never tell about the quality of the merchandise when you order online. Half the time, it's some cheap imported junk that falls apart the first time you use it. I'm looking for something a bit more heavy-duty."

"Okay," Gina said with a smile, "if I see Raphael, I'll ask him where he gets his spanking supplies."

"If you're serious about this, I'll introduce you to Suzie Lu," I said. "She lives in my apartment building, and she's a dominatrix. I'm sure she'd be glad to give you some tips on where to buy your equipment."

"You know," Sophie said. "Since big sister probably thinks she has an exclusive on the pool boy, I imagine the fur is gonna fly when it comes out that he's been nailing little sister as well."

"Well, they won't hear it from me," Gina said.

Lenny stuck his head out of his office. When he's with a client, he becomes very formal and sometimes even polite.

"Sophie," he said quietly, "would you please bring in the paperwork on the Jacquelyn Wade case?"

Sophie had the standard contracts and forms on her desk, already typed up and ready to sign. She grabbed the pile of papers and walked into Lenny's office.

I turned to Gina. A rising sense of desperation almost overwhelmed me.

"I really need your advice on this," I said. "I know Jackie had nothing to do with this, but all of the evidence is going to point her way. I don't even know where to start. Reno says to go after whoever made the phone call and whoever trashed the house. Assuming I can find out either of those things."

"It's a good plan," Gina said. "You'll probably find the two are linked. I'm sure the homicide detectives will also try to make a connection. Now that Lenny has the case, it will give it the visibility it didn't have before. I imagine the D.A. will be directly involved. It's not in his best interests to prosecute someone who won't be found guilty, and he's lost to Lenny too many times to go in with a hole in his story."

"That makes sense," I said.

"The detectives will look in all the places accessible to them. So, suppose you seriously want to bring something new to the investigation. In that case, you'll need to go after this from a different angle. You'll need to use sources they couldn't possibly touch."

No, no, no, not a good idea.

"What do you mean?" Although, as I asked, I got a twist in the pit of my stomach. I knew where she was going. I'd already briefly considered the same idea and then rejected it. I wasn't that desperate. At least not yet.

"There're a lot of coincidences revolving around the resorts," Gina said. "Scary people are buying and selling them, people are inheriting them, and people are possibly dying over them. As I recall, you have a direct line to the one person in Scottsdale who knows more about resorts than anyone."

Crap, she's right. But, damn.

"I know," I said. "Tough Tony DiCenzo. I've thought about talking to him, but I'm not really sure I can do that, at least not yet. The last time I worked with DiCenzo, I got away without being shot, slashed, or blown-up. I don't know if I'll be so lucky the next time."

"I know it won't be easy," Gina said, now with a motherly tone to her voice. "But I wouldn't put it off too long. Tough Tony may have some information you'll need. Murder investigations have a bad way of gathering momentum around one suspect. I wouldn't want to see Jackie get steamrolled."

I'd met with Tough Tony three times in my life, and each

time was its own kind of nightmare. He scares the hell out of me, and I have no desire to ever see him again.

Unfortunately, as fate would have it, Tough Tony not only seems to like me but feels he owes me a favor. This is not unlike the Godfather or Tony Soprano owing me a service.

I have no intention of ever using it. I know it would undoubtedly cause more trouble than it could ever fix.

But I also knew Gina was right. If there was a resort connection to the situation with Jackie, Tough Tony would probably know about it.

Damn.

~~~~

Jackie was going to be busy with the initial interview and paperwork for at least an hour. I didn't want to sit around doing nothing, so I called Terry Lennox to see if I could come over and talk.

When he answered the phone, he sounded like he'd been asleep but said it was okay to come over. I guessed his band had played the night before, and I briefly felt bad for waking him up.

The drive up to Terry's house took about fifteen minutes. Pulling into the driveway, it was as trashed and nasty as the time before.

Terry met me at the front door in grey gym shorts and a red T-shirt. They appeared to be the same ones he'd been sleeping in.

His long hair was a tangled mess, and his eyes had a slightly unfocused look. After opening the door, he turned and walked into the kitchen. I took this as a sign to follow.

He went to the fridge and pulled out a beer. He offered one to me, but I declined. He then popped the top and chugged half of it.

"I already heard about Jackie," he said. "Your office called yesterday and told me. Um, thanks for finding her and everything."

He drained the rest of the beer and let out a loud belch. "The news is saying she murdered her husband," he continued as he shook his head. "Can you imagine that? Husband? Seriously? She told me she was divorced, but go figure with chicks, huh? Some of them will say anything to get laid."

I took the note from Jackie and handed it to him. He tore it open and read it, although it seemed to take him a long time to do so. He then tossed the note on the kitchen counter and got another beer from the refrigerator.

"Well, so much for Jackie-D," he said. "Sucks, too. She was a tiger in the sack. I might need to consider older chicks more often. That woman had some serious bedroom skills."

He stopped to look me up and down, pausing to stare at my boobs.

"But, you know," he said. "This may turn out to be lucky for both of us. Seems like I don't have a girlfriend now. As it happens, I've been thinking a lot about you the past couple of days. I'm not scheduled to play again until tomorrow night. How's about you and me driving over to Palm Springs for the night? I'll get us a room overlooking the city."

"What?"

"Sure, if you turn out to be half as hot as you look, I'll take you shopping on the way back. There's a sweet outlet mall in Cabazon. I have money, you know? I'll buy you a couple of Versace dresses and maybe even some Ferrucci shoes. I'm sure you've always wanted to party with a real rock star. Looks like now's your chance."

Why me?

I fantasized about smashing the beer bottle against the side of his head and watching his eyes roll up into his skull as he slowly collapsed on the floor. But, since he was still a client, I restrained myself. Lenny tends to get fussy about me brutalizing the paying customers.

"Sorry," I said, "I have a lot of work to do tonight. Maybe another time."

~~~~~

I got back to the office as Jackie was finishing up with Lenny and Sophie. She had the dazed and vacant look on her face again. I've seen this several times before – when clients sign the paperwork and realize their situation is genuine and not some bad dream.

Gina was still there, so Lenny called everyone into his office.

"The detectives called, and I've scheduled an interview Monday morning at ten o'clock," Lenny said. "By then, they'll have completed their initial investigation. If the D.A. agrees there's enough evidence for a grand jury indictment, you'll probably be arrested and charged. But even if that happens, assuming no surprises come up, we'll be able to have you released from custody by the end of the day."

I looked at Jackie and saw she was focused on what Lenny was saying, but tears silently slid down her face. I looked at Sophie and saw she was crying as well.

"Between now and Monday," Lenny said to Jackie, "I want you to keep out of sight and stay out of trouble. If your friend Pam agrees, it would be good if you can continue to stay at her house. We can arrange with the police to gather some of your clothing and personal effects from your house. Let Sophie know what you need."

~~~~

I drove Jackie back up to Pam's neighborhood. As we went, I asked her what she remembered about the creepy guy who'd threatened her.

"I wish there was more to tell," she said. "Physically, he's tall, maybe six-two, and he's built very solidly, like a football player. He was clearly in command of his little group. I really didn't notice a lot else about him except for his scar and his anger issues."

As we turned onto Pam's street, I saw Jackie's car was now parked in front of the house. Pam must have gotten it from Jackie's house sometime during the day. I pulled into the driveway, then Jackie and I got out of my car.

As we walked up the driveway, the garage door opened. I was expecting to see Pam, but instead, three men rushed out, guns drawn.

Crap!

Jackie screamed and ran down the street, two of the men following closely behind.

The guy holding a gun on me was a small, nasty-looking hoodlum, about thirty years old. He had short dark hair, dark squinty eyes, and a thin black mustache.

His lips were curled back in a sneer, and he was twitching nervously. Apparently, his boss had run down the street, and he didn't know what to do with me.

Both my purse and my gun were sitting in my car.

Shit!

I ran into the garage, looking for something to help me defend myself. I found an old coffee can full of screws and bolts on a counter and threw it at him. He tried to move out of the way, but it hit his shoulder and bounced off.

While he was dodging the coffee can, I found a can of wasp spray on the same counter. I turned and sprayed him full in the face with it.

He screamed and fired off a shot that went wide. He was yelling in pain and waving his arms.

I kicked at the hand holding the gun, and it went flying. I went to grab the pistol, but it had slid underneath a tool cabinet, and I didn't have the time to go after it.

I ran back towards my car. I needed to get Jackie and get us out of here.

I got my car door open just before I felt something hard hit me in the back. I turned to see the hoodlum getting ready to throw another yellow quart-bottle of motor oil at me.

He then spotted a hatchet sitting on a shelf and grabbed it. Yelling like a wounded animal, he lunged after me.

I ran around to the passenger side of my car, trying to evade the guy and his hatchet. His face was already turning red from the contact with the wasp spray. His eyes were severely bloodshot and tearing.

As I dodged my assailant, a white van pulled up on the street alongside Jackie. I was amazed and impressed that she could run so fast in heels. The door of the vehicle opened, and two men jumped out and grabbed her.

Seeing movement out of the corner of my eye, I turned in time to see the hatchet flying directly at me. Quickly, I swerved and heard the hatchet thump against my car.

I then saw a yellow blur that I took to be the quart of oil. I felt the rough thump as it hit me squarely on the side of my head.

I saw lights dance across my vision just before I went down. I tried to shake it off, but I was fading fast. I tried one more time to stay awake, and then the world went black.

~~~~

I slowly came back to consciousness with the sun shining in my eyes. I must have hit the ground hard when I went down.

I couldn't move my head, so I tried to put my hand up in front of my face. Unfortunately, my arm wasn't working either.

After a few seconds, somebody's head appeared in front of the sun, and I felt grateful for the shade. As my eyes adjusted, I saw a police officer looking down at me.

Finally, I was able to slowly roll over onto my side and see I was still lying on the driveway. There was a lady in a yellow jogging suit sitting next to me. I assumed she was a neighbor of Pam's.

There was a group of about ten people at the end of the driveway, all looking at me. As I took in this strange scene, another patrol car pulled up, lights flashing.

The officer asked how I was feeling. After doing a quick inventory of my aches and pains, I decided that except for a bump on the side of my head, I was doing okay. He then helped me into a sitting position.

I looked into the garage and saw another officer helping Pam out of her house. She looked like she'd been in a fight.

Her hair and clothes were a mess, and her shirt was torn. She also had what looked like the start of a deep bruise on the side of her face.

I guessed the men had forced their way into the house and subdued Pam while they waited for Jackie to come back. I had no idea how they knew Jackie was staying with Pam.

An ambulance pulled up in front of the house, and a man and a woman hopped out. The man went to Pam, and the woman came over to where I was sitting on the driveway.

She flashed lights in my eyes, then took my pulse and my blood pressure. She held up her fingers for me to count and asked me if I knew what day of the week it was.

After about ten minutes of this, she determined I would live and took off to consult with her partner. I got unsteadily to my feet then walked over to Pam, who was sitting in a chair on her front porch.

"Are you okay?" I asked. "What happened?"

"It was horrible," she said. Her voice was distant, and she seemed to be on the verge of crying. "I got back with Jackie's car about an hour ago. Then somebody knocked at the front door. When I answered, three men barged in."

"Oh my God."

"I tried to get away, but they started hitting me, and then they tied me to a chair. When I heard your car pull up, I screamed as loud as I could. I was hoping you'd hear me and drive away. One of the men hit me in the face to shut me up, and then they all went into the garage."

Pam seemed to realize we weren't all here. She looked around in a panic. "What happened to Jackie?"

"The bad guys took her."

At hearing this, Pam visibly deflated and started to cry.

The patrolman walked over to us, clipboards in hand. Since we'd been certified to have no pressing medical issues, he wanted our statements. We each took a clipboard and started writing.

~~~~

About ten minutes later, an unmarked police car came screeching to a stop in front of the house. The only reason I knew it was a police car was the flashing red light on the dashboard.

The car door opened, and a livid homicide detective stepped out. He went straight to the senior officer on the scene and started asking a lot of angry questions.

One of the other officers walked over to see how we were doing.

"Do you know who called this in?" I asked him.

"It was a neighbor. We got a call for shots fired and a fight. We were here right away, but by then, the perps had already fled. I'm glad to see you weren't seriously hurt. I'm afraid your car wasn't so lucky."

What?

My heart sank. "What happened to my car?"

He pointed, and I saw the hatchet the guy had thrown at me was now embedded in the front passenger fender.

Damn it!

We walked over to my car and saw the hatchet was wedged three inches into the fender. The officer bent over to get a closer look at it.

"He must have really thrown it hard. Good thing it didn't hit you. You can pull it out after it's dusted for prints."

It figures he threw the hatchet on the passenger side. All the previous damage was on the driver's side. My car was now going to look like crap from any angle.

~~~~~

I drove back to my apartment. I was a mess, and I wanted to change my clothes before going back to the office.

While still in the car, I called Sophie and told her what had happened. I should have called Lenny directly, but my head was pounding with a bitch-kitty of a headache, and I didn't want to deal with his screaming.

I walked up the two flights to my floor, looking around to make sure no one was waiting outside my apartment. After seeing the three men rush out of Pam's garage, I was feeling a bit spooked.

I'd opened the door to my apartment and was about to go in when I heard the ding of the elevator arriving on my floor. As the doors slid open, I tensed. Then I heard the soft jingling of keys I recognized as belonging to Grandma Peckham.

"Hello, Laura," she said in her cheerful voice as she came around the corner. She was carrying a bag of groceries, so I took the bag while she opened her door.

Walking into her apartment, I set the groceries on her kitchen table. Marlowe was on his chair, and he woke up long enough to yawn and stretch.

It wasn't long before he closed his eyes and fell back asleep. Grandma went over to the refrigerator, pulled out two Diet Pepsis, and handed one to me.

"You look terrible," she said. "What happened this time?"

"It's been a rough morning. Some men tried to kidnap me."

"This wasn't like those brothers who kidnapped you and

handcuffed you to a bed a few months back, was it?"

"Sort of. But I don't want to think about it right now. Tell me about your day instead. How's the search for the new man going?"

"Well, I took the pictures like you suggested and put the ad on the internet."

I shivered at the thought of Grandma taking naked selfies but shook it off.

"Any luck yet?"

"I've gotten about a hundred responses so far."

"Wow, that's great."

"I guess I've still got what it takes to attract a man. Most of them are from out of state, but there are several local men too."

"Any of them spark an interest?"

"There're a few. I've been writing to three of them, and they all seem nice. Hopefully, I'll go out with one soon."

"How do you feel about dating again?"

"I can't wait. It's been a long time since I've had relations with a man. I hope I can find one who has a penis that still works."

"Maybe you should put that in as a requirement in your ad. It might cut down on the disappointments."

"That's a good idea. I wouldn't want to get all excited about having a new man, then go through that penis nonsense again. The last time that happened, I thought he was going to cry."

"Well, good luck, and let me know if I can help. If you get serious about anyone, I'll be glad to run a background check to make sure he isn't a serial killer or anything."

"I might do that. A girl can't be too careful when it comes to this sort of thing."

Chapter Six

I went back to my apartment and took a quick shower. I still had dirt and bits of grass in my hair from lying on the driveway.

Standing in the shower felt terrific and helped me deal with everything that had happened at Pam's house. I wished I could stand there all afternoon.

After the shower, I put on minimal makeup and pulled my hair back into a ponytail. I wasn't feeling fancy, and I wanted to get back on the job.

~~~~

I drove back down to the office. Jackie had been kidnapped, and I wasn't sure what to do next. I parked in my space behind the office and went in through the rear door.

I walked up to the front offices and saw Sophie hunched over her desk, furiously typing away on her computer. She always does this when Lenny is on the warpath, and she wants to keep out of the way.

"Hey, Sophie, how's Lenny taking the news?"

She motioned me to bend down and started talking in a low voice.

"The police called about ten minutes after you did. Apparently, the homicide detective thinks Lenny set the whole thing up. Lenny went ape shit and has been drinking and screaming ever since."

"Okay, let me go in and talk to him."

I walked into Lenny's office. He was standing at the window, looking out at the shoppers walking on the street.

He had a glass of Jim Beam in one hand and a cigarette in the other. From the half-full ashtray on his desk, he'd apparently been smoking most of the afternoon.

When he heard the door open, he turned and looked at me. When he's upset, Lenny speaks extremely slowly, as if he's talking to an idiot.

"All you had to do was to keep the client out of trouble until Monday. After they arrested her, she'd be in the system, and we could have better dealt with this. As it stands, the homicide detective is probably at the assistant DAs office, thinking up charges they can press against us when our client doesn't show up on Monday."

"Hey," I said. "We were jumped by three guys with guns. Unless you wanted a shoot-out on the street, there was nothing I could do."

Lenny took a long drink of his Jim Beam. He seemed to think about it for a minute, then he walked over and ground out his cigarette in the ashtray on his desk.

"Yeah, okay, you're right. But this is really bad. We need to somehow figure out how we can make this work for us."

He downed the rest of his Jim Beam. I could see he was thinking through how to best deal with this.

"Okay," he said. "On the negative side, our client, the obvious suspect in the Roger Wade murder, has disappeared.

Unfortunately, we only have your story about how it happened."

"Didn't any of the neighbors see anything?" I asked.

"Not a thing. Several people heard the gunshot and a woman screaming, but no one actually saw anything. The police on the scene believed your story, so that will help. It's a shame you weren't more seriously hurt. A gunshot wound would have gone a long way to helping us establish our story."

What?

I didn't bother getting upset over Lenny's comment. I knew from experience he wouldn't have a clue that he had hurt my feelings.

"On the positive side," Lenny continued. "If we can find out who kidnapped Jackie or even why she was kidnapped, it will most likely strengthen our defense. It's also possible the same people who kidnapped Jackie were involved in the murder. I want you to find that tie-in."

"And get the client back?"

"Yeah, and get the client back. Don't be surprised if everywhere you look, a cop will have already been there. It turns out that both our client and the deceased are well known in the Scottsdale social and celebrity scenes. There'll be plenty of press coverage on this, and you know how that tends to mess things up."

I nodded my head. Having random reporters following me around was never pleasant.

"The only thing in our favor is that our client isn't officially missing until she doesn't show up for her scheduled meeting with the detectives on Monday morning. Go find out what's going on and get her back."

Lenny pushed the intercom button.

"Sophie, set up a call with the deputy mayor. I need to start getting in front of this."

I took this as an excellent time to leave.

~~~~

I walked out of Lenny's office and went to the back. Grabbing a Diet Pepsi from the break room fridge, I downed four Advils and then sat down at my cubicle.

My head was still throbbing, but I needed to think of the best way to solve a problem with no obvious solution. I had no idea who took Jackie or why they took her.

I didn't know where she was being held. And, I had no clue where to even start looking. After about twenty minutes of getting nowhere, I did the only thing left to me.

Crap, I am so going to regret this.

I pulled out my phone and called Max. I'd met him a few months before while working on an assignment. He's the number two man in the DiCenzo crime family.

Even after working with him, Max is a complete mystery to me. I've only met with him a few times, and I don't really know anything about him, including his last name.

He seems to have an education, dresses well, and has impeccable manners. From the way he talks and acts, he appears to have some military in his background.

Where Reno has the body of a boxer, Max is more the long-distance runner. He's somewhere in his mid-thirties, tall, lean, and always seems to have endless energy. I can't help but wonder how that would translate in the bedroom.

Stop that!

In looks, Max reminds me of the former pro-wrestler, now actor Dwayne Johnson. The comparison to "The Rock" stops at Max's lips, which are larger and more sensual. I also knew from experience they were incredibly soft and delicious.

I'd had an immediate attraction to Max, which is very rare for me. Unlike Sophie or Gina, it usually takes me weeks of getting to know someone before I'm ready for any sort of intimacy.

With Max, it took all of ten seconds before we were in an embrace, his kisses fueling my desire. What was worse, he knew exactly how I felt about him.

Max answered on the third ring. His voice was soft and firm, but it also sounded surprised.

"Laura Black," he said. "I'd almost forgotten I'd given you this number. Not many people have my direct line. I'm glad you kept it."

Like I'd ever get rid of it.

"Max, I need to talk to you. I'm working on the Roger Wade murder, and I need some advice."

"Okay, do you want to meet somewhere public or private?"

Don't tempt me.

"We should probably keep it public," I said. "Actually, I've been meaning to get over to the zoo before it gets too hot. I hear they've added some new exhibits. I'll meet you on the bridge. When is good?"

"Tony called a meeting for later tonight, but I have some free time until then. I can meet you there in about half an hour. That will give us some time to talk."

"Perfect," I said, "I'll see you there."

Damn.

That only gave me ten minutes to run to the bathroom and fix both my hair and my makeup.

~~~~

The Phoenix Zoo is about fifteen minutes southwest of the office. It's one of the city's gems and is popular with both the locals and the Snowbirds.

The yearly highlight at the zoo is called Zoolights. Every night between Thanksgiving and the middle of January, the zoo lights up with millions of colored lights.

There are hundreds of animated lighting displays, from the comical to the beautiful. Every tree becomes a living light sculpture, and every path becomes a magical adventure.

To get to the zoo from the main parking lot, you need to cross a turtle-filled lagoon over a long bridge. This is where I was standing, waiting for Max.

It was almost five-thirty, and the sun was in the western part of the sky. From the angle, it was about a half-hour from going down.

I watched Max as he walked in from the parking lot and as he crossed over the bridge. He had on the same tinted sunglasses I remembered from the first time we met.

Seeing Max again was enough to speed my heart up several notches and give me a severe case of the butterflies. My hunger for him seemed to have gone up several notches.

I was glad we were somewhere public. Self-control was never my strongest virtue, and I'm not sure what would happen if we were ever to meet somewhere private.

Okay, so I knew exactly what would happen.

He walked up and gave me a hug. As we embraced, I felt a wave of heat rush up and down my body. I then clung to him for several seconds longer than I should have.

At last, I came out of it and let go. He looked down at me with a touch of amusement. As if he'd just read my mind.

"Come on," he said. "Let's go walk through the zoo."

We went in, and I picked a trail at random. After a few minutes, we found ourselves walking along a path with animals on one side and a beautiful lake on the other.

I love going to the zoo and seeing how they change it each year. I felt happy for the first time in days.

I didn't want to break the mood by jumping straight into murder and kidnapping. I was content just to stroll and chat for a bit.

"I talked to Danica the other day," I said. "She said Alex is doing okay."

"Actually, he's doing better than okay."

"How so?"

"At first, Tony and Mrs. Sternwood agreed to give him only a token role in the new resort, mostly to keep him out of trouble. But he's really thrown himself into it. He works seventy or eighty hours every week. He's already made a dozen suggestions. All of them will make the resort better, plus he seems to have real leadership abilities. He has a knack for getting people to work together."

"I thought Tony would still be mad at him for what he did."

"During the police questioning, Alex never even hinted at Tony's involvement in the affair. From what we understand, the police actively tried to make a connection. Tony values loyalty more than anything. Of course, we also heard Lenny helped shield Alexander from the worst of the police questioning. I know Tony appreciated his efforts."

"I'm glad Alex's working out so well. I never really got a chance to get to know him, but he seems to make Danica happy."

"Tony and Mrs. Sternwood have agreed to Alexander taking over the day-to-day running of the hotel portion of the resort once it gets up and running. In the meantime, he'll help oversee its construction, and he'll be in charge of hiring some of the senior staff."

"Wow, that's great."

"Of course, our guys will have his back and make sure things go smoothly. Family or not, building a resort this size is a serious business. If we were to fumble it, it could have repercussions for the other resorts and even the other side of the business."

We walked in silence through the beautiful trees and foliage, moving into a part of the zoo with a tropical rain forest theme. There were bamboo plants, palm trees, and broad-leafed banana trees everywhere.

"You wanted to ask about the murder?" Max asked softly.

Okay, back to reality.

"Yeah. Lenny is representing a woman named Jackie Wade. She's a wealthy Scottsdale socialite. Her husband, Roger Wade, was killed sometime last week, and Jackie's the prime suspect."

"I heard about that on the news. I guess I shouldn't be surprised you're involved."

"She was kidnapped this morning by a group of armed

men, and I need to get her back. Roger apparently was involved in some of the resorts, and now that he's dead, everything will probably go to Jackie. I was wondering if you or Tony know anything about Roger Wade that could help me piece this together."

"When it comes to Scottsdale resorts," Max said, "it's a relatively small group of people, and everyone knows each other, more or less. Even the resorts owned by the chain hotels are still built and run by the same local groups."

"So, you've heard of the Wades?"

"The Wade family's been involved in Scottsdale resort development since the beginning. We worked directly with Roger on a project a few years ago. On that project, Roger Wade and Howard Spencer were the two active partners. We were part of the financing, along with a couple of other groups. After the project was completed, we took the payout and backed out. Tony may have worked with him on other projects, but it's the only one which comes to mind."

"Jackie mentioned another man. He's the leader of a group of investors Roger's been working with over the last couple of years. He's tall and broad, with short black hair and a black mustache. He has a big scar on the left side of his face and speaks both English and Spanish. According to Jackie, he has some serious anger issues. She thinks this is the same man who had made threats against her a week before."

"No, he doesn't ring a bell. But again, Tony may know more. I'm assuming you'd like to talk with him?"

"Yes, I need to find out everything I can about Roger and what he was involved in. If Tony's available, I'd like a few minutes of his time."

"Okay, I'll pass along the request. Things are kind of busy at the moment, but he likes you, and I'm sure he'll want to fit you in."

"Thanks, I really appreciate it."

We were still walking through the middle of the rainforest. Off the main path, there was a small trail leading into a tropical jungle.

Max took my hand and led me down this trail. It went in about twenty yards, took a bend, and ended at an "employees only" gate. Still holding my hand, he looked down at me.

"Okay, enough business. Have you thought any more about my offer?"

Only every day.

"I'd still like to see if there's something between us," he said. "I'd be glad to start out slowly and see where things go."

Oh, I know where things would go.

"Maybe we could take off for a quiet weekend," he said. "Somewhere beautiful with a white sand beach, a blue ocean, and a lot of palm trees."

Yum!

"You don't know how good that sounds," I said. "But every time I think of being with you, I get visions of being asked to be on Mob Wives of Scottsdale. I don't think I could be part of that lifestyle."

"Wife, huh? Well, maybe someday I can make you change your mind."

With that warning, he put his arms around me and pulled me in for a kiss. I didn't even try to fight it. Actually, while he was leading me down the path, I was secretly hoping he'd kiss me. Kiss me, at the very least.

As with the first kiss with Max, I seemed to enter a dream

world. The noises of the zoo faded into the distance, and the sunlight seemed to dim.

I was only aware of Max's arms around me and his lips on mine. My breathing stopped; the whole of my being was taken over by waves of mounting pleasure.

As before, my lips took on a mind of their own as I kissed him back. He curled an arm around my waist, pulling my body tight against his.

My mind started racing, and my appetite, which Reno had awakened, now kicked into high gear. The fluttery butterfly feelings in my stomach now traveled throughout my entire body.

I felt like I was floating. I wanted him, and all the arguments about what he did for a living dissolved and were gone.

No, no, no. Damn it!

I pushed myself away from him. The sensations were starting to overwhelm me.

My breathing was fast, and I knew my face had turned a bright red. I lowered my head and hid my face in my hands.

After a moment, I started to calm down. I looked back up at Max, who still held me loosely in his arms. His knowing smile annoyed me a little bit.

"How can you do that to me?" I asked. "I tell myself I want no part of you, then you kiss me, and I'm ready to have your babies."

"Babies, huh? I'm not sure we're ready for babies, but I do like the way your mind's going."

"Shut up," I said. "Come on. Let's get back out to the main path. Otherwise, I'll make you do something to me that might get us both arrested. Neither one of us needs that right now."

Max held my hand and walked me back to the main path. We then meandered back through the zoo and out to my car. He told me he would give me a call when he could arrange a meeting with Tony, but it probably wouldn't be until sometime the next day or even the day after.

Although he didn't kiss me again when we parted, he also didn't let go of my hand the entire time as we walked back through the zoo. I wasn't sure what to make of that, but I know I liked it. I liked it a lot.

~~~~

Even though the sun had set, the western sky was still bright with fiery oranges and reds. The day had already been a long one, and I didn't have another move I could make until I talked with Tony.

Without thinking, I found I'd driven the fifteen minutes back to my apartment building. I parked and took the stairs to my floor. After the kidnapping, the thought of being alone in an elevator was still too much for me.

I went into my apartment and collapsed on the couch. Marlowe must have heard me come in.

I heard the cat door in the bedroom swing open. A moment later, he hopped onto the couch and flopped on my lap.

I'd been petting Marlowe for about two minutes when my phone rang. It was Pam.

"How are you doing?" I asked. "You were amazingly brave today. Thank you for trying to warn us."

"Thanks, but it didn't do a lot of good. They still kidnapped Jackie, and from what I heard, they almost killed you."

"I'm fine, and we'll get Jackie back. So far, you're the only one who's been injured."

"I'll be okay. My face hurts where they hit me, and I'll have a bruise for a few days, but I don't think they seriously injured me. I put an ice pack on it, and the swelling is almost gone. Do you have any news on Jackie?"

"I haven't heard anything yet. The police are sending out everyone they can spare to look for her. But honestly, I'm not sure they believe the kidnapping story. They're treating her more as a fugitive suspect than as a kidnapping victim. I'm spending my time looking into the places the police won't go."

"That's what we've been thinking as well. We were planning on hitting a couple of the clubs tonight and asking around. We know everyone worth knowing in Scottsdale, and maybe somebody will know something."

"What a great idea," I said. "When and where are you starting? I'd like to come along."

"We're planning to meet at the Maya Day and Nightclub about nine o'clock. You can probably find us near the pool."

"Perfect, I'll see you there."

I'd just put the phone down when Sophie called. She sounded annoyed.

"Hey, Sophie," I said. "What's going on? I thought you and Milo were going to the Rhythm Room tonight."

"We were, but he called to cancel. Seems his boss called a big meeting, and he can't make it."

"Sorry it didn't work out. Dating a henchman seems a lot like dating a cop. Neither one has a predictable schedule."

"That's so true. What about you? Are you working or playing tonight? I need to get out and do something."

"Actually, a little of both. The cougars and I will work a couple of the clubs tonight and search for more information about Jackie. We're meeting at Maya at about nine. Why don't you come along? I'm sure Lenny won't mind if I expense both of our covers for the night."

"That would be great, although I'm going to need to change and redo my makeup. I'm good enough for Milo and a blues club, but not if I'm going to hang out with cougars. Those women sorta intimidate me, you know, a little."

"You'll be fine. See you at nine."

After hanging up, a wave of exhaustion swamped me. This happens every time I schedule myself for a late-night after a long day.

I looked at the clock and decided there wasn't enough time for a nap, but maybe there was time for a quick dinner. I pulled out my phone and called Reno.

"Hey," I said after he answered. "You free for dinner?"

"Actually, I'm off duty for the weekend. I was going to call you and see if you wanted to make a night of it. I'm never sure with your crazy schedule."

Damn! Tonight?

"I'd love to do the whole night, but dinner is all I can squeeze in. I don't know if you heard, but Jackie Wade was kidnapped this morning, and I need to try and track her down."

"I've heard. And I've also heard several teams are working on the case already. I guess Jackie's some sort of celebrity in Scottsdale. Apparently, city hall has taken an interest in the case. Between that and the stories in the media, the department's going all out to find her. Are you sure you need to be out there too? I can think of a much better way for you to spend your Friday night."

Oh, yum!

"Trust me, I'd much rather be with you. But I was there when Jackie was kidnapped. Besides, she's a client. I have to try to get her back. I'm meeting up with Jackie's friends, and we're going to hit some of the clubs to see if we can pick up on any rumors."

"So, just dinner then?"

"Unfortunately, yes. What about Frankie's?"

"Frankie's would be good. I'll meet you there in about a half-hour."

"Let's make it an hour. Jackie's friends are all cougars, and I need to redo myself."

"Cougars, huh? Are you thinking about switching to young boys? Should I be worried?"

"Jerk."

~~~~

I went into the bedroom and pulled out several outfits. I finally decided on my short black skirt with the multi-colored rainbow sparkles.

I love this skirt. No matter what I do to it, it never wrinkles, plus the sparkles always make me feel special and sexy whenever I wear it.

I then settled on my second favorite red knit top with the plunging neckline. If I wear the right bra, it makes it look like I actually have cleavage. Unfortunately, my favorite red top had ripped when I was standing too close to a building that had blown up a couple of months before.

I spent the rest of the time trying to fix my hair and makeup. Like Sophie, I was starting to feel slightly intimidated at the thought of hanging out with a group of Scottsdale cougars all night.

~~~~

Frankie Z's is a small family-run restaurant off Hayden and Via Linda. It's one of those places that have been around for as long as anyone can remember.

Ever since Reno had taken me there on our first date, about a year and a half ago, I've come to regard it as "our" restaurant. It's run by Frankie Zappitelli, a small, ageless Italian woman.

When I walked in, Frankie was at her usual place at the hostess stand. When she saw me, she flashed her broad welcoming smile.

"It's good to see you back again. It's been almost a month. Where you been eating if not here? It's not so good as my cooking, eh?"

"Hi, Frankie," I said. "It always smells so good when I walk in the door."

"It's the essence," she said. "The garlic. With it, everything is beautiful. Your cute boyfriend is already here. I put you two in the corner on the patio, very romantic."

As she walked me through the lounge, I spotted Frankie's son, Little Zappy, working his usual spot behind the bar. Little Zappy is in his mid-forties and must weigh three hundred pounds.

He waved as he saw me walking through with his mom. Frankie continued on, leading me to the outdoor patio where fragrant jasmine vines covered the red brick walls.

It was beautifully lit with dozens of strands of white

Christmas lights. Italian love songs played softly in the background.

Reno was looking over the menu as I reached the table. When he saw me, his face broke out in a smile. I always take that as a good sign.

I sat next to him and leaned over for a kiss. As always, Reno smelled terrific.

"You look great," he said. "Maybe I should take you out to the clubs if you're going to look like that."

"Maybe you should. Has there been any word on Jackie?"

"None at all. But, as I was telling you, there are already several teams looking for her. Apparently, she has friends who are well connected in city politics, so this is getting a lot of visibility. Most everyone in the department agrees it was an actual kidnapping. But a vocal few think this was just a set-up to have Jackie disappear. The lead from homicide is all but accusing Lenny of having planned the entire thing."

"That's stupid. I was there, and it was legitimate. Plus, even Lenny wouldn't do that to one of his own people."

"Nevertheless, people know how Lenny works, and there's been some talk. It will be in everyone's best interest if she's found quickly."

Dominick, another one of Frankie's sons, brought over our drinks and breadsticks. We ordered dinner and then talked.

It was great being with Reno. Sitting next to him and talking about my day is always so perfect. Whenever we're together, I think about spending every night with Reno and how great it would be.

It kills me that we can't spend more time together. Sometimes I blame him, but with his cop schedule and my chaotic life, it's no wonder we only see each other once or twice a week.

I let out a sigh. Reno heard it and looked at me.

"Oh, that was just a sigh of frustration. We can't ever seem to be together for more than an hour or two at a time. It makes me wonder what it would be like to be two normal people with normal day jobs. We could have dinner together whenever we wanted and even spend the entire weekend together whenever the mood struck us."

"You think you're frustrated? I'm dating a beautiful and sexy woman, and we never have time for anything more than dinner. To be honest, I was getting more action back when I didn't have a steady girlfriend."

"Oh, really? You want to go back to dating normal women? Ones with normal schedules?"

"Nah, normal women are boring. But something's gotta change, or I'll go nuts. I keep hoping our schedules will match up someday soon, and we can actually spend some quality time together."

I held up my glass.

"Here's to hoping for better schedules."

He held up his glass and lightly clinked it against mine.

"Better schedules, soon."

~~~~

Reno walked me out to the parking lot. I'd parked in the back row, and now it was relatively dark where my car was sitting.

This, of course, started giving me some naughty ideas. My heart started beating faster, and my mind began to race.

Why can't I think of anything else?

I hit the remote and unlocked the doors. I got in the driver's seat while Reno took the passenger's side.

I tossed my purse in the back and then looked over at Reno. He looked back at me for a moment, then took me by the shoulder and leaned over to kiss me.

As soon as his lips touched mine, my heart sped up another notch, warming me all over. I had a bad case of the butterflies, and a pleasant tingling started climbing up my thighs.

When I felt his tongue touch mine, my hunger hit the red zone. I grabbed his body and smashed it against me.

His kisses deepened, and his body grew hot to the touch. At my not-so-subtle prompting, he started to gently touch and tease.

After two or three minutes of this, I literally started squirming with frustration. I knew there was no way I was letting Reno out of the car without him giving me some sort of relief.

"I want you," I said, my words coming out in gasps.

He was breathing hard, and his face looked flushed. He let out a low moan. "I want you too," he said. "Do you have enough time to come to my place?"

I looked at my watch. I had told the girls I would meet them in less than half an hour.

"Not enough time," I said.

"Hey, we talked about this not twenty minutes ago. You need to fix your schedule so we can be together, at least occasionally. Can we plan on tomorrow?"

"Maybe, but you aren't getting away yet. I need you to

make me happy – now."

"In Frankie's parking lot? What did you have in mind? It wouldn't be a good idea to be bouncing in the back seat like a couple of teenagers. What if someone was to walk by? We should probably think of, um, something else."

His fingers were gently touching my lips, and I knew what he had in mind.

"Well," I said, "there is one magic thing you do to me." I then took his hand and lightly kissed the tips of his fingers.

"Sure, great for you. But what about me? I'm a guy. I have needs too. Maybe more than you."

"I seriously doubt that. Besides, I'm wearing a skirt, and you have on a ton of clothes. It's not my fault you didn't plan better."

"Like how? Wear a kilt?"

I took one of his fingers and sucked on it for about ten seconds, sliding his finger in and out of my mouth to give him a nice mental image.

"Make me happy now, and I'll make it up to you," I said in my sexiest voice. "I promise."

"Oh yeah? When?"

"Soon."

"Soon's not an answer."

"It's the best I can do right now. Take it or leave it."

Chapter Seven

The Maya Day and Nightclub is one of the most popular bars in the city. It occupies the site of where the nightclubs Myst and Suede used to be.

It's on the same street as Nexxus, and ever since it opened, it's been one of my favorites. The inside is enormous, with great dance floors, hidden alcoves, and a VIP room, which I've only seen from the outside.

Setting Maya apart from the other Scottsdale clubs is the resort-sized swimming pool set in the middle of a huge outdoor patio. Seemingly floating in the middle of the pool is the main DJ stage.

The girls weren't hard to find. Even in a club this crowded, they seemed to have carved out a space of their own in a double-sized cabana next to the pool. Annie, Sophie, and Pam were there, along with four others. I was introduced to Elle, Shannon, Sonia, and Cindy.

Of the new ladies, Elle was the most striking. She had dark wavy hair that went halfway down her back, deep green eyes, and an infectious smile.

Seeing them together was an impressive sight, as if they belonged on the cover of a fashion magazine. Their makeup, hair, and nails were perfect.

Except for Annie, each had on forty or fifty thousand dollars' worth of jewelry. Each was dressed in an outfit screaming both money and class, expressing a passionate sensuality. As I walked closer, I caught the subtle mingling of several high-end perfumes.

I tried to get to know the new women, and I talked with each of them. When I told Elle I liked her name, she looked at me, a little surprised.

"Thanks, but it's actually Lynaé. For some reason, the club bouncers never liked my name. Maybe it was too hard for them to remember, I don't know. They shortened it to 'L,' and I've been Elle ever since."

I spent some time chatting with Sonia. She was very tall and athletic, with dark wavy hair down to her shoulders, flawless cocoa skin, and large brown eyes. I told her she looked familiar, but I couldn't place her.

"It's okay," she said with a laugh. "I get that all the time. Up until last year, I was married to one of the Phoenix Suns. I was always the girl in the background whenever he had a TV interview. I've known Jackie, Pam, and Elle for years. After my divorce, I started hanging out with them whenever they went to the clubs. They're all my best friends, and I'd do anything for them."

I asked Pam how she was holding up. She said she was okay, and now she only wanted to help get Jackie back. I saw she'd used makeup to skillfully cover the bruise she'd gotten earlier in the day.

The conversation in the group quickly turned to Jackie. I shared what I had, but it was nothing they hadn't already heard from Pam.

Everyone in the group had a different theory about what happened. Still, there wasn't anything said that brought a new flash of inspiration.

As we talked, I noticed several men in their twenties casually milling around our group. Each man appeared to be waiting for an opportunity to speak to one of the ladies, yet each was doing his best not to look like he was hovering.

At one point Shannon held up her empty martini glass in the direction of one of the men. He sped away, only to reappear at Shannon's side two minutes later with a fresh drink.

They sat together and chatted for a minute. From what I could catch, he was delicately propositioning her. She then leaned over and gave him a soft kiss. Shannon then smiled and caressed the man's face as he continued to talk.

At some signal I didn't catch, the man got up and resumed his place in the hovering crowd of men. A few minutes later, Sonia held up her glass to a different man, and the process was repeated.

After about a half-hour of warming up, the girls got up to work the crowd and ask about Jackie. Shannon, Elle, and Pam went straight to the entrance to the VIP lounge. They briefly chatted and joked with a huge bouncer, a bill was discreetly passed, and they were admitted.

Sonia and Cindy went onto the main dance floor. Annie and Sophie took off together, and I went out on my own.

I walked around the club, talking to the handful of people I recognized. Although everyone knew about the kidnapping, no one had any new insight on what had happened to Jackie or who had set her up.

After about an hour, we gathered back at the cabana. No one had anything new to report on Jackie. We then decided to walk across the street to Nexxus.

It was approaching eleven on a Friday night. As I expected, there was a line of about thirty people behind the rope.

Apparently, cougars don't ever wait in line. The girls casually walked up to the entrance and spent a few minutes chatting and laughing with the three huge bouncers, who they all seemed to know by name. The bouncers had pet names for each of the girls, except for Pam, who was known by everyone as Pammy.

Sophie and I were introduced as potential pumas, which seemed to amuse the bouncers. They said they were sorry to hear about what'd happened to Jackie-D, and they'd be willing to help any way they could. A bill was discretely exchanged, a bouncer then lifted the red velvet rope, and we were all admitted.

We walked into the cocktail lounge side of the club. After a brief discussion with the hostess, we quickly had an entire corner alcove to ourselves.

Within five minutes, a different group of men in their twenties began to hover around our group. A waitress appeared with a tray of drinks, apparently paid for by the men. We sat as a group and talked for about ten minutes.

Sophie looked over at me. "I've gotta try it."

She then looked at one of the men and waved him over. He was tall, athletic, and looked Nordic or maybe German with long blond hair, dark green eyes, and a great smile. He couldn't have been more than twenty-one or twenty-two.

He hurried over and slid into the booth next to her. They talked for a minute, her hand resting on his arm as she gave him a drink order. He then took off like a shot.

"Oh, I do like this," Sophie said. "Maybe we should be pumas full-time. Did you see him? That boy has an amazing body. I bet his butt's firm. I wonder what it'd be like to spank a butt that firm. No way I'd use my hand, though. I'd be sore for days. I should probably use a belt."

"I can tell you've spent a lot of time thinking about this," I said.

"You're right, and the more I think about it, the more I realize I need to find a leather ass-spanking paddle. I'm thinking I could get a paddle in the shape of a heart, so I could smack little red hearts all over his ass. Maybe even get a paddle with my name embossed on it so he'd have my name slapped onto his butt for a day or two."

"I'm thinking that might not be such a good idea when you date a married guy. Wives tend to get fussy about that."

"Nope, after the way the last guy kept canceling dates to be with his wife, I'm done with married guys. I don't care how cute or rich they are. From now on, they can figure out their lack of sex issues with their wives all by themselves and leave me alone."

"Well, what about if they already have a girlfriend? Are you going to stop dating those guys too?"

"Hell no. Girlfriends are a completely different issue. If a girlfriend can't keep her man's interest up, then it's time he finds a new girlfriend. At least for a few dates."

Two minutes later, the blond appeared with a drink in his hand. He slid back into the booth next to Sophie and started talking low into her ear. Within a few minutes, her face had acquired the soft pink glow she gets when she mixes alcohol and men.

After another five minutes, she dug out a card from her purse and handed it to the man. He took the card and then leaned over to give her a kiss.

Sophie grabbed him roughly by the shirt and pulled him in. She then spent a good thirty seconds with her face smashed against his.

Everyone at the table cheered and clapped as Sophie took control of the helpless man. When she finally allowed him to leave, we all held up our glasses in a salute to Sophie's incredible prowess.

After everyone had a fresh drink, the girls took off in pairs to hunt down any information they could get. Pam and I started off together, but she kept running into her friends.

Each one wanted to know the details on Jackie, but no one could provide any new information. After having the same dead-end conversation with three of Pam's friends, I struck out on my own.

As I walked by Annie, she waved me over. She was having a conversation with someone introduced as Jasmine, a friend of hers from college. She was somewhat older than most of the crowd but not yet old enough to be one of the cougars.

"Jaz," Annie said, "tell Laura what you just told me."

"Sure," Jazmine said. "I was telling Annie that if you don't count a few pissed-off girlfriends, the only person that's ever said anything bad about Jackie-D was Howard Spencer."

"Who's Howard Spencer?" I asked. The name sounded familiar, but I couldn't place it.

"He's a guy that hangs out at the clubs sometimes. He's not a regular. He's creepy old, but he's loaded, and he always buys our drinks and munchies. Sometimes he goes home with a girl, but usually not."

"What did he say?" I asked.

"Okay, so this was about three weeks ago. We were all

out at the Roxy when someone started talking about Jackie-D. For some reason, that set Howard off. He called her a scheming bitch and said she needed to be taught a lesson."

"Any idea what he was talking about?"

"None at all. Probably it was nothing though, we were all pretty drunk. I wouldn't even have remembered anything about it, except it's the first time I've ever heard a guy say something bad about Jackie-D. It sorta stuck in my mind."

"Do you know where I can find Howard?" I asked.

"No, but he shouldn't be too hard to find. As I said, he's seriously rich. I heard he has a house on the side of Camelback, or Mummy Mountain, or somewhere fancy like that."

"Thanks," I said. I handed her my card and asked her to call me if she thought of anything else.

I stuck around the club until a little after one. It was starting to thin out. Sophie and most of the cougars had already left. I called it a night and took off as well.

~~~~

I drove back to my apartment and took the elevator. I was too tired to take the stairs. It was slow, but I eventually made it up to my floor.

I was met at the door by Marlowe, who demanded to be picked up and held. As soon as he was in my arms, he went limp and started purring.

I walked with my cat to the bedroom. Leaving him on the bed, I put on some soft Phoenix Suns jammies and then collapsed next to him.

The last thing I remember was the sound of Marlowe purring as he fell asleep against the side of my leg.

~~~~~

I woke to the theme from the *Love Boat*, the old TV show from the eighties. It took me a few seconds to realize the sound was my phone ringing.

I looked at the caller ID and saw it was Max. At this, my heart took off. I answered with a voice I hoped sounded both sexy and awake.

"Hi, Max. Um, how are you today?"

"Laura, it sounds like I woke you. Forgive me. I should have realized you'd have been up late on a Friday night, chasing down the kidnappers."

So much for sounding awake.

"Not a problem," I said, as my heart beat a little faster. Laying in my bed and hearing Max's voice made me tingle in a lovely way.

"Have they found Jackie yet?" Max asked. "The morning news didn't have any new details."

"Not that I've heard. Maybe the police are getting somewhere, but I've run into nothing but dead ends."

"Well then, I have some good news for you. Tony's willing to meet with you today. He's playing the Kokopelli course at the Blue Palms. One of his meetings has canceled, and he has three holes open: the tenth, eleventh, and twelfth. We'll be starting at the tenth hole at about noon. You do play golf, don't you?"

"Um, I do, but it's been a while. I'll need to dig my clubs out."

Okay, so it's been like five years since I touched a club. This won't go well.

"Don't worry about being a little rusty. A lot of people

who meet with Tony on the course haven't played in a while either. No need to search for your clubs. I'll have a set of ladies' clubs for you. Standard right-handed, I assume?"

"You seem to know a lot about me. Can I assume you'll be there as well?"

"Yes, I always try to go out when Tony plays. Usually, to be the referee in case discussions start to get out of hand."

"Does that happen a lot?"

"Almost never. That's why I'm there. I've been told I have a calming influence."

You? Calming?

"No," I said. "I haven't seen that at all. In fact, you seem to have the opposite effect on me."

"Coming around to my way of thinking? I like that. Should I make reservations for a beach resort? I'm thinking maybe Puerto Vallarta. Next weekend?"

Oh, yum!

"It's kinda hard for me to plan ahead," I said. "So, maybe a rain-check on that. Where should I meet you tomorrow?"

"Go to the golf valet, and they'll bring you to us. I assume you'll be driving the same car?"

As he said the last, I could hear the smile in his voice.

"Jerk. Yes, I'll be driving the same car. It runs, and it's paid for."

"Okay, sorry," he teased. "See you at noon."

~~~~~

As I drove up Scottsdale Road to the Blue Palms Resort, I couldn't help but be nervous. In two of my previous three meetings with Tough Tony, there'd been violence and even death. I was hoping that on a golf course, on a beautiful spring day in Scottsdale, the violence and bloodshed would be held to a minimum.

I pulled into the Blue Palms. It was beautifully cultivated with palm trees, citrus trees, and tropical plants of every description. The thick grass was expertly manicured, the landscaping was graceful, and the buildings looked pristine.

The hotel reception building sat on a small hill surrounded by restaurants, pools, and a small water park. An enormous conference center was located further back from the reception building.

The clubhouse sat on a low hill in the distance. People everywhere were driving around in shiny blue golf carts.

I followed the signs to the golf valet, where a uniformed man opened my door and led me to a waiting cart. Here, another uniformed man drove me to Mulligan's, a fun-looking bar and grill located about fifty yards from the main clubhouse.

As I walked into the restaurant, I saw it had been set up for golfers coming in from the front nine and those preparing to play the back nine. There were about thirty people in the place, all talking, drinking, and eating.

In the center was an open-air grill where chefs in white coats were grilling burgers, ribs, and chicken. All the food was giving off a fantastic charcoal aroma.

Towards the back was a bar where two smiling men in blue Aloha shirts made cocktails and fruit drinks. On a small stage to the side, a three-piece band was playing light Mexican swing.

It was a wonderfully calming environment, no doubt set up to help the golfers relax before they went back out. It was also helping me steady my nerves before I met with Tony.

About ten minutes after noon, I heard the distinctive voice of Tony DiCenzo as he made his way into the restaurant. I also noticed the activity of the staff rose up a notch, everybody doing their best to look busy. It seems Tough Tony has this effect on everybody.

Max's smile was broad, and even Tony seemed to be in a good mood. Unlike the loud outfits of some golfers, they were both dressed rather conservatively.

Tony saw me and came over, his hand extended. "Laura Black," he said in his low gravelly voice as we shook hands. "It's nice to see you again. I'm glad an opening occurred so we could get together today. From what Max says, you've been having an interesting week. If you're ready, let's head out to the course so we can talk."

We walked out to our waiting carts. Instead of the usual two-person golf carts, two huge six-person carts were waiting for us. One was green, and one was red.

The drivers of the carts were Milo and Johnny Scarpazzi. I recognized them both from my previous meetings with Tony.

Johnny was driving the red cart, where Tony and I headed. Milo was driving the green one that Max climbed into.

Sitting in the red cart next to Johnny was a woman I knew only as Gabriella. She was somewhere in her thirties and was tall, athletic, and graceful. As with the last time I saw her, I wanted to describe her as beautiful, but there was something cold about her eyes that sent a shiver of fear down my spine.

I'd seen her twice before. Both times, she'd acted as a bodyguard for Tony. The second time, she ended up gunning down some nasty men, and I'd been more than happy to have her on my side.

As with the last two times, she was dressed in tight black leather, and her top was open to expose an eyeful of cleavage. Somehow it added to her overall look of danger.

I glanced around the cart as Johnny drove us to the tee boxes. Between the two seats in the back sat a sizeable built-in cooler. I lifted the lid and saw a full selection of beer, wine, and soft drinks, including half a dozen cans of Diet Pepsi.

"You've noticed I like to golf with some rather large and unusual carts," DiCenzo said as we drove. "They're good for conducting business, plus I like my people to be able to see when I'm coming. I want people to be ready when I visit them as they work. I've noticed when I show up unannounced, there's a tendency for accidents to happen."

~~~~~

There're three golf courses at the Blue Palms – the Kokopelli, the Anasazi, and the Hohokam. Of the three, the Kokopelli is considered the hardest and is usually used whenever a tournament is held at the resort.

We got to the tenth hole on the Kokopelli course, a long par five with a dogleg left, which meant the green was hidden from the tee. There were four tee boxes. Tony said he and Max would be hitting from the third tee box back, and he offered me one of the closer boxes.

I said no, I'd hit from the same box as them. Tony then gave me a slightly strange look I wasn't sure how to interpret.

I went to the back of the cart and found a set of Lady Pings in a white leather bag. The driver I pulled out looked brand new.

It had been a while since I'd held a new golf club, and it felt great. I took a deep breath and walked to the tee box.

I hit first, trying to ignore the fact that four men, and maybe even Gabriella, were looking at my ass. The distance was okay, but I sliced it a little.

All things considered, it was a good first shot. My time away from the game was showing.

Tony stepped up next and hit a nice shot. His ball went straight down the fairway, and his distance was reasonable.

Max stepped up and unloaded on the ball. Tony and I watched as his ball soared into the air, straight down the fairway, farther and farther, until it was lost from sight. I was amazed at the shot, but Tony didn't seem to think this was anything unusual.

Max said he'd go down the fairway to find his ball and took off with Milo in his cart. Tony and I walked down the fairway while Johnny drove the red cart a respectful thirty yards behind us.

"Max hit an amazing shot," I said, blurting out the first thing that popped into my head. My nerves were still getting to me, and I wasn't sure how to start asking Tony about Jackie and the kidnapping. "Most of the golfers I've known wouldn't purposefully outdrive their boss like that. At least not very often."

"Max is a scratch golfer, and he could've easily gone pro," Tony said, apparently not minding my indirect approach. "You know, I've never beaten him at golf. Someday I hope to. But when I do, I know it will be because I've truly beaten him. You see, I've never needed an ass-kisser who would let me win so that my self-esteem would somehow stay high."

"He seems to be a fantastic golfer."

"Matter-of-fact, one of the reasons Max and me get along so well is because of our first meeting, which happened to be on a golf course. I was still in the process of learning the game back then, but we still bet each other twenty dollars a hole. I told myself I would find out what the kid was made of. Now, understand he knew my position in the organization. Max also knew he was on a sort of informal job interview. Still, he beat me fifteen holes to none with three ties. It cost me three hundred dollars to find someone who would be honest with me, without all the bullshit. We've been working together ever since."

Apparently, Tony liked to walk the course rather than take the cart. I didn't mind. It gave us more of a chance to talk, which was probably as Tony intended.

As we reached our balls, Johnny pulled up even with us on the cart path, and we both retrieved a club from the bags on the back of the cart. Tony and I both hit decent shots from the fairway, and both of our balls landed a little short of where Max's first shot had landed.

"It's kind of funny that the job interview happened on the golf course," I said as we walked. "It seems like an odd place for business."

"Not at all. I hold most of my important meetings on the course. It helps me see the other person as they truly are. Do they get overly pissed off when they hit a bad shot? How closely do they choose to follow the rules of golf? Or even if they will cheat just to win a hole?"

"I guess I've never thought of golf that way."

"Besides, these courses are some of the most beautiful places on the earth. I make it a habit to walk every course in every resort I own as often as my schedule allows. I like to make sure everything is up to my standards. Everyone who works here knows I'll be on the lookout for something amiss. It's their job to see I don't find anything."

Max and Tony hit onto the green while my ball flew over and landed in a sand trap about twenty yards past it. Max again took off with Milo while Tony and I walked to the green.

"Tony," I said as we walked. "I guess Max told you I'm looking into the kidnapping of Jackie Wade. Roger Wade was her husband, and he was murdered sometime last week. I've learned Roger was heavily invested in some of the Scottsdale resorts. The control of these resorts will probably go to Jackie. Do you have any idea who would want to kill him or why anyone would want to frame Jackie for it? I get the feeling that whoever is responsible for those things is also involved in the kidnapping. I've reached nothing but dead ends searching for her. I've also run out of ideas for where else to find her."

"Max told you I've dealt with Roger Wade once before. In that deal, I was merely a passive investor. Before my close association with Max, I was also involved in a couple of deals with Roger and his partner, Howard Spencer. I came to know Roger as an honest but excitable person who didn't seem to have the temperament for developing the land his family owned."

"There's a temperament needed to be a developer?"

"I believe there is. Apparently, I was not alone in my assessment. Over the years, I heard Roger found it harder and harder to obtain financial backing to develop his properties. The only time he ever did a first-class job on a golf resort was in building the Scottsdale Saguaro Sky. To be honest, that was only because his father had part ownership and kept him from doing a crappy job. The last few years, I've heard he's mostly bought and sold undeveloped land."

"Did he completely stop developing resorts?"

"I know he was involved in one large development deal a

couple of years ago. That was the Rio Rancho Resort, just outside of Carefree. I never got the full details of who he was working with or how the deal was financed. Rumor was the major financing was from Mexico, which typically means drug money from one of the drug cartels, but that was the rumor."

"For some reason, I keep hearing the name, Howard Spencer. Someone told me last night he didn't like Jackie. What do you know about him?"

"Howard and Roger were partners for many years, so he would have known Jackie. About two years ago, Roger and Howard's Rio Rancho project collapsed, which led them both into a financial crisis. Since then, Roger and Howard have both been selling off properties as fast as they can."

"Any idea what happened to cause the collapse and crisis for Roger and Howard?"

"I have a good idea, and I was somewhat involved, although I was not the cause of the crisis."

I chipped out of the sand and back onto the green, and then everyone two-putted. As we walked to the eleventh tee, Johnny took a call on his cell phone and then walked over to talk with Tony.

They muttered to each other in low whispers, so I backed away. I had no interest in knowing what they were saying.

Besides, it gave me a minute to be alone with Max. As always, it was a great feeling.

"Nice move," Max quietly said. "Hitting from the same tee box as us. Most women would have moved up to the front box. I saw the look Tony gave you. It seems you can't help but charm him."

"Well, it wasn't my intent to charm him," I said, also

keeping my voice low so no one other than Max could hear. "I've never liked how some women claim to be as good as men at golf when they get a thirty-yard advantage on every hole. If I'm going to win a hole, I want it to be because I played better, not because I had an advantage. That's just me."

Max only smiled and shook his head.

I looked over and saw Gabriella standing next to the cart, watching over Tony, as well as the rest of the group. Her eyes were constantly moving, scanning, and assessing.

Hanging from her shoulder was a large and expensive-looking black leather bag. I suspected the bag contained her Uzi, along with enough ammunition to start a small war.

"Gabriella?" I asked Max. "I thought she was only for emergencies."

"Well," he said, "the thing about emergencies is you never know when one will come up. Better to have her and not need her."

I lowered my voice further. Max had to bend over to hear what I was saying.

"Can I ask you something about her? Something personal? The last time we were all together, you remember the time I mean, I watched her as she fired her Uzi. I could swear shooting at those guys actually turned her on. Like it *really* turned her on. Was I seeing things, or did that really happen?"

"Gabriella is a woman of unusual wants, needs, and desires," Max said. "But I've known her for many years, and Tony trusts her completely. Besides, we all have our odd little quirks."

He stood back up and started talking again in a normal

voice.

"You're hitting well for not playing for a couple of years. With a little practice, you could be terrific."

"The clubs you picked out for me are great. They look brand new."

"I grabbed a set, along with a putter, from the pro shop this morning. I hope they're alright."

"They're perfect. Thank you. By the way, the cooler in my cart is full of Diet Pepsi? How'd you know?"

"Oh, at our last, um, business meeting, the one with all the diamonds, you asked if we had any Diet Pepsi. This was after you already had three scotches. We didn't have any then, so I thought I could make it up to you by bringing some along today."

"Thoughtful," I said. "Are there any other secrets of mine you know about?"

"Not yet, although I would love to explore you and uncover one or two more."

Stop flirting with the crime lieutenant.

"Hmm," I said. "So now you want to uncover my secrets? Sounds interesting."

I can't help it.

Chapter Eight

Tony came back to the tee box, and we got ready to hit. The eleventh hole was a straight par four with the pin in the middle of the green.

Max had honors and belted a shot that landed a few yards short of the green. Tony hit a shot that was straight and landed about sixty yards short of Max.

I hooked it, and my ball landed thirty yards short of Tony's, off the fairway in the short rough. Max and Milo took off in the cart again, letting me walk the fairway with Tony.

"In talking with Jackie," I said, "she told me that about two years ago, Roger was involved in a deal with a guy who really scared her. She thinks this scary guy called her and threatened her just before Roger was murdered."

"This man. What do you know about him?"

"According to Jackie, this guy is big, arrogant, and has serious anger issues. He has short black hair, dark bloodshot eyes, and a full black mustache. She said he looks to be in his late thirties or early forties and has a big scar on the left side of his face. Like maybe he'd been in a knife fight or gone through a windshield or something. In addition to English, he speaks Spanish, and at least one of his associates does as well."

"I believe I know the man you're referring to. I was only in the same room as him once, and we were never introduced. He seemed to be a silent partner in the resort development deal I spoke of, the one that went south about two years ago. This particular deal was in the process of going down the toilet, and Roger asked me for a meeting to discuss additional financing."

"What happened?" I asked.

"Roger and Howard had run into financing problems on the project. By the time they asked for my help, the project was too far gone to save. As I said, Roger never had the temperament to develop his land into a world-class resort. The quality of the construction work was poor, and too many corners had already been cut. Property values were falling at the time, and several of the original investors either backed out or refused to provide any more financing to save it."

"Does that happen often?"

"It's rare, but if not managed properly, resort projects can sometimes end up in a death spiral. I could see that this deal was already there. I told both Roger and Howard I would not invest in something that was so far gone. It would be good money after bad. As I told you, I may have been involved in the split-up of the partnership because, as far as I know, that was the last deal they ever tried to put together as partners."

"What happened to the resort?" I asked.

"The project eventually collapsed, as I predicted it would. Roger, Howard, and all their investors took a bath on that one. It may be the reason Roger and Howard have been selling off so many properties to make up for the losses."

"Jackie said Roger had had mood swings for the past two years," I said. "I guess that would explain it."

"In my opinion, Roger's main problem was he had no

strategic vision. His group bought the land and started building back when property values were still relatively high. I'm sure he thought real estate values would continue to climb, and they would ride the bubble up and make an even larger profit when they sold. Unfortunately, property values tanked as they were in the process of building, so they didn't even get their original investment in the land back. Matter-of-fact, I was the one who eventually bought the land and the shoddy buildings they had started putting up on the property. I was able to salvage some of the buildings, and fortunately, the golf course layout was still in pretty decent shape. I tore down and rebuilt about half of the buildings, finished the project, and then sold it to one of the big hotel chains. You see, I ended up taking something that was garbage and making something useful out of it."

"What about Roger and the other investors? You made a lot of money on their loss."

"That's true. I imagine they were pissed, but that's just the way these things are done. If you don't have the balls for it, you should be in another business."

We reached our balls, and Johnny pulled up with the cart. Tony and I both selected a club, then we both hit. Tony's landed on the green, while mine fell short.

"Tell me more about the kidnapping," he said as we walked to the green. "Do you have any idea who they were or why they kidnapped your friend?"

"There were at least five of them, and three of them had guns. They looked comfortable with crime, and they seemed like professionals. I wish I could tell you more, but everything happened rather fast."

"I've started some inquiries," Tony said. "If I hear anything, I'll have Max relay the information to you."

"Thanks, Tony. I appreciate it. We can use this as my favor, so we'll be even again."

Tony stopped walking and gave me the same strange look again.

"Laura Black," he finally said. "The favor I owe you is for something substantial, since you risked your life saving mine to earn it. Please consider this as something one friend would do for another. Who knows, someday I might ask you for something similar."

Yikes!

Tony and I chipped onto the green. Max sunk his first putt while Tony and I both two-putted.

~~~~

We all walked to the twelfth tee box together. So far, Max had shot two birdies, Tony had shot par, and I had hit two bogies. Actually, considering whom I was golfing with, I was rather proud of myself.

The twelfth was a short par three with a sand trap guarding the green. My goal was to get the ball over the sand trap without having it sail too far over the green.

Max went first and hit a beautiful shot that landed ten yards past the hole, then rolled back to within three yards of the pin. Tony hit next and landed on the right edge of the green. I shot last and was thrilled when my ball stopped on the green, about ten yards from the hole.

I couldn't help but smile at the shot, and I might have let out a little squeal of delight. I looked over to see both Tony and Max smiling back at me. Max and Milo took off in the cart while Tony and I walked to the green.

"Tony," I said, "when I think of building a resort, I think of having someone like Arnold Palmer or Jack Nicklaus design the golf course and then building a big hotel in the middle. You talk about it like it's a bunch of bankers getting together to roll the dice in a big crapshoot."

Tony smiled and shook his head.

"Building a new golf resort is sort of like the Hollywood process of producing a movie. You need upwards of two hundred million dollars anymore to build a first-class resort. Most people can't open up their wallet and pull that kinda money out. You usually need to organize a coalition of people. Sometimes the investors want to help finance the project, get a quick return, and cash out. I like those people. It makes it simple for everyone. Some offer financing but only in exchange for a long-term piece of the resort."

"How is it going with Mrs. Sternwood? If I remember right, you said you're splitting the new resort with her fifty-fifty."

"I won't have a problem with Muffy Sternwood. I've known her for as long as I've been out in Arizona. She's both smart and sensible. Matter-of-fact, it was her late husband, the general, who was my mentor when it came to building and running resorts. Before I got together with him, I'd never even played golf, let alone built a golf resort."

"He sounds like a remarkable man," I said. "I only know Muffy, but she's a force of nature in her own right."

"General Sternwood was one of a kind. He not only showed me how to do it right, but he also tried to teach me about thinking for the long term. You know that piece of land Muffy and me are building the new project on? General Sternwood bought that back in the early eighties when it was nothin' but four hundred acres of dry ranchland in the middle of nowhere. Sure, he bought it for next to nothin', but even at that, I always told him he was nuts buying desert land twenty miles north of downtown Scottsdale. Now, here it is, almost forty years later, and we have four hundred acres of virgin land sitting between the Boulders Resort and Troon North. The man had true vision, no mistaking that."

"Tony, your resorts have to be doing well. Why don't you switch to running resorts full time and get out of the other business?"

Tony looked at me thoughtfully for a moment. "It's a question I've asked myself as well," he finally said. "Unfortunately, it's not as simple as that. I've concluded my resorts are profitable and run so smoothly, at least in part, because of my other ventures. Running a high-end resort is a cutthroat business. The other resorts would love to see us go down. No mistaking that. It's the other side of the business that ensures they don't make a move on us."

"What could they do?"

"All sorts of things – labor troubles, supply problems, even an occasional fire is not outside the range of possibilities. Plus, with us, it's more than a job. I believe you've already sensed we're truly more like a family. We count on each other, and I'd never give up on a guy if he screws something up once or even twice. However, if I lost my other ventures, we'd become another business. My top people would come and go like in any other company. I'd spend more time on human resources and staffing issues than anything else."

We walked in silence for a few steps. My time with Tony was nearing its end, and I wanted to get as much from him as I could. I asked him something that had been troubling me since our first meeting.

"When we were together before, you had talked about someone called Valentino. You said you felt like you were under attack. Whatever happened with that?"

Tony stopped walking and looked at me. His face had gone stony.

"I trust you, Laura Black, so I will be candid with you. Since the last time we talked, the situation has only been getting worse. It's like there's a cancer eating away at my interests in Arizona. I've reached out to my friends who control the activities outside of Scottsdale, and their reports are similar. There's something fucked up going on out there, and I've spent the last few months trying to get my hands around it."

"What kind of things?" I asked. I really wasn't sure if I wanted to know the answer or not, but I was the one who asked the question.

"As I told you, it started out small, maybe six months ago, with rumors of things amiss. But over the last couple of months, there've been too many things going wrong at once to be a coincidence. I'm certain I'm under a coordinated attack, but there isn't a pattern, and nothing makes any sense. Word on the street is something big is about to go down. Shipments of mine have disappeared. People I care about have been roughed up and abused. Entire warehouses of my goods have been cleaned out. People have even started to disappear. Truth be told, I think there're some new graves out in the deep desert."

"You still don't know who's behind it?"

"No, and that's the maddening part. If I knew who my enemy was, I could begin to confront the situation. But, as of yet, the only name I have to go on is Valentino. I don't know if that's the name of the group or the man in charge. Maybe it has something to do with the cologne he wears. Who knows? So far, I don't know shit."

"Is there anything I can do to help?"

"Keep your ears open. You're a smart and resourceful girl, Laura Black. It's why you're on my team. I think you'll know something is amiss when you hear it."

We walked up to the green without talking. Tony was furthest out, and he two-putted. I should have gone next, but Max had an easy shot, and I offered to let him putt out. Okay, so I thought it would be fun to watch him putt, then to watch as he bent over to pick up his ball.

I'm such a bad girl.

Max easily made his putt, leaving the last putt to me. I was a good ten yards from the hole and took my time lining up the shot. It felt creepy knowing both Max and Tony were watching my ass as I bent over and lined up the putt.

I hit the ball solidly, and it started out way too fast and too far to the right. Remarkably, it gradually curved towards the cup, slowed down, then fell in with a beautiful plinking sound.

I couldn't help it. I raised my fist into the air and shouted out, "Yes!"

I turned and saw both Tony and Max were laughing and clapping. Max took our clubs and walked them back to the cart, leaving me alone again with Tony.

"Laura Black," he said. "I had an enjoyable time with you today. We should play again sometime soon. I can tell you haven't played in a while, but your fundamentals are sound. If you need some pointers, you should give Max a call. He's a good teacher, and I'm sure he could help your game out. Plus, just between us, he still talks about you, and I know he would enjoy your company."

"Thanks for talking with me today, Tony. I'm worried sick about Jackie, and I wasn't sure whom I could even ask about it. I think I have some new directions to head now."

He held out his hand, and I shook it.

"Not to worry," he said. "If I receive any information or find out anything else that might help, I'll have Max give you a call. Now if you'll excuse me, I have another meeting. Milo will drive you back to the valet."

I glanced over at the thirteenth tee and saw two men standing in the tee box, nervously glancing at us. One was smoking, and the other was pacing. They both looked like they had on brand new golf outfits.

I waved goodbye to Max, and he waved back. I then got into the green cart, and Milo drove me back to the clubhouse.

~~~~

I drove back to my apartment house, climbed the stairs, unlocked the door, and flopped onto my couch. Thirty seconds later, Marlowe was on my lap, demanding attention.

After a minute of listening to my happy cat purr, I pulled out my cell phone. I called Sophie and let her know what my Saturday afternoon had been like.

"No shit," she said. "You met with Tough Tony again? Anybody get beat up this time? Was there a shooting? What about the buildings? Any of the buildings over there blow up?"

"It was pretty quiet on the violence and property damage side this time. Actually, it was kind of pleasant going out and playing golf with Max and Tony. It's a beautiful course, and I got a lot of information."

"Well, I wouldn't get too chummy with Tough Tony if I were you. He reminds me of this boa constrictor my cousin once had. My cousin would buy mice and drop them in the glass tank where the snake lived. Sometimes the snake would eat the mouse right away, but sometimes the snake would completely ignore the mouse. Sometimes they'd be together for days. The mouse would get over its fear, and play with the snake, and sleep all curled up next to the snake, like they were best friends. Then one day, the snake would reach over and swallow the mouse whole. The mouse never saw it coming, but it's what snakes do. Mess around with Tough Tony too many times, and you and the mouse may have a lot of things in common."

"So why are you dating Milo and always trying to talk me into dating Max? Besides, I'm hoping I don't need to talk with Tony anymore."

"Let's hope so. I'd be totally bummed if anything happened to you."

"From last night and today," I said, "the name Howard Spencer keeps coming up. Plus, I know I've heard it before last night. I'm going to look into him and see if it gets me anywhere."

"Howard Spencer? The name doesn't ring a bell with me, but then again, I don't get out as much as you do. Maybe Gina or Lenny will know. I'll be glad to do a search on him. Um, do you need the standard one, or do you need the up-close and personal deep-dive search? Do you need it today, or can it wait until Monday?"

"Well…"

"Okay, I figured that. I'll swing by the office and start the secret search in a few minutes. Milo and I will try and make it to the Rhythm Room again tonight, so I can work on it until about seven o'clock. Hurricane Carla and Johnny Guitar are coming up from Tucson to play tonight. It should be a good show, maybe you should come with us. You could invite Max, and we could make it a hoodlum's holiday."

"I'm not inviting Max."

At least not yet.

"Fine," Sophie said, "but you'll be missing out. Max is one fine-looking man."

"And speaking of Max, why does the theme to the *Love Boat* play when he calls me? Have you been messing with my ringtones again?"

"Well, maybe. But you're getting nowhere fast with Reno, and I know Max likes you. The *Love Boat*'s one of my favorites. Remember when we binge-watched a half-dozen episodes last year? It was nice seeing everyone fall in love."

"I think you liked the show more than I did. I thought it was kind of lame. Besides, I am too getting somewhere with Reno, and you know I can't date someone who's in organized crime."

"It's not so bad. When I'm with Milo, we never talk about business, and everyone's really polite to us."

"Could it also be that Milo's six foot four, weighs two hundred and twenty pounds, and is armed?"

"Well, I suppose that could have something to do with it. I'll call you when I have some information put together on Howard Spencer. You can swing by the office and pick it up." She then started singing the theme to *The Love Boat*.

I shook my head and hung up.

~~~~

Rather than let Sophie work alone late on a Saturday afternoon, I decided I'd keep her company. I drove down to the office, parked in the back, and went in through the rear door. Sophie was already working at her desk.

On her computer screen, I could see she was already deep into the background of Howard Spencer. The printer was churning out papers.

I could see Sophie had already started several small piles of paper containing his personal information, financial data, credit history, and anything miscellaneous she happened to pick up along the way. Sophie would eventually take the piles and combine them into an easy-to-read report.

"Hey, Sophie, what have you got so far?" I asked.

"Well, at least this one's interesting. Much better than most of the guys Lenny has me look up. From what I can tell, Howard Spencer used to be rich and right in the middle of the Snottsdale social scene. Up until about two years ago, he was at every charity party and social event in the city. His picture was in the paper at least once a month for an art gallery opening or some kind of charity fundraising event."

"Must be nice."

"He was also a partner in a real estate development company. Howard, Jackie, and Roger Wade were the only employees. He was making like over ten million dollars a year for as far back as I can go. He had a house on the north side of Camelback Mountain and vacation homes scattered around the world."

"Not bad," I said. "Sounds like a pretty good life."

"Well, about two years ago, something happened. The partnership collapsed, and Howard's fortunes went to hell. He started a new development company, with himself listed as the only partner. That company has lost money each of the last two years. Last year it lost over six million dollars. He sold the houses, and I don't even have a current address for him. He's completely dropped out of the social scene. His credit's gone to shit. And, if it wasn't for his financial trail, it would've seemed like he'd totally dropped out of sight."

"Wow, I'm always amazed at how much information you

can get on these people. Why don't you have Lenny set up your computer so you could do this from home? It would save you from having to drive down here at weird times."

"No way. If I had it at home, he'd have me working nights and weekends. I don't mind doing it for you and Gina sometimes, but Lenny would want it all of the time."

She then motioned for me to get closer. As I leaned down, her voice dropped to a whisper.

"To be honest, I've always been kinda suspicious at how easily I can get all of this really personal information on anyone, just by typing in a name and a couple of items of personal history. I'm not sure all this special software is completely legal. Lenny won't let me put it on the office servers, the only place he lets me keep it is on my desk computer. We got the software right after Lenny helped out with that DEA case last year, and I think it came from them. I need to enter three different passwords and then type in a six-digit random security code from a key-fob Lenny gave me. Once I get in, the database doesn't even have a name. It just spews out information on whoever I want."

"Well, if it came from the government that makes it legal, right?"

"I don't know, it sorta scares me, and I only use it when I have to, but it sure has made my job easier. I hope no one comes in the middle of the night and takes it away. For important things like this, I'd hate to rely on the standard searches that only go through the credit bureaus and the internet."

"According to Tony, Howard and Roger were both involved in a big resort project that failed about two years ago. They both lost a ton of money. Did you get any information on the creepy, angry guy Jackie saw working with Roger and Howard?"

"Not a word. It's like he doesn't exist either. Of course, once I get a name, it will probably make the searching a lot more effective. I'll need to do a deep dive into the history of Howard's new company. If Howard had a silent partner on the financing side, it would probably come out in those records. I don't do searches like that very often, but somehow I get the feeling this secret software will let me do it."

"I hope so. If it was his voice on the phone the day Jackie was threatened, he must somehow be involved in her disappearance. How long until you can get those records?"

"Even with the magic software, it will still take a day or two. Don't ask me why, but deep company financial records always take that long. Maybe there are elves on the other side who need to look up stuff in filing cabinets or something."

"What's Gina up to? I might need some help with this one."

"Lenny still has her booked solid. She's down to two cheating spouse patrols. That's counting Raphael, the pool boy. But she also has that drug guy where she's trying to establish an alibi. That's been taking up most of her time. From what Gina says, the guy is most likely guilty as sin. I think she's been building up a case for his guilt more than his innocence."

"Gina can't help but be a police detective. Even after all this time."

"Yeah, about once a year, Lenny loses a big fee because Gina won't let him represent someone that she knows is guilty of a major crime. She always makes them turn themselves in and plea bargain. It has to piss Lenny off, but that's just what you get when you hire a cop."

As we talked, Sophie organized the piles of paper she'd printed. In less than ten minutes, she handed me the report of everything she'd gathered so far.

She then took off to get ready for her date with Milo. I told her I might swing by the Rhythm Room and meet up with them later, assuming nothing else came up during the night.

I went back to my cubicle and started reading the file. The one thing that stood out to me was the same thing that had attracted Sophie's attention.

Up until about two years ago, Howard had been wealthy and among the city's elite. Then, something happened that had made it all crash down. From the information Tony had given me, I knew the crash resulted from a resort project gone bad.

I went through the rest of the file, but as Sophie mentioned, Howard didn't have a record of where he was currently living. He'd sold his house on Camelback Mountain six months before for seven million dollars.

The year before, he'd sold vacation houses in Belize and on the Kona Coast. He'd also apparently been in the process of selling a beachfront home in Jamaica when the property went into foreclosure, and he lost it.

Except for a single business account and a personal checking account, Howard had closed all his brokerage, savings, and checking accounts. His old business, the one he had with Roger, was apparently called Spencer-Wade Land Development, Inc.

As far as I could tell, it still existed, but I didn't see any more information on it. Howard's new business was simply called Howard Spencer Land Development, Inc. The company was registered in Delaware, and there was no local address given, other than the house he'd just sold.

I pulled out my cell phone and gave Gina a call. She

picked it up, and I could hear she was in the car.

"Hey, Gina. How's it going?"

"I've been busy. It's been one of those weeks where I won't get a lot of sleep. Are you getting anywhere on Jackie Wade?"

"I'm not sure. I took your advice and met with Tony DiCenzo."

"Good, I'm glad you talked with him. How'd it go? Did anything blow up this time?"

"That's so not funny. No, nothing exploded, but I did get a lot of background on Roger Wade and his involvement in the resort development business. But there's a name that keeps popping up. And I know what you always say when a name keeps coming up."

"If you hear a name once, remember it. If you hear a name twice, look into it. And if you hear a name three times, drag him in for questioning."

"That's the one," I said. "I keep hearing the name, Howard Spencer. Do you know anything about him?"

"Um, I remember a Howard Spencer as being one of the Scottsdale party people, but that was a few years ago. He was some kind of businessman."

"Yup, that's the one. But I know I've heard someone talking about him within the past few days, and it wasn't in connection with Jackie. It's nowhere in my notes, so I'm asking around."

"Sorry, partner, it wasn't me. By the way, keep your ears open for anything related to drugs, drug shipments, or major drug buys in the next week or so. Next Tuesday especially. Nothing small. I'm looking to hear of anything big."

"Is this part of your drug alibi guy?"

"Yes, and I'm running into a wall. Actually, worse than a wall. My guy has started to back off on telling me about the shipment. It's like establishing an alibi isn't as important now as protecting his sources."

"No problem. I'll let you know if I hear anything."

I disconnected and let out a sigh of frustration. I then punched in Lenny's number. The phone rang five times and was about to go into voicemail when Lenny picked up.

"What?" he growled at me. "Have you found Jackie yet? I got off the phone with the lead detective a few minutes ago. Just so you know, his mood hasn't improved."

"I'm working on it. I keep getting hits on somebody named Howard Spencer. He was the partner of Roger Wade. I know I've heard the name before, but I can't place him. Gina doesn't know him; I thought maybe you did?"

"Oh, I know Howard Spencer, and yeah, I told you about him. Matter-of-fact, that was who the detective wanted to talk to me about when he called. I'm starting to get a bad feeling about this. Where are you? We need to talk."

"I'm in the office. Sophie ran a deep-dive report on Howard Spencer, and there are too many coincidences."

"Perfect. Stay there, and I'll be down in about twenty minutes."

I went into the break room and pulled a Diet Pepsi out of the fridge. I then sat at my desk and flipped through the rest of the report on Howard Spencer while I waited on Lenny.

I went through the financial information, which told a bleak story of a once profitable businessman falling into bankruptcy and worse. He now owed millions of dollars to over a dozen large banks and creditors.

I went through his real estate holdings, which had gone from dozens of large tracts of land to a single tiny parcel. He was having a hard time even giving that away due to some sort of soil contamination issue.

The twenty minutes of waiting stretched into thirty minutes and then into forty. I only rolled my eyes.

So typical of Lenny.

I kept flipping through the file. The last section was the miscellaneous information.

Howard was born in Connecticut. He had degrees from both Harvard and the Wharton School of Business.

He'd been married twice. From the pictures, the first wife had been for love and the second wife was strictly trophy. The trophy wife had divorced him two years ago, about the same time as his finances took a dive.

And then I saw it. He had one child, a boy from the first marriage who had taken his mother's last name. Terry Lennox.

Dog Farts.

~~~~

An hour after he'd hung up with me, Lenny came in through the back door. I followed him into his office.

Without speaking, he went to his wet bar and poured himself a Jim Beam over ice. He asked me if I wanted a drink too.

I was about to say no. I needed to keep focused.

But then I noticed he'd absent-mindedly picked up his bottle of twenty-one-year-old Balvenie scotch. This was the scotch he only drinks to celebrate big money wins with his most exclusive clients.

Over the last few months, I'd picked up an appreciation of Balvenie. So, instead, I said, "Yes, please."

He handed me the glass, and I spent several seconds watching the single ice cube swirling around, slowly melting. Then I held the glass up and took in a deep sniff. I loved the complex aroma.

It was deep and fruity, with just a hint of raisins. I took a sip, letting the hot pleasure flow through my mouth. The scotch seemed to dissolve and evaporate on my tongue, leaving a long and gentle nutty taste.

I took another sip, a slight shiver leaving goosebumps on my skin. The scotch was absolutely fantastic.

Damn.

I looked up and saw Lenny giving me an annoyed look. I think he'd just realized which bottle he'd used to pour my drink.

"Well, if you're done having sex with your scotch," he said. "Let's get started."

Lenny sat at his desk, and I took one of the wooden chairs positioned in front. The legs of the chair had been chosen to be especially short. This had the effect of making Lenny look even bigger behind his desk.

"Why didn't you tell me Howard Spencer was the father of Terry Lennox?" I asked.

"I didn't make a connection between Howard Spencer and Jackie Wade until the police called me this evening. I knew Howard was involved in real estate development, but I didn't realize Roger Wade was his partner. This sheds a totally new light on events."

I started to piece together a scenario of what'd happened, but I wanted to get Lenny's take. So, I shut up and let him talk.

"It was a week ago now. Howard Spencer called and asked me to help his son find his lost girlfriend. I didn't ask any questions; I thought it would be a chance for me to pay back an old debt. Now, of course, I'm starting to think he set me up to find Jackie with his son as an excuse. The reasons for him doing this are unknown."

"What happened tonight?" I asked.

"Well," he said as he lit up a cigarette. "The police called me about an hour and a half ago and started asking me about Howard Spencer. They asked if I knew him. Seems he and Roger Wade were business partners, and they want to talk with him about both the murder of Roger Wade and the disappearance of Jackie Wade."

"What did you say?"

"I said, sure, I know him. Matter-of-fact, we took on his son as a client about a week ago. They wanted to know why we would do that. I told them it's privileged. They asked if I knew the current whereabouts of Howard Spencer. I told them I hadn't seen him in several years. They asked me where he was currently living. I told them I didn't know. They asked what his phone number was. I said he was the one who called me. They started to imply I was impeding the investigation. I started to imply they can take a flying fuck. And then, some heated words were exchanged on both sides."

"That doesn't sound so good," I said.

Lenny shook his head and waved his hand in dismissal. "Bottom line is, by helping Howard's son find Jackie and then by taking on Jackie as a client, it appears I've opened us up to an awkward situation. The fact that Jackie was about to be charged with murder and then disappeared has only made the situation worse."

"What can I do?" I quietly asked.

"Okay, here it is. In addition to finding Jackie, I need you to find Howard Spencer. I also need you to find out what the hell is going on with both him and Jackie."

I sat back in my chair, blew out a breath, and I may have rolled my eyes.

"The police are also looking for both of them, so try not to step on their toes too much. And work through me to make sure we feed them any material we dig up along the way. You know how pissy they get if we don't."

Chapter Nine

I went back to the break room and grabbed another Diet Pepsi from the fridge, then took a seat in my cubicle. I sipped the soda and tried to think.

First things first. I pulled out my phone and called Terry Lennox's number. It rang several times and then went to voicemail. I left a message for him to call me right away.

I tossed my phone on my desk with a deep sigh of frustration. I really disliked this part of the assignment. It always starts out as something easy that I think I have a handle on.

This time, my task was simply to find a wealthy Scottsdale cougar called Jackie Wade – something I sort of know how to do. She wasn't trying all that hard to hide, and it was relatively simple to find her.

Then there was a murder, and she got kidnapped. But that was okay. I've dealt with that before as well.

It wouldn't be as easy as finding a Scottsdale cougar who'd recently dumped her boy-toy and was simply hanging out in Mexico. However, it was still something I could probably do.

But now, in addition to finding Jackie, I also needed to

find a guy who'd been off the radar, possibly for months. Someone who the police, with all their resources, had no clue where to find him.

I took a deep breath in and then let it out.

Okay, not a problem. I have better resources than the Scottsdale Police Department. I'll find them both.

I picked up my phone and called Annie. She answered right away.

"Hey, Annie," I said. "Have you or the girls heard anything new on Jackie?"

"No, I was hoping you had. We were out all night, and the girls have been hitting the Saturday weddings to see if they can pick up anything new. Pam and Sonia went to a charity auction at the Scottsdale Museum of Contemporary Art this afternoon. About half of the Snobsdale elite showed up, but so far, we haven't heard a thing."

"Is everyone going back out tonight?"

"Oh, sure. Saturday night is always prime time for the girls, and we'd be out in any case. But I have to be honest. Having Jackie missing is really starting to overcome me. I'm so worried and scared for her."

"I am too," I said, "but we'll find her. There's one new thing. In addition to Jackie, I'm also looking for Howard Spencer. Do you know if anyone saw him last night?"

"I'll ask the group. I didn't see him, but then again, I really wasn't looking for him."

"Let everyone know if they see him to call me right away."

"Will do, and that won't be a problem. Everyone has your number in their phone, and everyone promised to call you first when they find out anything. You'll also get a group text if any of us discovers anything helpful."

"I need to talk to Terry Lennox. I rang him on his cell, but there was no answer. Do you know where he's playing tonight?"

"I think he's at the Venue. There's a big charity event going on, and everybody will be there. I'm pretty sure *Dog Farts* is the entertainment. It's probably started already, but you can always catch him after the show or maybe even between sets."

"Thanks, Annie. I don't know what I'd do without your help."

~~~~~

Venue Scottsdale is a warehouse-sized building at the south end of Craftsman Court, just down the street from Dos Gringos and about two blocks from the office. I first went there to see a rock concert with George Thorogood and the Delaware Destroyers while I was in high school.

I've been back many times since. The name on the building has changed a couple of times over the years, but it's always been a great place to see a show.

~~~~~

As I walked down Craftsman Court, I passed Dos Gringos, and the smell of grilling carne asada hit me. I took a brief detour into the bar for a quick Diet Pepsi and a three-pack of street tacos.

~~~~~

Twenty minutes later, I stood at the box office at Venue Scottsdale, paying an outrageous cover so I could get in and talk to Terry Lennox. As I was paying, I heard the muffled booming sound from inside the club, indicating the band had already started its first set.

I stopped briefly before going in and tried to figure out which charity would be getting the money being collected. I looked over all the posters and asked several people.

All I could discover was the name of the foundation, which was apparently run by one of the old-money Scottsdale elite. No one had a clue what the charity actually was.

Included in the price of the cover charge was a looped "awareness ribbon" pin. The ribbon, green and blue with a yellow stripe, was apparently the symbol for whatever disease or social injustice the event supported.

Almost everyone had one on to show how much they cared about whatever charity it was. I put mine in my purse and walked in.

The interior of Venue Scottsdale is a large atrium surrounded by oversized open balconies that ring the second floor. The stage sits at the front of the atrium.

Off to either side are tables, game areas, and well-stocked bars. The club was over half-full, and more people were coming in by the minute.

As I walked through the atrium, I saw that Dog Farts were on the stage, under a dozen colored and flashing lights. They were playing a lively cover of an old Nelly song called *Hot in Herre*, a great piece about dancing and partying until you got so hot you had to take your clothes off.

The crowd was really into it, and the dance floor in front of the stage was packed. But, as far as I could tell, everyone still had their clothes on.

Looking at the band, they looked like a mix of an eighty's hair band and a contemporary pop group. Most of the band members were dressed in coordinated and stylish outfits of shiny purple shirts and black pants.

The exception was Terry, who was dressed in skin-tight white leather pants and a billowing, long-sleeved, crimson silk top. The shirt was unbuttoned down to his navel, exposing his well-developed chest.

Terry's blond hair was loosely curled and hung down to his shoulders. When Terry smiled, his teeth were a bright white that showed all the way to the back of the atrium.

I could see why so many women were initially attracted to him. If I hadn't already known he was a total idiot, I might have fallen for him myself.

Like Terry, the other band members had long curly hair. Several large electric fans had been placed around the stage, causing everyone's hair to blow in the breeze as they played.

It sort of made them look like a music video from the eighties. It was a nice effect.

As the band played, they spent a lot of time dancing around the stage with exaggerated movements and a lot of hair flipping. Personally, I've always liked a band that pays more attention to the music than to the onstage antics, but that's just me. The crowd really seemed to love their clowning around.

The Nelly song ended, and the band launched into one of their own tunes. It was good, and I could see why Sophie had bought their CD. It was a ballad, and Terry sang with sweetness and genuine emotion.

As I moved closer to the stage, I noticed several of the women near the front looked up at Terry with mingled looks of adoration and lust. Unfortunately, I knew these women would make my task of talking to Terry tonight that much harder.

Obviously, I wasn't going to be able to get near Terry while he was playing, and I wasn't even going to try to get his attention while he was on stage. Instead, I went up to the bar to wait until the set was over.

Beer and soft drinks were included with the cover charge. I asked for a Diet Pepsi, but all they had was Coke.

My lips were still burning and tingling from the hot sauce that I had dumped on the tacos. I drank the Coke in big slurps until the fire on my lips was mostly out.

The band's first set ended at about ten-thirty. I'd been hoping they'd circulate through the crowd during the break. Unfortunately, Terry and the rest of the band quickly disappeared backstage.

I went around back, trying to figure out a way to get to the dressing room. When I got there, I saw the door leading to the back was blocked by a group of ten or fifteen women, all of whom were trying to talk their way past two large and extremely bored-looking bouncers.

Damn.

I started feeling a little down at my lack of progress, so I made my way back to my stool at the bar and ordered another Coke. As I sipped it, I kept glancing around to see if I knew anyone in the club, but I didn't recognize a soul.

After about half an hour, the band came back on stage to a loud round of cheering and applause. If anything, the crowd had grown between sets, and the club was now packed.

As the band played, I noticed there were two distinct groups in the room. The first was the older and better-dressed group, most likely associated with whatever charitable cause the foundation supported. They all had their awareness ribbons proudly displayed on their chests, and most of them had a mixed drink of some sort in their hands.

The other group was clearly here for the music. They mainly were drinking the complimentary beer in red Solo cups. Their awareness ribbons were stuck wherever they thought would look the most outrageous. Both groups were doing their best to stay apart from the other, even on the dance floor.

Half an hour into the set, I saw Pammy, Annie, Sonia, and Elle come into the club. As usual, each was dressed with a mix of class and sexy sophistication.

Their hair and makeup were as perfect as if they'd each spent an hour in front of the mirror, which maybe they had. They made walking in five-inch heels look effortless.

I waved, and they came over to the bar. As always, they arrived surrounded by a delicate cloud of mingled high-end perfumes.

"Have you heard anything new about Jackie?" Pam asked.

"Not a thing," I said. "I suppose that Annie told you I'm also looking for Howard Spencer. He might have some additional information for us."

"Annie told us," Elle said, "but so far, there hasn't been any word on either Jackie or Howard."

"Sonia and I were at an art auction and a wedding reception today," Pam said. "Everyone's worried sick about Jackie. Nobody thinks she had anything to do with Roger's death, of course. In fact, most people are worried Jackie will be next if she's not found soon."

"Did you have any luck with that?" I asked.

"Unfortunately, we didn't hear anything helpful. Annie told us you'd want to talk to Terry Lennox tonight, so we thought we'd come here and report to you in person. Besides, about half of the old-money charity crowd in Scottsdale will be here tonight. It'll be a good chance to ask around about Jackie."

"Thanks for your help," I said. "The tip you dug up about Howard last night could possibly lead somewhere. Well, that's assuming anyone can find him. He's been keeping a pretty low profile lately."

"Do you know what Howard has to do with Jackie?" Pam asked. "I know Howard and Roger used to be partners, but I thought they dissolved the company a couple of years ago. I've seen Howard around the clubs occasionally, but that's about it."

"I don't know anything yet," I said. "But his name keeps coming up, and even the police are taking an interest in him. Talking to him could help us find Jackie."

"We're keeping an eye out and asking around," Annie said. "If he's out there, we'll find him."

The women all got mixed drinks, then went off to work the room. I nursed my Coke for another ten minutes while scanning the crowd, looking for anyone I knew.

My eyes suddenly focused on a group of the charity sponsors. In the middle of the group was Margaret Sternwood.

Margaret, or Muffy to her friends, is the widow of General Sternwood, one of the original Scottsdale cattle barons and land developers. She's now in her eighties but still seems as sharp as ever. As always, she was decked out in at least a hundred thousand dollars' worth of jewelry.

During an assignment a couple of months before, I helped free Muffy's grandson, Alex, from some Russian thugs. Since then, Alex has proposed to my friend, Danica Taylor, and the wedding isn't far off.

Muffy is also in the process of building a new golf resort with Tony DiCenzo. She's a blend of old money toughness and old lady charm.

I walked over to the group, and Muffy recognized me right away.

"Well, Laura Black," Muffy said. "I haven't seen you since we met at the auto auction, and that was months ago. How have you been? You know, I never did get a chance to thank you properly for what you did for Alexander and me."

"I've been good, and I was happy to help. Actually, I'm glad you're here tonight. I'm working on something new. Do you have a minute to talk?"

"Well, of course, dear," Muffy said. "Let's find somewhere quiet where we can chat."

We left the group and went over to an empty table on the side of the atrium. It was quiet enough so we could talk without having to yell at each other.

"How's the car you bought at the auction?" I asked. "It was a 1953 Ford Vega Roadster, wasn't it? Have you taken it out for a road trip yet?"

"Cars like that don't go on a road trip," she said with a laugh. "Unless there's a crew filming it for a movie. That car's going into the lobby of the new resort I'm putting up. I assume you've heard the details of that particular deal?" As she asked the question, she gave me a sly smile, and her eyes lit up with a mischievous twinkle.

"I've heard all about it," I said. "And, I hear Alex is going to play a part in running it."

"You heard right. You know, Alex really seems to have come around the past couple of months. He's more mature and responsible than ever. If I'd known then what I know

now, I would have hired a couple of Russians to beat the tar out of him years ago. It would have saved everyone a lot of trouble."

Fortunately, from her smile, I could see she wasn't being serious. At least, I hoped she wasn't serious.

"Muffy," I said. "I'm looking into the kidnapping of Jackie Wade. Her husband was murdered, and now everyone's concerned about her safety."

"I heard about the poor girl. I'm so sorry for her. The whole thing sounds like a real mess for everyone involved."

"Did you know Roger Wade?"

"I've met Roger, although I was more familiar with his father and grandfather. The Wades were one of the original families who came to Scottsdale after the war."

"Tell me about that."

"We all started out in the cattle business, of course. But when Anne McCormick died, her ranch was bought out by Kaiser-Aetna and then turned into the McCormick Ranch golf resort. That was the start of the boom. We all thought maybe there was something better to do with our ranchland other than simply raise cattle."

"What about the Wades?"

"Like us, Roger's grandfather thought the valley could be transformed into something special. Certainly, more than just the ranching and agriculture that was here when we started."

"Do you know of anyone who would want to harm Jackie or Roger? Maybe someone who had a grudge against one or both of them?"

"I never got to know Jackie, but Roger seemed like an honorable man, even if his work was sometimes shoddy. His father was the same way. My late husband worked on a couple of deals with him back in the eighties."

"What about Howard Spencer?" I asked. "Do you know anything about him or where he could be now?"

"We never had any dealings directly with Howard, but again, we did a few deals with his father and grandfather. The Spencers have been in Scottsdale almost as long as the Wades, but to be honest, I never really trusted them."

"Why not?"

"They were always more concerned about making money off a deal rather than in developing the property. Most of the buildings they put up in the seventies and eighties were cheap junk, and many have already been torn down. Plus, they always wanted to be creative about the accounting."

"Creative, how?" I asked.

"As in, they always kept two sets of books. One for the taxman and one that showed what they were really doing. It was not an uncommon practice back then before everything was computerized. But we never went along with it, and after a while, my husband stopped doing business with the Spencers altogether."

"How do you remember this after all these years?"

"I was the bookkeeper for the business, dear. I remember everything about the financing."

"I'm looking for Howard Spencer. He might have some information that could be useful. Do you know anywhere his family had houses or other properties? Somewhere he could hole up now that his personal finances have taken a bad turn?"

"Now that's stretching my memory. Let's see. I remember his father bought a place in Hawaii, somewhere on the Big Island, I think. He had a vacation home somewhere on the coast in Central America, El Salvador, or maybe Belize. He had a cabin up by Payson, and he talked about buying a villa in Tuscany. I also heard he had built a lovely house across the valley from me, on the north side of Camelback, but I never was there, so I don't know exactly where it is."

"The villa's new to me. So is the cabin. Do you know where in Payson it is?"

"It's a few miles west of town. He called it a cabin, but it was more like a small house built on the side of a mountain. His father bought several hundred acres in the valley where the cabin is, back in the sixties. Of course, when land values started to rise up there, I'm sure he would've sold most of it off. We went there once for a party Howard's father hosted. This must have been in the late eighties or the early nineties."

"You wouldn't still remember how to get there, would you?"

"My husband was driving, and I don't remember exactly where it was, somewhere past where they rebuilt the Zane Grey cabin. I remember the Spencer's cabin had a lovely redwood deck and had a great view of a heavily wooded valley. When we were up there, I remember Howard's father hinted the cabin wasn't on the books, so his creditors wouldn't be able to find it."

"Thanks," I said. "That sounds promising. I'll check into it."

"I'm sorry I can't be more helpful. I don't get out as much as I used to, and I'm starting to lose touch with who's who in Scottsdale. In fact, I probably couldn't name more than a dozen people in this entire nightclub, and that's including you."

"Okay," I said. "One last question. Do you know which charity this event is raising money for? Is it for a disease, or is it for buying shoes for poor children or education for minorities? No one seems to know."

Muffy looked at me with a blank stare, then down at her awareness ribbon, then over at her friends, who were all wearing their ribbons, and then looked back at me.

"I haven't the slightest idea. Well, I'll be damned."

~~~~

Dog Farts finished their last set at about twelve forty-five. The crowd slowly left the club or hung out to have one last drink before the bar closed.

I walked around to the backstage area and found Terry. He was in a dressing room between two skanky-looking women; one was a blonde, and the other was a brunette.

I had seen them both up against the stage, looking up at Terry most of the night. From the way they were talking and laughing with each other, I got the feeling I wasn't going to be able to speak with Terry alone.

As I got closer, Terry saw me. He put an arm around each of the nasty women and looked directly at me.

"Yo, Laura," he said, "I saw you in the crowd. So, how'd you like the show?"

"It was great. Hey, I need to talk to you, alone. It's about Jackie and the murder. It won't take more than five minutes."

"Hey, check this out," he said, ignoring me. "Jessica and Maria here are two of my biggest fans. We're going over to my house for an after-show party. Why don't we make it a foursome? It's still not too late for you to have some sweaty sex with a rock star."

Seriously?

"Um, thanks, but I think I'll just stop over tomorrow. When will you be up?"

Terry looked at the blonde and then at the brunette.

"These girls both look pretty healthy, and I can just sense the pent-up sexual frustration in both of them. I get the feeling we're going to be at it most of the night."

At this, both girls started giggling. The one he called Maria reached down and gave his package a firm squeeze through his leather pants. At this, Terry gave a slight nod of appreciation. This set the girls giggling again.

"Come by around one o'clock," he said. "We should be up by then."

~~~~

I couldn't help but feel a little discouraged as I walked back to the office. The bars and clubs were in the process of winding down for the night. There was the usual after-closing mix of laughing groups, snuggling couples, and lonely singles wandering the streets of Old Town Scottsdale.

I thought about Reno and his offer to spend the night with me. If I hadn't had to work, this one night could've easily turned into an entire weekend. Who knows what could've happened between us then?

I got back to my car and drove back to my apartment. Since I was so late getting home, I knew Marlowe would be sleeping next door at Grandma Peckham's. I changed into some soft pink pajamas then fell into bed.

~~~~

I woke up about eight o'clock and lay in bed for almost half an hour, trying to decide what more I could do to help find Jackie. Once again, I was out of leads and didn't know what to do next.

I looked at the clock and decided that eight-thirty on a Sunday morning was still too early to call the Cougars. I'd need to wait an hour or two before I called to see if they'd picked up anything new.

I took a shower and got dressed in a pretty outfit. Unfortunately, it didn't do a lot to improve my mood.

I knew Reno was an early riser, and he'd be up by now. Maybe he'd be able to help cheer me up.

I punched in his number and listened as the phone rang. He picked it up before it got to the third ring.

"Hey, handsome," I said, trying to sound cheerful despite being depressed about Jackie.

"Well, good morning. I figured you'd have been out all-night hunting down the bad guys."

"I was, but now my next move isn't until this afternoon. I was thinking I could come over and make you a big breakfast."

"I wish you could. Unfortunately, I'm teeing off with three guys from the fraud division at noon. If I'd known, I would much rather have spent my morning with you."

"It was a spur of the moment thing. Do you have time for a quick breakfast somewhere before you tee off?"

"That'd be great. You can have me until eleven. Then I'll need to head into Mesa. Meet at the Morning Squeeze?"

"Perfect, see you in twenty minutes."

~~~~

The Morning Squeeze is where Reno and I would go

whenever we went out for breakfast. It's on Scottsdale Road, just a couple of blocks from the office. The décor is friendly, and they do a great eggs Benedict.

I got there first and grabbed a big yellow booth towards the back. I was facing the front door, so I saw Reno when he arrived.

As usual, several of the women in the restaurant also saw him as he walked in. I noticed their eyes follow Reno as he walked to our table. Some of the women were less discreet with the staring than others.

I stood up as he got to the table. Reno hugged me and gave me a kiss. As always, it was terrific, but I was vaguely disappointed it didn't immediately lead to something more.

Our waitress appeared with two mugs of coffee, and we ordered right away. We both knew the menu.

"How goes your hunt for Jackie Wade?" Reno asked.

"I'm getting nowhere. She's been missing for two days, and all I have are rumors. Howard Spencer, Roger Wade's former business partner, may be involved, but I still don't see how. I've got a few leads on where to find him, but nothing solid. I'm going to spend the rest of the day looking for him."

"I haven't heard anything new through the grapevine. If I do, I'll let you know. Kidnappings happen all the time in Phoenix between the Mexican drug gangs, but they're rare in Scottsdale."

"Jackie wasn't involved with a Mexican drug gang."

"I assume you're right about that. I also heard the lead detective in the Roger Wade murder investigation almost blew a fuse when he heard his prime suspect had suddenly disappeared. I hope you can find her soon. I can see it getting sticky for Lenny since his client disappeared right before they charged her."

"She didn't disappear. She was kidnapped."

"I know that, but the lead doesn't see it that way. I'm just saying."

Our waitress came out with our breakfasts, and we dug in.

"Where are you playing golf today?" I asked.

"We got a tee time at a public course in Mesa."

"That's a long drive. Why not golf here in town?"

"Mostly because I'm a cop, and I don't have the two hundred dollars to spend on a round of golf."

"Wow, is it that much? No wonder the course looked so nice."

"I take it you've played up here recently?"

"Um, well, yeah. But it was only three holes, and it was strictly business. At least I didn't have to pay for it."

Reno looked at me for a second with his stony-faced cop look. I expected more questions. Instead, he shook his head and ate his breakfast.

~~~~~

Since I was so close to the office, I stopped in, going in through the rear security door. I sat in my cubicle and flipped through the paperwork on Terry Lennox and Jackie Wade. I then went through the paperwork on Roger Wade and Howard Spencer.

Feeling frustrated, I turned on my desktop computer to do some more research on Howard Spencer. As the computer started up, I heard the theme to the *Love Boat* coming from my purse.

I knew Max was calling, and I experienced a surge of happiness. I dug through my bag and pulled out the phone.

"Good morning," I said, trying to sound happy and cheerful.

"It's almost good afternoon. I'm glad I didn't wake you this time. I wanted to tell you what we've been able to gather so far regarding the information you wanted."

"That was quick."

"Well, you know us. Unfortunately, we still have almost nothing on the kidnapping. We think we have a name, but that's it."

"What name?"

"Carlos."

"Just Carlos?"

"Apparently, he's involved in one of the Mexican drug gangs. We're not sure which one. Does that ring a bell with you?"

"Not at all."

"We're trying to get more. The Mexican drug gangs kidnap members from each other's gangs all the time, and we seldom get involved."

"That's the second time I've heard that theory today. Jackie isn't involved with Mexican drug traffickers. She's just a wealthy Scottsdale woman who likes dating guys half her age."

"No one has any information on Jackie Wade being involved in the drug trade," Max said. "Before the kidnapping, she seemed to be completely outside of whatever she's involved in now."

"That still doesn't give us a lot to go on. Do you have anything on our creepy, angry man?"

"Nothing directly, at least not yet. Tony also remembers the man, assuming he's the same one. If we assume this man is Carlos, it will give us a direction to find him. The resort investment community is relatively close and tight-knit. Everyone seems to know everyone else. We have inquiries out."

"Thanks for doing that. So far, I haven't found a thing."

"You also asked about Howard Spencer, and you wanted to know when the company he owned with Roger Wade dissolved. It turns out that Spencer-Wade Land Development, Inc. is still legally intact. In fact, the company still owns several properties. Most of the properties that they own with clean titles are currently for sale. Tony said he gave you some background on the final deal that brought the company down."

"Yes, and it's amazing how an entire business can fall apart with one bad deal. I can see why everyone's always so careful. Thanks for all the information. I still don't know how any of this ties into Jackie's kidnapping, but the more I can find out, the better it usually is."

"Glad to do it. When we find out any more, I'll call you right away. And don't forget about my offer. I can still get us some plane tickets, and we'll be strolling on a Mexican beach next weekend."

Sweet!

"That sounds wonderful, but I'm going to be kinda busy the next few days. Makes it sort of hard to make plans."

"Yes, I suppose it would be."

~~~~

It was almost one o'clock when I drove into Terry Lennox's neighborhood. As always, pulling into his driveway and seeing the condition of the house was a little depressing. On the positive side, this was the one place in Scottsdale where I wasn't embarrassed about how my car looked.

When I rang the front doorbell, I expected that Terry and the two girls would still be naked and asleep on the couch. I was surprised when Terry came to the door, awake and fully dressed. A mug of steaming coffee was in his hand. The girls were nowhere to be seen.

"Yo, Laura," he said as we walked into his living room. "Hey, one o'clock on the nose. You're prompt. I got a new K-Cup machine. Would you like a coffee?"

"Um, sure, that'd be great."

As Terry went into the kitchen and made the coffee, I looked around the living room. It was now cleaned, vacuumed, and organized. It even smelled a little like fresh flowers.

I glanced into the kitchen, and it was spotless. I could only assume he had a professional cleaning service.

Terry came back with the coffee, and we sat on his couch.

"Look," I said. "I need you to be totally honest with me. There's been a murder and a kidnapping. Everything seems to revolve around your dad. Can you tell me everything you know about the relationship between you, your dad, and Jackie?"

He seemed to think about it for a minute, and then he nodded his head.

"Yeah, okay, you're right. Something fucked up's going on. So, check it out, here's the thing. I'd dated older babes a few times before, and they were usually okay. At least they didn't want me to buy 'em stuff, like the young chicks do. Jeez, with some of these girls, you nail 'em once, and they think you should buy 'em a fricken department store."

"Jackie?" I prompted.

"I've known Jackie D and her crew for a while, like everyone else does. Dad gave me a call about two months ago and told me to start dating her. He said he wanted me to find out where she kept her important papers and stuff. He said he didn't want me to steal anything. He only wanted to know where she kept them."

"So, what happened? Did you find out where she kept everything?"

"Oh yeah, I was really smooth with that. I asked her once if she had, like, a safety deposit box. I made up a totally bogus story about how I had one for papers and stuff. I asked her if she had one too. She said everything she had was in a little fireproof box she kept in her bedroom at the house. I looked for it a couple of times, but I never found it."

"What happened then?"

"It was like, out of nowhere, she says she doesn't want to see me again. Can you imagine a chick not wanting to see me again? It only shows maybe she's kinda mental after all. So, I called my dad and told him we'd stopped seeing each other, and I couldn't look for the box anymore. He said not to worry about it, so I didn't."

"Okay, that makes a lot of sense. But what about when she went missing? Was it your idea to call Lenny?"

"I'd never heard of Lenny. He was some lawyer dude my Dad knew. A few days after Jackie dumped me, dad called again. He said Jackie had disappeared and he needed to talk to her about something important. He said he'd called a lawyer friend, and one of the law firm's investigators would probably want to talk to me so they could find Jackie. I wasn't supposed to mention my dad, but to just go along with it. Besides, like I said, Jackie's hot in bed, and I really wouldn't mind getting back together with her."

"Any idea where I can find your Dad? I need to understand what's going on."

"I'm not sure where he's been staying the last few months. He sold his house, you know. I assumed maybe he was living with a lady friend. You know, my Dad always did have a way with the ladies. Like father, like son."

"Do you know if he still has a cabin up by Payson? Do you think he could be living there?"

"You mean Granddad's cabin? I haven't been there since I was a kid. I assumed Dad sold it years ago, but he never said."

"This is probably a dead-end, but do you remember how to get up there? I'd like to take a look around."

"Um, maybe. I kinda remember the area, but there are a lot of roads going in a lot of different directions up there."

"Can you come up with me? It shouldn't take more than about four or five hours total to run up and check it out."

"Okay, sure, I'm not playing tonight." He then fixed his eyes on my boobs. "But if Dad isn't up there, you'll owe me a favor. A wet sloppy favor, if you catch my drift."

"Um, didn't you have sex with two women all night last night?" I asked.

"That's why they call me the Love God. I'm always ready."

Gross.

"We'll take my car."

Chapter Ten

Payson is a peaceful mountain town about eighty miles northeast of Scottsdale. It sits at the base of the Mogollon Rim, a line of cliffs that extend across central Arizona for almost two hundred miles.

The cliffs of the Rim are three thousand feet high. They are the dividing line between the warm deserts of southern Arizona and the colder Colorado Plateau to the north.

During the nineteen-twenties, the famous western writer, Zane Grey, owned a cabin outside of town. He'd come up in the summers and write about Arizona and western life in general.

After his death, his cabin became a popular museum, but it was later destroyed in a forest fire. The town of Payson then built an exact replica in a park west of town and again made it into a museum. According to Muffy, this was the starting point in the search for Howard's cabin.

Terry and I drove up the Beeline Highway, which connects Scottsdale to points north and goes directly through Payson. In about an hour and a half, we'd made it to the town. We turned west at the sign that pointed to the park that held the Zane Gray cabin.

From the park, we followed the Doll Baby Ranch Road

west for several miles. Terry had his face pressed to the window, looking for anything that seemed familiar. A few rough cabins were dotted along the hills, but nothing that could be described as a small house.

I had a flash of inspiration. I pulled over and called Muffy Sternwood on a private number she'd given me a few months before. After ringing five or six times, Muffy answered the phone.

"Well, Laura Black, you're the last person I expected to call me today. What can I do for you, dear? Is this about the kidnapping?"

"Yes, I'm still looking for Howard Spencer. We're up in Payson, and I'm looking for his father's cabin. Do you remember anything that could help us find it?"

"Well, I remember we drove past the park where they rebuilt the Zane Grey cabin. I told you that part last night. We drove west for a while, then turned onto some road. I wasn't driving, so I wasn't paying attention to road names. Now that you mention it, I seem to remember something about peaches. Does that help?"

"We passed Peach Orchard Road about a mile back. Does that sound familiar?"

"It could be, but it was a long time ago, and I don't remember the road names. I do remember the cabin was built on the side of a hill facing north. It had a beautiful view of a wide valley. We came up to the cabin from the road below and got a good view of the deck and the picture windows facing north. It was quite dramatic, as I recall."

"Thanks, Muffy," I said. "You've been a huge help."

We drove back to the turnoff for Peach Orchard Road. It didn't look like more than a side street, but as I went down it, the road continued west into the mountains.

After about two miles of slow twists and turns, the road started to crawl along the side of a mountain. There was a broad valley visible to the north.

We'd gone another mile when I saw a house come into view. It had been built a little way above the road, and I could see a large deck and picture window that looked over the valley.

"Yo, that looks like the place," Terry said.

I turned into the drive and went the fifty yards up to the house. We parked next to a building that looked like a garage and walked up to the door.

We knocked, but there was no answer. We peered in the windows and walked around to the deck, but we didn't see anyone.

It was a gorgeous day with a deep blue sky, big fluffy clouds, and a cool light breeze. Temperatures were somewhere in the upper sixties. Since Terry and I were both Scottsdale natives, we each had on a light jacket.

The deck had a lovely view of the valley. Terry and I spent a minute smelling the pine trees and taking in the scenery.

"Stay here," I said. "I have some lock-picking tools in the car. It doesn't look like anyone's been here, but let's find out for sure."

I walked back to my car. My tools were in the trunk, and it took me a minute of digging around until I found them.

When I stood up and closed the trunk lid, I saw a man standing next to the garage. I also noticed he was pointing a gun at me.

Crap.

"Who are you, and what do you want?" he said, still pointing the gun at my chest.

"My name's Laura Black. I'm an investigator for the law firm representing Jacquelyn Wade. She was kidnapped two days ago, and we're trying to find out what happened to her."

"And why should I believe you? How do I know you weren't sent by Carlos?"

"Dad?"

We both looked over and saw that Terry had walked around the corner of the house. He had a puzzled look on his face. It was likely he'd never seen his father point a gun at anyone before.

"Terry," the man said. "What are you doing here?"

"We're looking for Jackie D. Dad, the gun is totally uncool."

The man I now took to be Howard Spencer looked down at the pistol and slowly lowered it.

"Look," he said, "I'm sorry about the gun. But I'm in some trouble, and I have people looking for me. I was on the deck when I saw your car coming up the road. I came out to the garage and waited for you to go away. When I heard you digging around in your car, all I could think was that you were getting out your guns, so I came out. But I still have the same question, how do I know you're who you say you are."

"Dad, she's the one from Lenny Shapiro's office who tracked down Jackie D in Mexico. We've been working together for over a week."

At this, Howard relaxed and slipped the gun into his waistband behind his back.

"Alright, let's go sit on the deck. I want to keep a watch

on the road."

We all walked back to the deck. Howard took out a set of keys and unlocked the cabin. He got three beers from the fridge, came back out, and passed them around.

There were several comfortable wooden chairs scattered across the deck. We sat in the three that had the best view of the road below and the valley beyond.

We made small talk as the sun went down over the mountains. The clouds across the valley lit up and glowed with the bright reds, yellows, and oranges of a beautiful Arizona sunset.

We sipped three more beers as the sky darkened and the stars came out. Across the valley, lights from a half dozen cabins twinkled between the pine trees.

No one spoke for several minutes. I got the feeling Howard was gathering his courage to explain what was going on. I didn't interfere, and finally, he spoke.

"I'd like you to understand what happened," Howard said. "In case something happens to me, the truth about the murder will still need to come out. I've been watching the news, and Jackie's in enough trouble as it is. I don't want to see a murder charge hanging over her head."

"Alright, what happened?" I said. Glancing over at Terry, I saw he was closely following the conversation. "Um, maybe you'd like to discuss this in private?"

"No, it's okay," Howard said. "Terry's old enough to learn life isn't all about parties and getting the girls. He should know how I screwed up, so maybe he'll do things differently when it's his turn to make an important choice. Even with the most optimistic outcome, it's likely I'll be charged with several crimes. He should hear about it directly from me before he reads about it in the papers."

"Okay," I said. "Tell it however you think best."

"Before I go into what happened with the murder, you'll have to understand that my family has been buying land, selling land, and involved in development projects in Scottsdale for over sixty years. The land my grandfather raised cattle on in the fifties is currently where some of the most prestigious golf resorts in the state are located. In the seventies and eighties, my father and grandfather developed dozens of tracts of virgin ranchland. It was the work they did that has made Scottsdale the vacation destination it is today. After business school, I gradually took over the family business. I then proceeded to run it into the ground."

"What happened?" I asked.

"Well, it took a long time to ruin what they'd built. In fact, I started out with a hot streak. For the first ten or fifteen years, everything I touched turned to gold. I got financing whenever I needed it, and I almost always sold at a large profit."

"Sounds like things were going great. What happened?" I asked.

"About ten years ago, I was offered a chance to get involved in a huge project, the Scottsdale Saguaro Sky Resort. The lead in the project was Roger Wade. His family had held the land since the fifties."

"What led you to get involved?"

"Roger needed financing to develop the resort, and at the time, I happened to have a pile of money I needed to put to work. We decided the best way to handle the project would be to put together a separate company. We called it Spencer-Wade Land Development. Honestly, I don't think Roger ever fully trusted me, but we worked together well enough. After we finished the Saguaro Sky, we decided to keep the partnership going, and every year we cranked out a good profit."

"I've been to the Saguaro Sky," I said. "It's a beautiful resort. I especially like the huge tropical pools there."

"Roger eventually bought out my share of the resort. I know I asked too much for my side of the project, but Roger gladly paid it. He said he felt the Saguaro Sky would be his family's legacy."

"So, what happened then?"

"About three years ago, we were about to take on the biggest project we'd ever attempted. Unfortunately, we were seriously short of the backing we needed to see it through. That's when we picked up an investment group from Mexico. At the time, they seemed like an answer to our prayers. Roger initially didn't want to have anything to do with them. His instincts were pretty good, as it turns out. But I finally convinced him they could provide the money we needed."

"What happened with the project?"

"Unfortunately, as we started to get into the heavy construction phase, there was a sudden drop in property values across Arizona. People who'd promised to provide financing backed out almost overnight. We called in every favor we could, but the whole project eventually collapsed. We were forced to sell out to Tony DiCenzo for pennies on the dollar. The bastard's probably still laughing at us."

Terry got up and stretched while Howard continued talking.

"We lost everything we'd put into the project, of course, plus we lost several properties we'd put up for collateral. That was bad enough, but it turns out the investment group from Mexico was only a front for a major drug syndicate. Investing with us was a way for them to launder some of their drug money back into the US. Turns out the guy we were working with is their local representative. His name is Carlos, but we later found out his men call him *El Carnicero*, which they say translates into the Butcher. I don't know how he earned the nickname, and I honestly don't want to find out."

"Jeez, what a mess," I said.

"Unfortunately, the syndicate wanted their money back, all of it, plus interest. Over the last two years, I've sold everything I could sell, and I've given it to Carlos. The only thing I have left is this place, and I couldn't sell it, even if I wanted to."

"Why not?"

"It's officially owned by a foundation that legally doesn't exist anymore. There's a non-revocable trust paying the taxes and utilities. My family will have it forever or at least until someone challenges ownership of the property in court."

"What about Roger?" I asked. "How'd he handle the problem?"

"I know Roger's been doing the same things as me," Howard said. "He certainly had a lot more to sell, so I knew he was going to come out of it okay. Unfortunately, Roger had taken several of the most valuable properties from Spencer-Wade Development and had transferred them into Jackie's name. He did this both for tax purposes and to keep them safe from creditors in case something unforeseen happened. And, if we're being honest, he also did it to keep them away from me. He even did this with the Scottsdale Saguaro Sky. As I said, he'd always considered it to be his family's crown jewel, and I know he was hoping to find a way to keep it. But it eventually became clear he would have to sell most of it to pay off Carlos and the Mexican syndicate."

"Do you know how everything was going to work?"

"The first step was for Roger to sign over the bulk of the Saguaro Sky to Carlos. Unfortunately, the resort was still in Jackie's name. So, Roger had Jackie sign the paperwork to transfer the Saguaro Sky back to Spencer-Wade Development. This was a few days before she moved out. Roger always had her sign documents, and she always went along with it. She knew she was only a legal placeholder for our company. But when Roger went to file Jackie's paperwork with the county, he couldn't find it. That document, along with the deeds and ownership paperwork to a dozen other properties in her name, had disappeared. Roger kept them all in his home office safe in a file he called his Jackie file. He assumed Jackie had gone in and taken the file without really knowing what was in it."

"Wow," I said. "What'd Roger do?"

"Well, it would have been relatively simple to have Jackie sign some new transfer documents. Unfortunately, after she moved out, she started having a real estate lawyer review any paperwork Roger gave her before signing anything. I think she became concerned Roger would try to take advantage of her. Jackie never knew what she was sitting on, of course. Still, I can imagine the stink her lawyer would make if Roger presented her with papers to sign away roughly three hundred million dollars' worth of property. Since then, he's sold several other properties his family had worked for years to acquire. Unfortunately, without the Saguaro Sky, it still didn't come close to covering what he owed."

"I can see why Roger was so stressed," I said.

"Roger needed to get the original transfer document back. Actually, he needed to get the entire file back from Jackie. In addition to outright ownership of the Saguaro Sky, other documents in the file show her as a partial owner of five other resorts along with several undeveloped properties scattered around Scottsdale. I know Roger casually mentioned it a few times to Jackie, trying not to raise her suspicions. Still, she kept referring him back to her lawyer. Finally, I got the idea that if we could somehow find out where she kept the document, we could go in and take it."

"What was your plan?"

"I knew Jackie had started hanging out in nightclubs, and she'd turned herself into some sort of sex cougar. I asked Terry if he'd start dating her and find out where she kept her documents. Since Terry and Jackie had never met before, I didn't think he would mind dating my business partner's wife. Terry discovered Jackie kept her documents in a fireproof file box in her bedroom. He said he'd looked for it but wasn't able to find it."

"Sorry, Dad," Terry said. "I searched her bedroom the best I could, but I didn't see anything that looked like what you were talking about."

"I understand," Howard said. "It was a longshot. You tried, and it didn't pan out. I'm sorry I got you involved in this. I never thought it'd go beyond getting the file from Jackie's house."

I watched as Terry nodded his head. He seemed to accept this wasn't his fault.

"Two weeks ago," Howard continued, "Carlos called us in for a meeting. Roger and I went and told him we were in the process of getting the document from Jackie. He flew into one of his rages and said he knew how to get Jackie out of her house, then we could go in and take the file. He drove down the street to a payphone, called her up, and threatened her. Later that night, the three of us went over to Jackie's house and turned the place upside down, trying to find the documents. We found a small file box in her bedroom, but it didn't have anything inside except for the deed to her house and a few tax documents. Carlos called up a couple of his men, and we all spent the rest of the night tearing up Jackie's house looking for the damn thing. We even started ripping into the walls to see if she had hidden the file there. But even though we turned the house inside out, we didn't find a thing."

"That explains a lot about what happened," I said.

"Finally, we went back to Jackie's bedroom to look one more time. We'd flipped over the mattress and gutted it when Carlos flew into yet another rage. He screamed that we weren't even trying to find the document. He then took a gun we'd found in the nightstand and shot Roger three times in the chest. He told me if I didn't find the document soon, he'd kill me too."

"That must have been horrible," I said.

"His next step was to kidnap Jackie and make her give us the document. It wasn't my idea, and I didn't want to be involved, but Carlos was now in control. Unfortunately, after Carlos threatened her, Jackie bolted out of Scottsdale, and we didn't have a clue where she went. They'd already put a tracking device on Jackie's Jaguar, but they lost her when she started driving in the deserts where there's no cell service. While we waited for Jackie's signal to reappear, Carlos had his men out searching for her, but that got us nowhere."

"She was in Mexico by then," I said.

"I needed Jackie to be found as quickly as possible, so I called up my shyster friend, Lenny Shapiro. I knew he had people who could find her and get her back without involving the police. I didn't think it would be hard to track her down since she always uses credit cards for everything. I didn't think she'd be smart enough to live off of cash for a week."

"If I hadn't talked to her friends," I said, "it would have been impossible for anyone to find her until she decided to come back."

"Well, I heard you'd found her in Mexico, and she came back into Arizona. Carlos was again able to track Jackie's car, first to her house and then to her friend Pam's. They kidnapped Jackie when you dropped her off Friday afternoon."

Howard hung his head and spoke in a whisper. "I believe after Carlos gets what he wants from Jackie, he'll probably kill her. I'm sure I'm on that list as well. I know too much."

Howard sighed and drained the rest of his beer.

"There it is. I've been hiding since right after the kidnapping. I thought I'd be pretty safe up here. I didn't think anyone knew about this place. Plus, I figured even if someone remembered my family once had a cabin in the woods, I didn't think anyone would actually be able to find it. You must be pretty good to track me down in only three days."

"You've got to go down to Scottsdale and tell the detectives what you know," I said. "They're not even convinced this is a real kidnapping. They think Jackie murdered her husband then ran. We're going to need the police's help if we want to get her back."

"I know," he said. "But when I do, I'll become a sitting duck for Carlos and his men. I'm sure they're already looking for me. If the police arrest me, there's no way they can protect me in jail. Carlos' boss is the leader of the Black Death, and he has a strong relationship with the Mexican prison gangs."

He paused and looked at Terry and me. After a moment, he spoke again.

"Anyway, I'll go down and talk to the police. Jackie was

always nice to me, and this isn't her fault. Besides, it's partially because of me that her husband is dead and she was kidnapped. I screwed up big time, but maybe this way, I can partially make up for it."

"It's too late to drive down to Scottsdale tonight," I said. "I'll make some phone calls, and we'll go down first thing in the morning."

~~~~

My first call was to Lenny to let him know what I'd found out.

"Okay, that's good," he said after I gave him the summary. "Get Howard down to the district station as soon as you can before he changes his mind. Make sure he's open and candid with the detectives. With his statement, the DA will be less likely to charge anyone with obstruction when Jackie doesn't show up for her interview tomorrow."

"And then maybe the police will work harder to find Jackie and get her back?" I asked.

"Yeah, that too. We need to get our client back."

I then called Reno so he could let everyone in the department know what was going on.

"Reno, I've found Howard Spencer."

"What? How'd you find Howard Spencer?"

"Long story. Call the lead detective and let him know Howard's coming into the Foothills district station first thing in the morning to make a statement. Jackie didn't murder her husband; it was a Mexican national named Carlos, AKA Carlos the Butcher."

"What? How do you know Carlos the Butcher killed Roger Wade?"

"Like I said, it's a long story. I also know for sure Jackie was kidnapped and is being held by Carlos."

"What? How do you know Jackie was kidnapped by Carlos?"

"Are you going to question everything I say, or are you going to get things moving?"

"Fine. I don't know how you always end up in the middle of these things. I sometimes wonder why Scottsdale even has a police department since you're out there doing everything for them."

"Hey, it's not my fault. I'm just doing my job."

"Alright, I know. But speaking of jobs, when are we going to get together? You still owe me big time."

"Soon."

"You always say soon. I've had the weekend off, and you've spent the entire time working."

"I know, it's been kinda busy. Maybe I should have come over and taken care of you this morning rather than us going out to breakfast."

"Really? Was that an option? Sure, now you tell me."

"I'll make up for it. I promise."

"When?"

"Soon."

~~~~~

We all woke up early, and I made everyone a quick breakfast from the things Howard had brought up to the cabin. Fortunately, he had coffee, and I found a working coffee pot.

It was one of the old percolator types, but it worked well

enough. When I drank the boiled coffee, I had a flashback to my grandparents' house in Phoenix and how their coffee tasted when they let me sip it as a kid.

Terry agreed to ride down with his dad to the police station in Scottsdale and also be there when Howard gave his statement. I said I would follow behind them and help if I could.

We arrived at the district police station about nine-thirty. Howard, Terry, and I were each interviewed by a separate detective for about an hour.

We were then asked to wait while the detectives met to discuss what they'd heard. Our stories must have matched up okay because Terry and I were told we were free to leave.

They wanted to interview Howard again to see what else they could learn. Still, the detective in charge thought he would probably be done later in the afternoon. Terry said he'd come back and pick up his dad.

~~~~~

I drove back to the office. Sophie had finished running the quick checks on Carlos the Butcher. As expected, all that came back was a grainy photograph that could have been anyone, along with a single-paragraph report.

Carlos, also known as Carlos the Butcher, was a prominent leader in the *Muerte Negra*, or Black Death syndicate. His last name was listed as unknown, as was his age, his residence, and his birthplace. According to the report, the only known associate of Carlos was the head of the Black Death, a vicious-looking man named Escobar Salazar.

"This isn't what we need," I said. "Can we use the secret software on him?"

"Well, okay. But it's starting to give me the creeps

whenever I use it. I keep expecting the Men in Black to bust through the door whenever I run it. You know, I sometimes want to type my own name into it, just to see what the government knows about my family and me. So far, I haven't gotten up the nerve."

"I don't blame you," I said. "It would make me sick to find out a close relative was a wanted felon. On the bright side, maybe a relative is actually a rich criminal mastermind, and you could hit them up for a loan."

"So far, I've been okay with not knowing. If times get tough, maybe I'll change my mind."

My cell phone rang. I looked at the caller ID and saw it had a Phoenix area code. I wasn't expecting a call, and I didn't recognize the number.

My heart sped up as hope sprang into my chest. Could this be Jackie? Maybe she had escaped. I answered and tried to ask three questions at once.

"Jackie, is that you? Where are you? Are you alright?"

"No," a man's voice slowly answered back. With one word, a horrible feeling settled in my stomach, making me feel like I would throw up. I told myself to breathe and tried to keep myself together.

"Who is this?" I asked. I had a bad feeling I already knew the answer.

"You may call me Carlos." He spoke slowly and distinctly with a heavy Spanish accent.

"Where's Jackie? I need to speak with her."

"Jackie is with me. She is safe. For the moment."

"I need to talk with her."

Suddenly the voice on the phone became livid.

"What you need to do is shut up!" the man screamed. "If you ever want to see your friend alive again, you will do exactly as I say! Tell me you understand!"

His fury was so intense that I could envision his face turning red and his body shaking with anger.

"Okay, okay, I understand," I said, trying to calm him down.

There was a pause for almost thirty seconds. I heard him breathing hard, hopefully trying to calm himself.

"First of all," the voice said, now in a more normal tone. "If you go to the police, your friend will die. Even if you do everything else I tell you to do. If there is even the hint of police involvement, I will kill her first and look for explanations later. Tell me – do you know I'm telling the truth on this?"

"Yes," I said. "I know you're telling the truth."

"She says you're clever. So, by now, you must be fully aware of who I am and what I'm looking for. I want a paper Jackie has signed. You know the one I mean, yes?"

"Yes, I know."

"Ah, so you are clever. That is good. Now listen carefully. She lied when she told Howard's son she kept her papers in her bedroom. She had only the unimportant ones there. The paper I need is located in a safety deposit box at her bank. The key to the box is still at her house. There is a policeman on guard to protect the crime scene. You'll need to get the key, go to the bank, and get the paper. Then you will bring the paper to me. Do you understand?"

"Yes," I said. I was trembling all over. "But where is the key? You searched the entire house."

"Yes!" he started screaming again. "But we were not

looking for a key! We were told the paper was in the house! We walked right past the key, many times!"

There was another pause, and I could hear him breathing heavily and again trying to compose himself.

"The key is in plain sight in the kitchen," he finally said in a normal tone. "There is a wall hanging with many keys on it. The key you need has a Scottsdale National Trust Bank ring on it. The keyring is blue, and you will know it's the right key because it looks unusual. You will need to sign papers at the bank to get to the safety deposit box, and the signatures must match exactly. You are a clever girl, so I know you can do it, no?"

"I can do it. When I get the paper, where do you want me to take it?"

"I have people watching the bank. I will call you when I know you have it."

The phone went dead, but I spent almost a minute with it still held up to my ear. I needed more information, and my mind was desperately thinking of what to do.

My first thought was to call Reno and ask for advice. He'd know police procedure and the best way to get the key without a fuss.

But Reno wouldn't let it stop there. He'd need to know why I needed it. He'd also want to make it official business, and we'd have yet another argument about letting the police handle police business.

But I'd talked with Carlos the Butcher. I knew if I screwed this up, Jackie would be hurt or killed, and it would be my fault.

I made a decision and called Gina.

"Hey, I need your help." I then downloaded her on my

conversation with Carlos.

"This is the part of the job I always have a problem with," she said. "We're obligated to go to the police with anything like this. They're better equipped to handle this type of situation, and legally it's the only thing to do. On the other hand, morally, our first duty is to our client. I don't doubt what Carlos says. At the first sign of a cop anywhere near where he's holding Jackie, I believe he'll kill her."

"What I can't understand is why there's a police guard on the house," I said. "Getting into a crime scene has never been a problem before."

"Anytime there's a major crime at the home of someone who's considered a celebrity, it's guarded. Otherwise, people break in and steal souvenirs to sell on eBay."

"Okay, so how're we going to do it?"

Gina thought for a moment.

"As an investigator for the law firm representing Jackie, you could make a case for entering the murder scene. Homicide and forensics have already gone through the house, so they probably won't object."

"What about the cop?"

"Chances are there's only one officer on the scene, and he'll regard it as a low-value assignment. If two people go in the house, I imagine you could distract the officer and pilfer anything you wanted."

"Okay, that could work. I'll get Sophie to help."

"Yes, but it's only step one."

"What's step two?"

"You need to get into the safety deposit box."

"I'll have the key."

"Yes, but you also need to sign to get into it. If the signatures don't match, they won't let you near it, or it will raise a red flag at the very least."

"Okay, I'll work on that. Is there a step three?"

"Step three will be finding out where Jackie is. You said Carlos would call you back. He'll probably use the same phone again, and he'll likely be somewhere close by Jackie when he does."

"That makes sense."

"Let's set it up with the cell carrier to get a location on the phone when he calls. Maybe they can even give us a general idea of where the first call was made from. It'll give us a starting point of where to look."

"How do you want to split it up?"

"You work on getting the key and going to the bank. I'll make the calls and set up the location trace with the cell phone company. When he calls back, we'll have an address."

I walked back up to the reception area and collapsed onto one of the red leather wing chairs next to Sophie's desk.

"What happened?" she asked. "I hate to tell you, but you sorta look like crap again."

"I'm going to need some help," I said. I then told her about my conversations with Carlos and Gina.

"Damn," she said. "Why do the crazy ones always call you? Oh well, what can I do to help?"

"My first step is to get the key. Gina's right. The police probably won't object if we say we need to take some pictures of the murder scene."

"I'll grab the camera," she said. "And since we're trying to distract the cop guarding the house, let me take my car separately. I'll stop by my apartment first and put on something that'll help distract him."

Sophie took off in her car, and I took off in mine. My first phone call was to the detective in charge of the murder investigation. We'd chatted a few hours earlier, and he'd given me his card

He still wasn't happy I'd shed doubt on his lead suspect, but I could tell his mind was occupied elsewhere. He was probably thinking about Carlos the Butcher and what it could mean to his murder investigation.

Going after a pretty Scottsdale cougar was one thing. Going after an international drug smuggler and known killer was something completely different.

After talking for about five minutes, he gave permission for me to enter the scene and take pictures. This was with the understanding I would be escorted by the officer, and I wouldn't touch anything.

I mentally crossed my fingers when I said I wouldn't. He then said he would radio the officer on the scene and give permission for me to enter.

My next call was to Pam. I said I had to go to Jackie's bank and get some things from her safety deposit box. I asked her if anyone in the group knew what her signature looked like.

"Oh, sure," she said. "I can do Jackie's signature. We sign each other's credit card receipts all the time. But you know they need more than a signature. I have a box at the same bank, and they also compare photos."

Photos? Crap.

My heart sank. "Damn, how are we going to get the papers now?"

"I think I know a way," Pam said. "I have an old wig I can wear. The color is close to Jackie's. The length is too short, but it should be close enough. Jackie and I both wear the same size, so it should work."

"Are you sure you want to go into a bank and impersonate Jackie? I'm not sure doing this is exactly legal."

"Do you think it will help get her back?"

"I can't make any promises, but it might."

"Then, of course. Why are you even asking? I'd do anything for her."

"Okay, perfect. I'll give you a call before I come over, but it shouldn't be too long."

Chapter Eleven

I pulled up in front of Jackie's house and parked behind the patrol car. I got out and told the officer who I was. Fortunately, the detective had already called, and I was expected.

About five minutes later, Sophie pulled in behind my car. She got out holding the big digital camera from the office.

She hadn't been kidding about dressing to distract. She'd put on a low-cut red knit top and a Wonder-Bra, so her boobs were all but falling out. As she walked up to the officer, I saw he'd taken notice and was indeed being distracted.

The officer led us through the garage and then had us both put on a pair of blue plastic booties as we walked into the kitchen. I saw the rack with the keys hanging on the wall, just as Carlos had said.

"Why don't you two go up and take the pictures," I said. "We all don't need to go up, and there'll be less chance of disturbing the scene."

The officer took another look at Sophie's distractions and eagerly agreed. They disappeared into the living room, and I heard them climb the stairs. I went to the rack and found the key.

It was just as Carlos had described. It was an unusual round shafted key on a blue Scottsdale National Trust Bank ring. I took the key off the rack and slipped it into my pocket.

In less than ten minutes, Sophie and the officer came back into the kitchen. They were chatting like old friends.

Sophie thanked the officer, and he said it was his pleasure. He then pulled out a card and handed it to her. She dug one of hers out of her purse and gave it to him.

Sophie extracted a promise from the officer, whose name turned out to be Michael, to call her. He promised he would.

As we got to our cars, I started laughing.

"You were supposed to distract him, not set up a date with him."

"Well, why not? He's cute, actually single, and besides, you're dating a cop. I was thinking maybe I should start dating one too."

Sophie left to go back to her apartment to change her clothes while I headed over to Pam's house. Before I left, I called to let her know I was on my way.

I made it to Pam's and knocked. When the door opened, I had to look twice. It appeared Jackie was standing in front of me.

"Well," Pam said as she posed for me. "What do you think?"

"That's amazing. You could be her twin."

"It's not so amazing. I know how she does her hair and makeup. This wig won't hold the style for more than an hour or two, even with all the products I used, but it should work long enough for us to get what you need."

~~~~~

We pulled into the bank parking lot at four-fifty. I looked around but didn't see any of Carlos' men.

Since the bank closed at five, we hurried into the lobby and went straight to the receptionist. She didn't look happy that customers had appeared minutes before she was leaving to go home.

Pam placed the key on the receptionist's desk, apologizing that it was so late, but she needed to grab something from her box. The receptionist typed the key number into her computer, and I saw a picture of Jackie pop up.

I had a terrifying thought – maybe the woman would recognize the name of Jacquelyn Wade from the news reports. If that was the case, I was hoping she didn't have a way to summon the police before we could get to the box and leave.

But who was I kidding? This was a bank. If she suspected anything amiss, the police would be there within minutes.

Fortunately, the receptionist just wanted us out of there as soon as possible. She asked Pam to sign an electronic pad with an oversized stylus, which made her signature all but illegible.

So much for their high-security system.

Since the guard, or whoever was supposed to lead us into the vault, had apparently already gone home for the night, the receptionist motioned for us to follow. She asked us to stand at the entrance to the vault while she went in.

The vault was smaller than I thought it would be, with only about fifty safety deposit boxes, all in a group on one of the walls. The receptionist went to one of the boxes, inserted Jackie's key, and then inserted a key dangling from a plastic bracelet on her wrist.

My heart pounded, and I was practically hyperventilating as I waited anxiously to see if we would get the box. So many things could go wrong.

Pam was apparently having similar thoughts. She grabbed my hand and squeezed it, to the point my fingers were going numb.

The receptionist smoothly turned both keys, opened the small door, and slid out a long metal box. She handed it to Pam, then hurried back to her desk.

Pam and I went into a small room next to the vault. She set the box on the table in the middle of the room, and we both spent a few moments staring at it. Finally, I reached out and lifted the metal lid.

Inside was a thick file holding maybe a hundred pieces of paper. The bundle had been folded in half to fit into the small box. I carefully lifted the file so the documents wouldn't all fall on the floor.

I put the file in my bag. Pam went back to the receptionist and told her she could have the box back. We then walked out of the bank and hurried back to my car.

When I dropped Pam off at her house, I thanked her and told her I'd call with any news. I then drove back to the law office in Old Town.

Sophie had beaten me back and was in the reception area, talking with Gina. I walked in with a big smile and told them I was successful. Lenny must have been waiting because he came out of his office as soon as I started talking to Sophie and Gina.

"Well?" Lenny asked.

I reached into my bag and pulled out the file, carefully placing it on Sophie's desk, making sure none of the loose papers fell out.

"Sophie," he said as he picked up the file and started flipping through it. "We don't know how long we'll have these documents. I want you to make a copy of everything in the folder."

"I've set it up with the cell carrier to trace the location of the next ten calls made from Carlos' phone," Gina said. "The first call was made from somewhere in south Scottsdale. With the next call, we'll be able to get the location of the phone down to about three hundred feet."

"Okay," Lenny said. "That's good. Our best bet is to make the exchange as quickly and smoothly as possible." He looked over at me. "Stick by your phone and answer it right away when it rings. Plug it in, so it has a good charge. This Carlos sounds a little insane, and I don't want an incident because your battery went dead."

Lenny went back into his office. Nervous, I made small talk with Gina while Sophie sat at her desk and started organizing the documents to be copied.

Every few seconds, I looked at my phone and imagined it was about to ring. I half wished it would, so we could get it over with. But I was also half hoping that it wouldn't.

Sophie mentioned she'd used the secret software on Carlos. But other than a few up-to-date pictures, there wasn't a lot of new information.

She also said she left the single-page report on my desk in a folder. I was about to walk back to my cubicle to read the document when my phone rang.

I looked down and saw the same Phoenix number displayed on the screen. I looked back and forth between Sophie and Gina. Lenny came out of his office and twirled his finger, giving me the hurry-up signal.

"Hello," I said as I answered the phone.

"Listen carefully," a voice I now knew as Carlos' said. "By now, you should have the paper I want. This is correct, no?"

"Yes, I have it."

"Very good. You will bring me the transfer document, undamaged. If everything is correct, I will give you your friend, and you may leave. If you try to deceive me, or if I see any police, you will both be killed. Do you understand?"

"Yes, I understand."

"I will call you tomorrow morning with the time and location of where to bring the paper. Make sure to answer your phone when I call."

The line went dead, and I fell into one of the red leather chairs. The brief conversation with Carlos had mentally wiped me out. I was already starting to worry about the exchange, even though it wouldn't happen until the morning.

Gina got on the phone and called her contact within the phone company. She wrote down the location, thanked the person, and hung up. She looked at the address for a few seconds, then her eyes got big.

"Oh, shit," she said. "That's my abandoned grocery warehouse in south Scottsdale, the one just south of Curry Road."

I'd had some experiences with the industrial and warehouse district of south Scottsdale, and they weren't fun memories.

"Why 'oh shit'?" I asked. "And how do you know it's an old food warehouse?"

"Because that's where my drug exchange is supposed to

take place tomorrow."

"Oh, shit."

"Exactly," Gina said. "Up until now, I didn't know or really care who got the drug shipment. Our only interest was in establishing an alibi for our client. Who, by the way, is obviously deeply involved in the drug trade and should turn himself in then throw himself on the mercy of the court," she said, looking at Lenny.

"Yeah," he said. "We should consider that." His tone told me he wasn't ready to give up his fee from the client quite yet.

"Well, I think we can now assume Carlos is the one who'll be receiving the drug shipment," Gina said.

"Oh, shit," Sophie said.

"Why 'oh shit' now?" I asked.

"Are we sure Tough Tony isn't involved in the drug delivery or exchange?"

"Hold on," Lenny said. "Do you think DiCenzo's part of this drug deal? If he is, we're going to need to back away. He's still legally a client of the firm. If we go to the authorities with this drug delivery thing and DiCenzo's involved, it could boomerang right back to us."

"I don't think he's involved," I said. "When I talked to Max and DiCenzo, Tony seemed truthful when he told me he didn't know who Carlos was. I think he would've at least told me this was something they were involved with, and we'd need to stay out of it."

"What?" Lenny asked. "Do you have some sort of hold over Tough Tony, so he has to tell you the truth?"

If you only knew.

"Just because Max is a panty dropper," Sophie said, "it still doesn't mean he's telling you everything he knows about the drug thing. Maybe you should ask him about it directly."

"That wouldn't be a bad idea," Gina said. "Tell him we know about the drug exchange and that we may be obligated to go to the police on it. See how he reacts."

"Yeah," Lenny said as he pointed at Gina. "I like that. Talk to him and find out for sure. I don't want to be at the top of Tough Tony's shit list."

I had to agree. Talking to Max made sense. I walked back to my cubicle, took a deep breath, and made the call.

"Max, I need to see you."

"Change your mind about Puerto Vallarta?"

Oh, yum!

"I still need a rain check on that one. I have a question, and it's something I don't want to discuss over the phone. Would you have any time to meet tonight?"

"Sure. Do you have time for dinner? How about Different Pointe of View? That restaurant has the best view in the city."

That would be so romantic.

"Definite rain check on that. Unfortunately, I don't have a lot of time tonight. Could we just meet for drinks somewhere close, like the Casablanca?"

"Of course. When can you meet?"

"As soon as you can get there. What's your schedule tonight?"

"I can be there in half an hour."

"Perfect, I'll see you there."

I hung up the phone and realized meeting Max in a half-hour gave me almost no time to fix my makeup or hair. Good thing it would be dark in there.

~~~~

It was less than a five-minute walk from the office to the Casablanca. When I got there, Max had already picked out a table with a great view of the city.

I felt a pang of regret that my job kept interfering with my love life. Maybe if I had a regular office job, I could also have a normal personal life.

I briefly envisioned going out on a date on a Friday night and the date lasting the entire weekend. I knew this was something ordinary people did, and I was a little bit sad that it didn't happen to me.

Max stood up when I reached the table. As I sat, he pushed in my chair. When the waitress came over to our table, Max ordered a Tanqueray and tonic while I requested a Diet Pepsi.

"Diet Pepsi?" he asked. "You must be busy tonight."

"Oh, you don't know how good a scotch sounds right now. But you're right, I do have a lot going on tonight, and I need to focus."

"It was nice seeing you on Saturday. We should do it more often."

"It was great playing golf with you. Why didn't you tell me you're so good?"

"Now, you want to know my secrets?"

"Well, I imagine you have some interesting things to uncover," I said with a smile.

Stop flirting.

The waitress came back with the drinks, and Max handed her a twenty. We each took a sip of our drinks and waited for the other to start talking.

"Okay," he said after a moment. "You wanted to ask me something?"

"Yeah, um, this is sort of a delicate question." I leaned close to Max and dropped my voice almost to a whisper. "Um, do you have anything in terms of a big shipment of, um, anything, coming into the country tomorrow, specifically into Scottsdale?"

"Why do you ask?" His voice had also gone down almost to a whisper level.

"Gina's working on an assignment, and she's stumbled onto a large shipment of, something, coming into the country from Mexico. If it's not yours, we'll probably need to go to the police. If it were yours, well, we'd need to reconsider. It somehow ties into Jackie Wade's kidnapping, and things are starting to get complicated."

"About Jackie and the kidnapping," he said, sitting up and talking just a little louder. "We still have inquiries out on Carlos. I told you we picked up a rumor that he's with one of the local drug gangs. So far, he's only a name. Like Keyser Söze in the movie *The Usual Suspects*. The only new thing we know about him for sure is that he drives a flashy red sports car."

"I've got more to add then. His name is Carlos the Butcher. He's the local leader of a drug cartel from Mexico called the Black Death."

"Really? You seem to have better sources than we do. We've heard of the Black Death over the last few months. But about all we know about them is they're one of a growing number of groups running drugs up from Mexico. So far, they've kept a low profile, and no one knows a lot about them. We don't know how big the group is or exactly what they're doing here. We assume it's small-time drugs, but who knows."

"Small-time? With a name like the Black Death? It sounds like they're pretty nasty."

"Oh, they all have names like that. When you deal in drugs and guns, no one would take you seriously if you said you were from the Fluffy Kitty drug cartel."

"I suppose you're right. Well? What about tomorrow?"

"No, tomorrow isn't anything we're involved in."

"Okay, thanks for letting me know. Although, I'm not sure if that helps or not. Jackie's been kidnapped by Carlos. We think he probably has her in the same old grocery warehouse in south Scottsdale, where the shipment will arrive. He said if we involve the police, he'll kill Jackie, and I believe him. I've talked to him, and the man seems to have a lot of issues."

"Well, we're not the police. Do you need any help with this?"

"Um, thanks. But probably not. Yes, we need all the help we can get, but I hope you understand I can't actually get involved with your group or what you do. That would be crossing a line I don't think I can do."

"We've had this conversation before," he said. "And of course, I understand. You're a nice girl, and you're probably right to stay away from the business side of what we do. But, it's there if you need it."

"Thanks, Max. It's nice knowing I have a friend out there."

"Just a friend?"

"Well, for now, anyway."

As we finished the drinks, I reluctantly mentioned I had to leave. We walked out of the lounge and down the stairs, Max leading the way.

Halfway down, he stopped and turned. Since I was still a step above him, our height was now about the same, and I found myself looking directly into his eyes.

He wrapped his hand around the back of my neck and pulled me in for a kiss. I hadn't been expecting this, but I instinctively responded by wrapping my arms around his waist and kissing him back.

Unlike some of Max's previous kisses, this one didn't drive me toward an immediate climax. This one was more about affection and romance.

It was a slow deep kiss, one I wanted to go on forever. It was a nice change, and I couldn't wait to see what the next kiss would bring.

I'll probably burn in hell for this.

~~~~

I walked back to the office. Gina and Sophie had gone for the night. Lenny was still in his office, working through a stack of papers.

"Well?" he called as he heard me walk into reception.

"Max says they don't have anything to do with it, even after I told him we were going to go to the police."

"Alright," Lenny said. "That settles that. If and when we contact the authorities, we've given DiCenzo a fair warning. I hope he remembers that if things turn to shit."

Even though it was starting to get late, I still didn't want to go home. The thought of meeting Carlos in the morning was playing havoc with my nerves.

I started thinking it would be good to learn as much about him as possible before the meeting. I went back to my cubicle and opened the folder Sophie had left on my desk.

Even with the magic software, there wasn't much in the file. As in the standard report, everything they knew about Carlos fit on a single page. But at least there were three recent pictures. Two were even in color.

Looking at the pictures of Carlos the Butcher made me shudder. Carlos looked big, mean, and his eyes looked a little insane. I started reading the report, and suddenly I couldn't breathe. My heart sped up, and I broke out in a sweat.

Oh, shit. Oh, shit. Oh, shit.

My hand shook as I took the piece of paper and slid it back into the manila folder. I then took out my cell phone and dialed Max.

He answered on the third ring with his usual confident and powerful voice. I felt like crying.

"Well, that was quick. Change your mind about dinner?"

"Max?" I said. I knew that my voice was trembling.

"Laura, what's wrong?"

"I need to talk to Tony. Right away. It's important."

Max grew serious. "I assume this is about business?"

"Yes."

"Okay, keep by your phone. I'll call you back as soon as I can."

~~~~

Less than ten minutes later, my phone rang. When it started playing the theme from *The Love Boat*, I answered right away.

"Tony's working in his office at the Tropical Paradise tonight," Max said. "He said he'll meet with you. I'll meet you in the lobby and take you up. Maybe thirty minutes?"

~~~~

I tried to stay focused as I drove up Scottsdale Road to the Tropical Paradise. It was one of a handful of high-end resorts Tony DiCenzo owned outright, and I'd been there several times before.

I turned into the main entrance and drove past the resort's huge tropical-themed fountain. The main reception building was located at the top of a small hill.

I knew this building contained the main lobby, several high-end shops, an art gallery, and some outstanding restaurants. It also apparently held the offices for Tough Tony DiCenzo.

Without thinking, I pulled up to the main entrance. A man in a red uniform opened my door and helped me out of my car.

Usually, I never use the valet. First, I can't afford it, and second, I always need the exercise I get from walking in from the parking lot.

But tonight, I didn't even think twice. I let the man hand me a claim token, and I walked into the lobby.

I briefly registered the beauty of the enormous indoor space of the main reception area. It normally gave you the feeling you were on a tropical island in the middle of the South Pacific.

The center of the space consists of a large waterfall splashing down into a lava rock basin. Several colossal fish tanks, filled with thousands of colorful tropical fish, were embedded in the lava rock making up the room's walls. Vines and lush tropical plants were everywhere.

Max stood near the main reception desk, talking with one of the hotel employees, a woman wearing a red pants suit. I noticed the woman was rather pretty. I was also somewhat surprised when I felt a pang of jealousy.

So, what's up with that?

Max saw me walking toward them. He lightly touched the woman's shoulder and quietly told her he'd talk to her later. Again, there was the slightest twinge of jealousy.

Stop with the jealousy. You have a boyfriend. Don't you?

"Are you okay?" Max asked as we walked across the lobby.

"Not really, but I have some information Tony needs to hear. I won't be able to sleep until I pass it on."

Max didn't press for more information. As always, I was impressed he let me work through things in my own way.

He led me up a wide curving stairway that went up to the second floor. We went past several ballrooms and conference rooms.

At the end of a wide hallway was a large pair of glass doors with Scottsdale Land and Resort Management, Inc. stenciled in large gold and black letters. A security podium stood on either side of the doors, each with a beefy, armed, and uniformed guard.

We went through the glass doors and into what was a large and luxurious office reception room. Max led me down one of the hallways branching out from reception.

Although it was getting to be later in the evening, a few people were still working in various offices and cubicles.

Turning a corner, we went down a long hallway that was much nicer than the other areas.

We passed several large offices, each housing the vice president of some department or another. At the end of the hallway was a living room setting, complete with black leather sofas and a large wooden desk.

On the walls hung several original oil paintings, all of which depicted a southwestern theme. Beyond the desk was a large and ornate door leading into yet another inner office.

Even at this late hour, an admin was at her desk, typing some memos into her computer. She turned her head, and I was startled to see it was Gabriella.

This was the first time I'd observed her dressed in anything other than skin-tight leather. Apparently, she had other duties in addition to being Tony's personal bodyguard.

As we walked by her desk, she glanced up at us. I saw and felt her eyes zero in on me. As always, her stare gave me a cold chill.

She reached under her desk and pushed a button. There was a faint click, and Max pushed open the heavy door, ushering me inside.

Tough Tony DiCenzo was seated behind an enormous desk. He had several papers spread out in front of him and was in the process of signing one when we walked in.

Tonight, he wore a white button-down shirt and a pair of black-rimmed reading glasses. It made him look less like a gangster and more like a businessman.

DiCenzo looked up as we moved further into the room.

"Laura Black, welcome. Please take a seat."

I sat in one of two wooden chairs in front of Tony's desk.

As with the chairs in front of Lenny's desk, these chairs were relatively short and uncomfortable.

The word *hot-seat* went through my mind. Max sat a respectful distance away on a black leather couch.

"Max says you have something you'd like to discuss with me," Tough Tony said in his gruff voice. "But, before we start, is there anything new concerning the situation with Jackie Wade? As you know, we've done business with her late husband, and I've met her socially several times. If there's anything we can do to help, please let us know. I hear she's being held by a man called Carlos the Butcher. I believe Max told you we know almost nothing about Carlos or his group."

"Actually, it's Carlos I need to talk to you about."

I took the folder out of my purse and handed it to Tony. He opened the folder and held up the single page of paper.

He scanned it for about ten seconds, and then his eyes opened wide. He continued to stare at the paper for a good minute before he set it down.

When he spoke, his voice had taken on an overly polite tone with traces of anger. It was more than a little unsettling. I'd never heard him talk like that, and it scared the willies out of me.

"The man in the photo on this page appears to be the same man I saw two years ago, in my meeting with Roger Wade and Howard Spencer," DiCenzo said. "The same man we talked about as we walked the golf course on Saturday."

"Yes," I said. "Everything fits together. He's the same man."

"I assume you believe the rest of this information is accurate?"

"As far as I know. It comes from some sort of government database. Actually, I'm not sure the information was ever meant to leave the law office."

"This is not a problem. You can return this to your office. A lot of things have become clear that were not clear before. Would you mind if I showed this to Max?"

"Of course not," I said. It still struck me as odd that Tony was being so polite at a time like this.

Max got up and walked over to the desk, standing next to my chair. Tony handed the paper across to him. He took it and started reading aloud:

"The Muerte Negra, also known as the Black Death narcotics cartel. Current operational territory: Widely throughout central Mexico, north-central Mexico, and Arizona. Current status of group: Attempting to consolidate cocaine and heroin importation and distribution throughout southern and central Arizona, including Phoenix and Scottsdale. Group organization and structure: Cartel leadership is located in central Mexico under Escobar Salazar. Field commanders are located in northern Mexico and central Arizona. Arizona field commander is identified as Mexican national Carlos Valentino, also known as El Carnicero, also known as the Butcher, also known as Carlos the Butcher.

Max glanced up at Tony. As often happened between these two, they didn't say a word, although I could sense a lot of information going back and forth between them.

"Carlos Valentino," Tony said quietly. "Well, Laura Black, it appears I now owe you two favors."

Chapter Twelve

I drove home and tried to go to sleep. I was exhausted from the events of the past week, but I was also scared to death about what would happen in the morning.

~~~~

I was in the twilight stage between being awake and almost asleep when I was jolted awake by a scream. It was a woman's scream.

I sat up in my bed, my heart pounding, listening hard, trying to figure out what it could be. I heard the scream again and then heard a loud thump

It took me a second to realize it originated from Grandma Peckham's apartment. It sounded like she was in trouble.

Still groggy, I got up and pulled out my pistol. I walked from my bedroom to the living room when I heard a sound from Grandma's apartment that sounded like giggling.

What the hell?

I stood against the wall separating my bedroom from Grandma's. There was another thump of something hitting the wall, then another, and then another.

I heard the scream again, but this time I realized it was

actually more of a moan. The screaming and moaning went on for several seconds, followed by more thumping against the wall.

Oh, okay. Good for you, Grandma!

I put the gun back in my purse and lay down on the bed. The thumping and moaning went on for a few minutes, then quieted down. But by then, I had fallen asleep.

~~~~

Even as exhausted as I was, I had a hard time sleeping. I woke up about two o'clock after having a nightmare about the last time I'd been involved in an exchange with a bunch of criminals.

In that one, I'd gotten shot at, and a building had exploded. Several people died, and I'd been lucky to escape with only a nasty bump on the head.

I got back to sleep around three, but by four-thirty, I was up again. Adrenaline was pumping through me to the point I knew rest was over for the night.

I went to the kitchen and put on a pot of coffee. It was more to have something to do than the need for caffeine.

As soon as I turned the coffee pot on, Marlowe appeared at my feet, demanding to be fed. I told him it was too early and he could wait, mostly because I didn't want to watch him throw up his breakfast.

I went back to the bedroom, took a long shower, and then put on what I consider to be my combat outfit: Black boots, black cargo pants, and a black T-shirt. I knew it wouldn't protect me from bullets or bad guys, but putting it on made me feel better and somewhat more in control, which was good enough for me.

I walked into the kitchen and poured a cup of coffee.

Marlowe was still harassing me, so I plopped a spoonful of Ocean Delight into his bowl. As always, he sucked up the food like he was starving, and three other cats were trying to take it away from him.

I went into the bathroom, put on a few swipes of makeup to cover the dark circles under my eyes, and pulled my hair back into a ponytail.

From the kitchen, I heard the *Aaaaaaaaaak!* sound of Marlowe throwing up. In my current nervous state, this really grossed me out. I grabbed my purse and hurried out the door.

~~~~

When I reached my car in the parking lot, I glanced off to the east and couldn't help but notice that the sunrise was going to be beautiful. I drove over to the office and parked but realized I didn't want to sit around an empty office waiting for everyone to come in.

Getting out of my car, I again noticed it was a beautiful spring day in Scottsdale. The day was already warm, and thousands of birds were singing. I decided to walk over to the Morning Squeeze.

It was still early enough to walk in and get my pick of tables. I ordered the eggs Benedict and coffee, but I really wasn't hungry. I tried to read the paper, but I kept losing focus.

The thing that really got to me was that the rest of the world treated this as just another Tuesday. People were getting ready to go to work. Students were finishing up homework assignments. Nobody knew what a truly shitty day this would be, at least for me.

I walked the three blocks back to the office, and it did me a world of good. It relaxed me and got me ready for whatever was going to happen. By the time I arrived, I was itching to go out and take on Carlos and his entire gang just to get Jackie back.

I walked in the front door. Gina and Sophie were standing in reception, both hysterical with laughter.

"How can you two be laughing?" I asked. "Don't you remember what's going on today?"

"I know," Sophie said between chuckles. "But Gina was just telling me what happened yesterday with Raphael, the pool boy." She looked over at Gina and started laughing again.

"Well," I said to Gina. "Go ahead and tell me. I need to hear something funny today."

"Well," she said, "you remember the assignment. Our client, dad, needed to get evidence that his mom was having an affair to break the prenup. Since I wasn't having any luck with the cameras in the bedrooms, I got permission from the client to install a few more around the rest of the house and the grounds. After I left the office last night, I went home and reviewed yesterday's videos. Long story short, it turns out that mom gets together with Raphael while little sister's at school in the morning. Mom spends an hour or so getting her needs filled, then she takes off to do her charity events and shopping, leaving the house empty for little sister to have her turn at Raphael when she comes home from school. Apparently, Mom's favorite place to play is in the cabana by the pool. It's a beautiful and secluded setting, and I can see why she likes it so much. But that also explains why I haven't been able to get any evidence on her before."

"Come on, tell her what happened," Sophie said, still with tears in her eyes from laughing.

"So, yesterday morning, mom and Raphael are going at it hard in the cabana when little sister suddenly appears. I still have no clue why she just showed up. She walked right up to them and just stood perfectly still with her mouth hanging open. Mom's back was to the pool gate, so she didn't see her daughter come in. Little sister watched her mom grinding Cowgirl on Raphael for about two minutes. Then little sister starts yelling and screaming at mom. Mom hops up, and before long, they're both yelling at one another."

"Tell her about Raphael," Sophie said, now laughing again.

"The funniest part was Raphael. Little sister and mom are yelling at each other, and our pool boy is standing between them. He's still naked, has an incredible erection, and a huge grin on his face. For him, it was like watching a tennis match, with his head going back and forth between the women as they yelled at each other. I imagine he was hoping to have one last go with one or maybe both of them."

"So, tell him about dad."

"After about five minutes of yelling, like out of nowhere, our client shows up. So now, they're all there, dad, little sister, naked mom, and naked Raphael, still with his monster stiffy. Dad quickly gets the not-so-subtle drift that both his wife and his daughter have been having a go at the pool boy, and he starts yelling, right along with mom and little sister."

"And Raphael? I asked. "What about him?"

"Oh my God," Gina said. "It was hilarious. If anything, Raphael got even bigger and harder watching all three of them yelling and screaming at each other. Like maybe he was getting visions of a family orgy."

Sophie was laughing again, and tears were rolling down her face. "Now, tell her the best part."

"Okay, so it's about an hour later, and things seemed to have calmed down a bit. Little sister's still fuming at her mother, and I guess she wanted to vent to someone."

"So, who does she call?" Sophie asked with a fresh burst of laughter.

"No," I said. "She didn't."

"Oh yes, she did," Gina said, laughing again as well. "She got on Skype and called big sister up in Flagstaff. She spent a good ten minutes crying and telling her big sis all about Raphael, how much she loved him, how their mom had ruined it all by sleeping with him, and how she thought mom had been doing him for months if not years. The entire time, little sister doesn't notice big sister's about to blow a gasket. When the explosion came, it was like an atomic bomb going off. Big sister called her every nasty name I've ever heard of. She was so mad she started making up new words to call her sister."

"She's an English major," Sophie said. "Probably took some creative writing classes."

"Well," Gina said, "I imagine things are going to be a bit tense at the client's house for the next few months. But Lenny will certainly get his fee. There's no way the wife can deny infidelity now."

Lenny heard the laughing, and he stuck his head out of his office.

"Laura, glad you could make it. Nice outfit. You look like a cat burglar. Okay, it's time to save the world, or at least save the client. Everyone, come into my office. We need to go over this one more time."

The three of us went into Lenny's office. He sat at his desk, and we sat in the three short wooden chairs.

"The document Carlos wants is in this folder," he said, holding up a blue file folder. "We need to give this to him as quickly and as smoothly as possible. Has he called you yet to tell you where to go?"

"Not yet," I said. "He said he'd call this morning. He didn't say when."

"We're assuming it'll be somewhere near the warehouse, if not actually inside it," Gina said. "Apparently, Carlos wants to get all of his crime done in one day."

"What's the latest information we have on the drug drop-off?" Lenny asked Gina.

"From what our alibi client says, it's between one and two o'clock this afternoon. He's been careful to say he doesn't know for sure where it'll take place, but he infers it'll happen at the loading dock of the south Scottsdale food warehouse. He's also made it clear he's going to be in Tucson all day. He still believes if he isn't at the scene of a major drug exchange today, then it will shed doubt on whether he was present at the previous crimes."

"As soon as we get Jackie out of the building," Lenny said, "we'll notify the police that we believe a major drug exchange will take place today between one and two at the warehouse. Sophie will go down the street to a payphone and make an anonymous call to the police. On the other hand, if something goes wrong, I'll need to call the police directly. I'll tell them about the exchange and that Jackie is in there, presumably as a hostage. You got all that?"

I nodded, and Lenny continued. "I don't need to tell you that informing the police directly that we know a major drug delivery is occurring will open us up to a lot of awkward questions, so make sure things go smoothly. I want you and Jackie out of there with plenty of time for the police to properly set up for the bust. That way, they can take down Carlos and his crew. It'll save us some worry that he might somehow be able to track down our involvement and seek some sort of retaliation."

Lenny looked right at me.

"Are you sure Tough Tony has nothing to do with this? We've had him as a client, and we're still under retainer from the last time. I can see this whole thing going downhill fast, on multiple levels, if the police bust in and see DiCenzo sitting on a pile of heroin."

"As far as I know," I said, "he's completely out of it."

"Okay then," Lenny said. "Now we wait."

The three of us left Lenny's office and went out to reception. We'd just started talking about the meeting with Carlos when I heard the front door open. We all turned to see Amber stroll in.

She'd ditched the pajamas and was now back in the slutty teenager outfit. She walked to the middle of the reception area, then stopped and stared at us.

We stared back. Within a few seconds, we were surrounded by the stench of burning dog pee.

I saw Sophie was gagging, and then she started to cough. I think she'd just thrown up a little bit in her mouth.

"Yeah," Amber said. "Like, I'm ready to work now, and stuff, you know?"

"About that," Gina said. "Lenny wanted you to have something."

Sophie opened her drawer, pulled out an envelope, handed it to Gina, who then passed it to Amber.

"What's this?" Amber asked.

"It's your termination letter and a check with two weeks' severance."

"What? Seriously? Oh, you gotta be shitting me. You can't fire me. I have like, rights and stuff, you know?"

"Not really. The employment papers you signed last week waived any rights you might have had. Plus, you're on a strict ninety-day probation period in which Lenny can discharge you for any reason without recourse. Which he just did."

Amber grew angry, and her face turned red.

"You wait," she shouted. "You can't treat people like this. I have rights, and I'll sue you. I've been sexually harassed at this workplace, and you're all in on it. You'll see. I'll sue your asses off."

She then turned and stomped out of the office.

Lenny opened his office door and stuck his head out.

"Hey, what's going on?"

The foul odor reached his nose, and the look of disgust on his face was priceless.

"Is Amber here?"

"She just left," Gina said.

"You fire her yet?"

"Yup, problem solved. At least for now."

"Good. Now let's go and get the client back. Did you get the phone call yet?"

As if by magic, my phone rang. I looked and saw it was the same Phoenix number as the day before. Sophie, Gina, and Lenny all gathered around me as I hit the answer button. I put the phone on speaker so everyone could listen.

"Hello," I said.

"There is an old warehouse on Mary Street, south of Curry Road," the frightening voice of Carlos said. "The warehouse has large pictures of vegetables painted on the side of it. Do you know the one I mean?"

I looked over at Gina. She nodded her head up and down and gave me a thumbs-up.

"Yes, I know the warehouse."

"Good. Be at this warehouse at ten o'clock and enter through the red door next to the loading docks. You will give me the paper, and I will give you your friend. Do you understand?"

"Yes."

"If I even see a police car drive by the warehouse, I will kill your friend, and then I will kill you. Do you understand?"

"Yes."

The call disconnected.

~~~~

The drive to the warehouse district only took about fifteen minutes, but the area was a world apart from the rest of the city.

Scottsdale primarily consists of world-class golf, beautiful housing, and exclusive shopping. Still, there's also a part of the city reserved for heavy industry. This is the warehouse and manufacturing district south of Curry Road.

The warehouse district is a tangled jumble of cinderblock buildings and chain-link fences topped with rusty barbed wire. It's as if Scottsdale decided to put all of its crappy buildings in one secluded spot so no one would ever have to look at them.

I drove down Curry Road, then turned south on Mary Street. About halfway down the street, I saw the warehouse. There were buildings on either side of it, and none of them looked like they'd been used for some time.

I pulled into the warehouse parking lot and saw large pictures of a tomato, a stalk of celery, and an ear of corn painted on the side of an otherwise white wall. Unfortunately, the paint was so chipped and faded that it gave a dead feeling to the building.

I parked my car in one of the twenty empty spaces next to the building. As instructed, I walked around to the dock.

There was a faded red door next to the loading bays. I gave it a push and found it was unlocked.

I went in the door and was met by two goons. One goon was enormous, and one was small. They both had dark hair and black mustaches.

The smaller one was the jerk who'd thrown a hatchet at me and tried to shoot me when they kidnapped Jackie. I saw his left eye was bloodshot, and his face was still discolored from the wasp spray I'd used on him.

Seeing him like that made me smile, just a little bit. He saw the smile and went into a rage, screaming at me in Spanish.

I readied myself and would've been glad to get into a fight with him. My adrenaline was pumping, and I felt like I could've taken on both goons at once.

Unfortunately, the bigger goon got between us and started yelling back at the smaller one. After a few moments, he had the smaller goon calmed down. They took me to Carlos, with the smaller one leading the way and the bigger one trailing behind me.

The loading dock had six bays where trucks could back up to the building and load or unload their cargo. From the outside of the building, I'd observed that none of the bays were in use. From the inside, it looked like the building had been shut down for some time.

The shipping area was almost empty, with only a couple of broken-down forklifts and a rack of old machines of some type remaining. As I looked around, I saw nothing on the warehouse shelves but a few dusty boxes.

The goons led me around to the office area of the shipping department. Large dirty glass windows overlooked the entire loading dock. The office had the same abandoned and unused look as the rest of the building.

One of Carlos's men came out of the office. He patted me down and went through my bag, looking for weapons or recording devices, I assume. Since I hadn't brought anything in, he found I was clean.

About a dozen guys lounged around the shipping office. Most of them were smoking cigarettes. A couple of them were on their cell phones, and others stood around in a small group talking.

Carlos was standing next to an old wooden desk. It was likely used by the warehouse shipping and receiving clerk, once upon a time. He talked in Spanish to another man, and I couldn't help but notice they both used a lot of hand gestures.

When Carlos noticed me come in, he pointed to a chair. I went to the chair and sat obediently. After finishing with the man, he turned his attention to me.

"You're Laura Black?" he asked.

"I'm Laura Black," I confirmed. "I think you have something for me."

Carlos made a signal to one of his henchmen. He walked across the office to the door of an inner storage room. He unlocked it and went inside.

The open door revealed bare metal shelves holding only a few old boxes of copier paper and office supplies. A minute later, the henchman reappeared with Jackie, her hands cuffed behind her back.

She looked better than I'd expected. True, her shirt was stained, her hair was a tangled mess, and she had large dark circles under her eyes, indicating she hadn't slept a lot.

But her eyes still had the fire and determination I was used to seeing. She looked like she was still more pissed off than scared.

I took it as a good sign. I knew if we got out of this in one piece, she'd end up being okay.

"Now then," Carlos said. "I think you have something for me."

I removed the blue folder from the otherwise empty bag hanging over my shoulder. I opened the folder, took out the single document, and held it out to Carlos.

He grabbed it from my hand, almost ripping it in the process. He sat down at the desk and bent over the papers, closely examining them.

He read over the document a couple of times, then closely scrutinized the signatures and the notary stamps under a large magnifying glass. Even though I knew the papers were genuine, my heart furiously beat in my chest.

I reached behind Jackie's back and held her cuffed hand. From the way she gripped it, I knew she was as frightened as I was.

What would happen if Carlos thought the document was a fake? Would he let us go out and try again? Or would he simply shoot us and go to some sort of plan B?

After five long minutes of watching Carlos search for a

flaw in the document, he sat up, apparently satisfied. He gestured to two of his men. The goons lifted us both up by our arms and quick-marched us into the same storage room where Jackie had been held.

"Hey," I shouted. "We did our part. Let us go."

One of the goons pulled out a pair of handcuffs and tried to put them on me. I put up a good fight, but between both guys, they eventually forced my hands behind my back and cuffed them.

As one of the goons was about to slam the door in my face, I yelled out to Carlos, "Hey! I did everything you asked. I brought you the damn document. Now let us go."

"I think not," Carlos said as he stood at the entrance of the storage room. "I think if I let you go now, you'll only cause me further trouble. When this whole affair is over, I'll let you both go. If you want to live, you'll shut up and do as you're told. Of course, if you've deceived me, or if I find you're working with the police, I'll personally kill you both."

Carlos moved out of view, and the goon closed the storage room door, locking it from the outside.

Damn.

The light in the room was dim but was still enough to see by. I spent two or three minutes walking around the storage room, looking for a way out. Unfortunately, there were no windows and only the one door, which was now locked from the outside.

There was a clear space against the wall in the back of the room. This is where Jackie and I sat.

"We may be here for a little while," I said. "Talk to me. It's been four days since you were kidnapped. Where have you been? What did they do to you?"

"It's only been four days? I've sort of lost track of time, but it seems a lot longer than that." Jackie paused to gather her thoughts. "Well, after they shoved me into the van, they drove me to a house. I don't know what part of the city it was in, but it was a fairly long drive, and it wasn't in the best neighborhood. They made me go inside, and they locked me in a bedroom. It had an adjoining bathroom, so that part was okay. But there were thick burglar bars on the windows, so I couldn't get out. They left me there for a couple of days. I didn't see anyone but a woman who brought me food. I tried talking to her in both English and Spanish, but she wouldn't talk to me."

"I can't imagine what that was like," I said.

"It totally sucked. But then, it must have been on Sunday, Carlos showed up. That was even worse. A man came into my room and handcuffed me. He took me into the kitchen, where Carlos was sitting at the table, holding a long knife. At first, he didn't threaten me with it. He just sort of played with it. They sat me in a chair next to him, and he started asking questions. While he was talking to me, he kept waving the knife around."

"What did he ask?"

"He kept wanting to know about a document I had in my bedroom. I told him I didn't have anything in my bedroom other than the deed to the house and my tax forms. He said he knew I was lying, and he would cut me unless I told him what he wanted to know. It was terrifying. I had no idea what he was talking about. He kept getting mad, and when he started yelling, he would hold the knife close to me, like he was about to slash at my face."

"What happened then?"

"After he asked me the same question about the document three times, and I gave him the same answer each time, he exploded. He started screaming in Spanish and ended up breaking everything breakable in the kitchen. He picked up anything he could find and smashed it on the floor or threw it against a wall."

"Did he hurt you?"

"No, for some reason, he never hit me or cut me. After he finished breaking everything possible, he calmed down and started from the beginning. He said I'd signed some papers to transfer a property to Spencer-Wade Land Development, and he needed them back. I told him I knew all about those papers and he could have them. I couldn't help but think to myself, this would have gone a lot quicker if he'd told me what he wanted in the first place."

"You knew about the transfer documents?"

"Well, sure. When I moved out, I went into Roger's safe and took my file. It had my birth certificate, the kids' birth certificates, my will, and my passport. I also knew it had a bunch of other papers, but at the time, I was just trying to pack everything, so I could move out. I didn't have a lot of time, and I didn't want to sit at the desk and try to sort everything out. Honestly, I didn't even look at what was in the file until Roger started bugging me about it, a few months after I moved out."

"Then you finally looked at it?"

"Actually, I took the file to my lawyer and had him look at it. He said many of the documents were quite valuable. Apparently, Roger had moved several properties from his business into my name. I knew he often used my name as a placeholder for things he wanted to keep separate from his company and from Howard. One of the papers I'd signed transferred a property back to his company. I assumed at some point, Roger would want the papers back or have me sign some new ones to transfer everything over to Spencer-

Wade Development. I would've been glad to do it, but he never asked. Since I was having him send everything to my lawyer first, it might've spooked him. But really, since I was now on my own, I just wanted to know what I was signing, so I could keep everything straight in my mind."

"You had the papers in a safety deposit box. Terry said he talked to you about it, and he didn't think you had one. What happened?"

"Well, I wouldn't tell Terry Lennox any of my secrets, but no, I didn't have one before about a month ago. Terry mentioned he had one for his stocks and bonds. I started thinking if the papers in the file were as valuable as my lawyer said they were, I probably shouldn't keep them in the house. I asked Pam about it, and she said she had a safety deposit box at her bank and I should get one as well. I went down to her bank and put the file in a box."

"What happened with Carlos?"

"Well, once I knew what he was looking for, I told him the papers were in a safety deposit box at the bank. Carlos started yelling and screaming at me again. He was so angry I thought for sure he'd start hitting me or even cutting me this time. He wanted to know how to get into the box. I told him the key was in my kitchen. At first, he was okay with that, but he got pissed again when I told him I'd need to be the one who went down to the bank to get it since they verify both the signature and the picture. He said I wasn't going anywhere, and I needed to think of another way for him to get the papers.

"I was so terrified, I thought he was going to kill me. I didn't know what to say, so I started talking about you. How you were smart and clever, and you could probably figure out how to get the papers. For some reason, he liked the idea of you helping him get the papers back, which seemed to calm him down."

"What'd you tell him about me?"

"That you were the one who found me in Mexico. I'm sorry I dragged you back into this, but I was so frightened. I wasn't sure what else to do."

"No, it's okay. I understand, really. We've been trying to get you back ever since they kidnapped you. In a way, Carlos calling me made it easier."

Jackie looked at me, locked up with her in a dimly lit room with my hands cuffed behind my back. She gave me a look that clearly read, *Oh, really*?

"I've talked to Howard about all of this," I said. "Roger didn't ask for the papers back or never sent over new paperwork for you to sign, because he thought you wouldn't do it."

"It goes to show how much Roger never really understood me. I never held a grudge against him, and I wouldn't have done anything to mess up his business. I already have more money to live on than I'll ever need. Roger and I weren't together anymore because I couldn't stand living with him. It wasn't that I'd stopped caring about him."

Jackie took a moment to think about it, then looked up at me with growing apprehension in her eyes.

"So, you're saying Roger was killed, my house was destroyed, and we're being terrorized, all because Roger didn't think I would give him back his papers?"

I shrugged my shoulders.

Jackie shook her head and let out a sad sigh. "So much misery over a stupid misunderstanding."

A commotion coming from what sounded like the main

shipping dock interrupted our discussion. Shouts from several men and the rattle of a large metal door being lifted filtered into the room.

I heard Carlos yelling what sounded like *descargue el camión.* This was beyond my vacation-level Spanish. I knew Jackie's Spanish was good, so I looked at her.

"He's shouting at them to unload the truck," she said. Her voice started to sound slightly far away and dreamy. I was hoping she'd be able to stay focused for a bit longer, at least until they figured out what they were going to do with us.

"The truck's early," I said. "I heard it wasn't supposed to get here until one o'clock. It can't even be noon yet."

"After they unload the truck, I wonder what they'll do with us," she said, still in that dreamy tone of voice.

"They'll probably take us back to the house where they kept you before. I can't see why they'd want to hurt us. It doesn't gain them anything."

I was trying to be brave for both of us, but I started to get a terrible feeling about all of this. Carlos now had the document, and Jackie was already listed as missing.

He could simply kill us and still have everything he was after. In fact, it would probably make things simpler for him.

Chapter Thirteen

We sat in the dark storage room for another fifteen minutes. Carlos had left the office when the truck arrived, but now he was back.

We heard his voice on the phone as he talked to someone in rapid-fire Spanish and then again as he yelled at one of his men about something.

Finally, the noise in the outer office dwindled down to background talking. All we could do was sit there and wait.

Five minutes later, we heard a frantic commotion coming from what sounded like somewhere beyond the loading dock. Men were yelling from far away, but they quickly got louder and closer.

I made out the words *fuego* and *incendio*. I looked over at Jackie for a translation.

"Something's on fire," she said rather too calmly. "I wonder what it could be?"

All of the emotions had been drained out of her, and she had mentally gone into a quiet and private place. I sometimes envy people who can do that.

Everyone in the room outside became silent for several seconds as they listened to the shouting. Then everyone started talking and yelling at once. We heard the sound of chairs scraping against the floor as everyone in the room seemed to scramble and go into action at the same time.

In the distance, probably even outside the building, we heard the sound of gunshots. I heard Carlos yelling loudly in Spanish, fury in his voice. The voices then receded into the warehouse.

Within a few seconds, the shipping office seemed to empty out, and everything was silent. I heard more shouting in the distance and possibly a few more gunshots.

I started to get a bad feeling. Carlos had said that if there was even the hint of police involvement, he would kill Jackie and me first and ask questions later.

I'd believed him when he'd told me this on the phone. Now that we were here, handcuffed in a dark storage room in a dingy warehouse, his words really started to send a cold chill through me.

My heart was racing, and my breathing was fast. When I looked over at Jackie, I could see her eyes were wide, and she was gasping with fear.

The room outside had been quiet for almost two minutes when we heard footsteps in the outer office. I quickly realized they were heading for the storage room, where we were trapped and pretty much helpless.

Unwilling to settle for being a victim, I got to my feet and frantically looked around for some kind of weapon. There were boxes and papers everywhere, but nothing I could use to defend myself, even if my hands weren't cuffed behind my back.

Damn it.

From outside, footsteps approached the door, then

stopped. I knew if Carlos was standing there when the door opened, we'd probably be killed.

I positioned myself in front of Jackie. If Carlos the Butcher was about to kill us, I'd at least get one good charge at him first. I took a deep breath and held it.

Crap.

The handle of the door wiggled back and forth, but it was still locked, and it would not turn or open. There was another pause, and then a loud crash as the door was kicked in.

Shit.

I looked in the doorway and saw Max casually walk into the storage room, a pistol in his hand. Behind him, in the outer office, I saw Gabriella. Her hair was pulled back in a ponytail, and she was dressed in a skin-tight, black leather jumpsuit with blood-red trim.

Her Uzi was in her hands, and her face was flushed pink with pleasure. She smiled in a way that made me think she was becoming aroused.

What's up with that?

"Let's get you both out of here," Max said. His voice was deep and steady, but there was a definite urgency to it. "It looks like about half of the police in Scottsdale will be here soon. Tony was worried Carlos might want to take that fact out on you two."

Max helped Jackie up and walked us back into the shipping office. It was probably a good thing my hands were still cuffed behind my back. With the way I was feeling, I probably would have wrapped my arms around Max and not let go.

True, I was scared half-to-death, and Max had just saved us, but it was more than that. Even though we were handcuffed and trying to escape from some truly evil guys, I couldn't help but notice how good Max looked and how fantastic his cologne smelled.

Jeez, what's wrong with me?

Max led us to the door leading out of the shipping office when I had a sudden thought.

"Wait! There's a paper in that blue folder on the desk," I said, using my elbows to point to the desk Carlos had been using. "I need it."

Max hurried over to the desk with a look of exasperation on his face and opened the blue folder. I was relieved to see the document was still there. Carlos must not have had enough time to do anything with it.

Max quickly folded the document and shoved it in the back pocket of my pants before hustling us out of the office. I heard the shouting of men in the distance and could smell something burning. It gave off a terrible plastic and gasoline odor that caught in the back of my throat.

Max took the lead, with Gabriella guarding our rear. Her smile was wide, and the pink glow on her face had turned into more of an erotic red flush. She was almost panting with excitement as she scanned the area, looking for men to shoot.

Max cautiously led us out through the empty warehouse and into a front office area. There didn't seem to be any power in this part of the building, and the only light came from a couple of dirty skylights.

There were about a dozen cubicles and several enclosed offices. These all had doors with big glass windows, so you could easily see into each one.

Max tried two of the offices and found they were both locked. At the third one, the door opened. Max led us in.

"Okay, stay in here," he said. "You should be out of harm's way, and this will be a good place for the police to find you. There's no reason any of the bad guys should come up here, but lock the door and stay hidden behind the desk anyway, just to be safe. Sorry about the handcuffs, but it'll add credibility to your story."

"You're taking off?" I yelled, unable to stop the panic rising in my voice.

"Sorry gorgeous, it can't be helped."

With that, he bent down and kissed me. As soon as his lips touched mine, all thoughts of bad men, guns, and death faded into the distance. All I could think about was Max and how wonderful his touch made me feel.

And then Max was gone, and we were alone again.

"Who was that?" Jackie asked.

Damn. What do I tell her?

"Um, I'm guessing one of Carlos' men must have had a change of heart and wanted to help us get away."

"Well, he was cute, whoever he was. And why didn't he kiss me too? Although, the woman with the machine gun and the S&M outfit was a little terrifying. I don't understand what's going on, but she looked like she was enjoying herself."

You don't know the half of it.

We managed to lock the door, then went around to the far side of the desk. We sat on the floor to be less obvious to anyone walking through the outside room.

There was a battery-powered clock on the wall, and we watched as the hands slowly went to one o'clock, then to five after, and then to ten after.

At one fifteen, a series of loud noises came from the direction of the warehouse. We heard several loud thuds, bangs, and crashing sounds, as though metal doors were being ripped off their hinges.

Men were yelling, and several shots were fired. Next, there was a loud explosion, causing the building to shake.

We heard faint voices over walkie-talkie radios and listened to a bullhorn in the distance. This went on for several minutes, but fortunately, none of it came near us.

Even though we were both still in handcuffs, I'd pulled the phone off the desk and was working with Jackie to call 911. We needed to tell the police where we were before Carlos came looking for us.

Unfortunately, it was dark behind the desk, and it was a complicated office phone with several buttons. With our hands behind our backs, Jackie whispered to me what buttons to push, and I was trying to press the correct ones. It wasn't working very well, and it felt like we were Lucy and Ethel doing a bad comedy act.

After five minutes of pushing buttons with no results, I decided either the phone wasn't connected, or we needed power in the office to make it work. Either way, we couldn't call the police.

After two or three more minutes had passed, we heard the sound of men yelling in the outer offices. It soon became clear the voices were coming closer. As they got nearer, I realized they were shouting in Spanish, and they sounded angry.

Jackie and I smashed ourselves against the side of the desk away from the outer room. We each tried to make ourselves as small as possible.

I checked to make sure nothing was poking out where

someone looking into the office window could see. After a minute, I heard the men in the cubicles outside the office door.

Again, I looked around the office for something to help us defend ourselves. Unfortunately, there wasn't a thing I could use, even if my hands were free.

I looked over at Jackie and saw she was again gasping and shaking with fear. Her eyes were open so wide it would have been funny if we weren't about to be gunned down.

From outside the office door, there was more shouting. It sounded like at least three men, and they didn't sound happy. One man, in particular, seemed to be barking orders in Spanish to the others.

Suddenly, the walls of our office shook as one of the office doors next to us was kicked in. We heard them rush into the office and quickly toss it, no doubt looking for us. They went back out to the hallway, and we heard them get extremely close.

The walls shook again as they kicked in the door of the office next to us. The men quickly ransacked the office, seeming to throw around anything they could find. Then they were outside our door, and I knew we were next.

I tensed and waited for the door to be kicked in. I knew they'd have guns, and Carlos had probably given them orders to find us and kill us.

I looked over at Jackie. Her eyes were still wide open, and her body was visibly shaking. I've never seen anyone so afraid.

A wave of intense emotion suddenly washed over me. I went from being frightened to being incredibly sad and frustrated.

After everything, I wasn't able to save Jackie. I felt totally responsible.

I was about to cause her death, and the feeling was heartbreaking. I'd never failed anyone like this before, and I was overcome with guilt and shame.

I looked into her eyes and spoke as quietly as I could. My lips were barely moving.

"Oh, Jackie. I'm so sorry."

I held my breath, closed my eyes, and waited for death to crash through the door.

And I waited.

And waited.

Hurry up and get it over with, you jerks. I don't have all day.

In the distance, I heard more men shouting, but there was still no crash from the office door. There was movement and quiet discussions from Carlos's men just outside our door, but for some reason, they left it alone.

I took another breath and held it.

As the new men got closer and the yelling got louder, I finally heard what they were shouting: "Scottsdale Police."

I didn't hear when Carlos's men took off, but they must have done so pretty quickly. It became deathly quiet outside of our office door.

When it sounded like the police had made it into the cubicle area, we both started yelling that we were in the office. I thought Jackie sounded a little hysterical, but after everything that'd happened, I probably did too. We then both slowly stood up from behind the desk.

Two men in full SWAT combat gear easily kicked in the door and rushed into the office. Two more SWAT team members checked the rest of the cubicle and office area. When they had given the all-clear, they helped us out of the building.

~~~~

We were searched for weapons and then taken to a mobile command center van, the size of a city bus. An officer removed our handcuffs, and we were helped into two office swivel chairs and handed a couple of water bottles.

We'd just started explaining to the officers who we were and what had happened when Reno burst into the van. He wore his blue windbreaker with the bright yellow "*SCOTTSDALE POLICE*" lettering stenciled on the back.

He saw Jackie sitting in her chair, and he smiled. It was a look of triumph I'd never seen on him before.

I immediately got another intense flash of lust and desire. This one was even worse than the one I'd just had with Max.

Damn, that man is beautiful.

Reno looked over and realized I was also there. His face twisted into a look of shock.

"You!" he shouted.

Oops.

His face flashed to anger and then slowly to acceptance.

"Why is it always you?" he asked sadly. "Why are you always in the middle of everything we do?"

"Hey, I just came here to find Jackie. I found her, but then they captured me. It's not my fault."

He hung his head down, and I heard him release a deep

sigh. He walked over to where I was sitting and bent down. His voice became quiet and serious.

"Are you okay?"

"Yeah, I'm okay. I've been so worried about Jackie, it made me forget about what kind of danger we were really in."

He paused for a moment. He dropped his voice further, and he leaned close to me.

"Half of the Scottsdale PD is about to come into this van. Before they do, is there anything else I should know about this?"

Why does he always do this to me?

"Um, nope, nothing else you should know about."

Reno looked at me for a moment. I could see my answer didn't make him happy, and I could tell he wanted to keep asking questions. Instead, he stood up and started talking again in a normal voice.

"I'm glad you're both alright." He looked at Jackie. "A lot of officers and detectives have been looking for you over the past few days. There'll be a lot of smiling and happy people as soon as we make some phone calls."

Reno took off to notify everyone about what'd happened, leaving Jackie and me by ourselves. I was suddenly overcome by a wave of relief and happiness.

I finally realized Jackie was free, and we weren't going to be killed. I looked over at her, and she must have felt the same thing.

She had a big smile even though she was crying. I realized I was crying as well, and we gave each other a long hug.

"Thank you," she said. "They would've killed me if you

hadn't been there."

I wanted to tell her I was sorry I'd messed up everything so badly. I wanted to say it was my fault she'd been kidnapped, and it was also my fault she'd almost gotten killed.

Instead, I said, "Sure, glad I could help."

~~~~

Jackie and I were checked out by a couple of EMTs. We were then transported under police escort to Scottsdale General for further checkups. I know a medical check is standard police procedure for something like this, but it's still a pain in the ass.

Before we took off, I went to my car and grabbed my purse. On the way over to the hospital, I called Sophie and let her know the basics of what had happened.

I knew both Gina and Sophie would want the complete story, but she could hear how beat I was, and she didn't press too much. I asked her to tell Lenny.

She wasn't thrilled, but she said she would do it. I know I should have called him directly, but I was mentally drained, and I didn't want to deal with his endless questions and cross-examination.

Next, I called Pam to tell her the good news and that we would be down at the hospital for a while. She said she'd let everyone know, then she'd come by the hospital to pick up Jackie. Since Jackie's house was still a crime scene, Pam said she would have Jackie stay at her house for the next few days.

While we waited in the emergency room for the third doctor to examine us, the lead detective in the Roger Wade murder investigation came in. As soon as Jackie saw him, her body tensed. Apparently, she'd forgotten about the murder and that she'd been the lead suspect.

But as the detective started talking, I could tell from his body language and the way he spoke to her, he now doubted she'd committed the murder. Of course, I could also tell he was too much of a professional to let that interfere with his job.

He said he was glad Jackie had been released from her ordeal, but he still had a couple of things he wanted to get cleared up about the murder. He said he didn't want to rush her, but if it was alright, he'd already arranged with Lenny for an interview the following day at ten o'clock.

Ten minutes after the detective left, Sophie and Pam came in together. There was talking and hugging all around for the next few minutes.

They both wanted to know what'd happened, and I tried to tell the basics of it without going into too much detail. When I thought about everything we'd experienced over the past few hours, a hard knot settled in my stomach.

~~~~

We said our goodbyes, and then Jackie left with Pam. It would still be another week or two until the police released Jackie's house and allowed her to return. I was glad Jackie would have someone to stay with until things calmed down.

Sophie drove me back to the warehouse to get my car. As we drove up to the building, we saw there were still a dozen police cars surrounding the scene, along with three news vans.

The reporters and cameramen from the news vans milled around and chatted with each other. I guessed they were between news broadcasts. I could envision all of them standing in a line, everybody giving a similar report, at the same time, to the three local TV stations.

Seeing the warehouse and remembering what'd happened in there gave my stomach another hard twist. After explaining to the officer at the perimeter who we were, we were allowed into the scene. Fortunately, the incident commander from earlier was still there.

He didn't consider my car to be part of the crime scene. I thanked him and drove my car back to the office.

~~~~

Sophie and I reached the office at the same time. Lenny was holed up in his office, and Gina was waiting for us in reception.

"Are you doing okay?" Gina asked.

"Yeah, but it came close to going completely to hell."

"But it didn't, and you never gave up. I'm glad you got our client back."

Lenny heard us talking and came out from his office. He was in a good mood since his client wasn't dead, and he'd be able to collect his fee.

"Good work on getting the client back," he said. "From what I hear, Carlos wasn't too keen on letting you go, even after he had the transfer document. He sounds like a man who can't be trusted. When you and Jackie didn't come back out of the warehouse, I called the chief of police directly. I let him know about the drug shipment and that I also believed Jacquelyn Wade was being held captive there. I thought that by calling the chief directly, I'd get an immediate response. I'm also hoping he will keep my name out of the official reports. But either way, he now owes me a big one."

"Did you happen to tell him I was in there too?" I asked.

"Well, mentioning you were in there ahead of time would've opened us up to some questions I didn't want to answer. I thought it'd be best if they found you along with Jackie. Now that they've seized the drugs and Jackie's been rescued, they won't need to ask a lot of questions about how you got in there. I hope it wasn't too much of a shock to them when they had to rescue both of you."

"I don't think Reno will talk to me for a few days. He was more than a little upset I happened to be in there with Jackie."

"It couldn't be helped. Besides, he should be happy you're still in one piece."

"The lead detective in the murder investigation stopped by to see us in the hospital," I said. "It seemed strange he was there, but he didn't even try to press us for any information."

"Not to worry," Lenny said. "I had a conversation with him before he went to the hospital. I imagine he wanted to see with his own eyes that Jackie was free. Since my conversation with him, I've gotten some inside information. The police no longer consider Jackie to be a suspect in the death of Roger Wade. Howard did a good job of implicating Carlos. It was a class move on his part. Unfortunately, he'll need to keep low for a while. He might even need to go into some sort of witness relocation program until this Carlos thing gets straightened out."

"So, Jackie is off the hook?"

"There'll be some formal questioning, but then she'll be a free woman." Lenny got a wistful look on his face. "It's a damn shame we had to give everything away to free the client. We still might challenge the transfer document, but it was signed over a year ago, and Jackie won't be able to show it was anything out of the ordinary. Even after all of this, Jackie's still going to lose the resort."

"Oh," I said, "about that." Reaching into the back pocket

of my pants, I pulled out the folded and wrinkled document. In the excitement of almost being killed, I'd completely forgotten about it.

Lenny's eyes got big, and his mouth dropped open. Gina and Sophie started laughing, then Gina gave me a high five. I handed the document to Lenny.

"No shit?" he asked as he unfolded the paperwork. "I don't believe it. You rescued the client and saved the resort? Damn, you're getting good at this."

A terrible thought suddenly occurred to me.

"What about Carlos?" I asked. "Won't he just kidnap Jackie again and make her sign more documents?"

Lenny looked at me as though he was disappointed that I missed something obvious.

"Having Jackie sign a transfer now wouldn't do him any good. The previous document would've held up because there was a long history of Jackie transferring properties between herself and Spencer-Wade Land Development, with little financial gain to herself. However, there is now ample evidence that any transfer document Jackie signed after the date she was kidnapped would have been signed under duress. Carlos could make Jackie sign a dozen documents, and none of them would be valid. I'm sure he knows that."

"So, Jackie's safe? I mean, really safe."

"Yes, Jackie's safe."

I looked over at Gina, and she was nodding her head. Relief and happiness washed over me.

"Perfect," I said with a big smile. "It's finally perfect."

~~~~

Sophie, Gina, and I spent the next hour talking about the

events of the past two weeks, and I filled them in on all the details. The only thing I left out was the rescue by Max and Gabriella.

Gina would have problems with it from a legal standpoint, which was something I didn't even want to try to sort out. Sophie would see it as yet another sign that Max and I were meant to be together. Since I already had a lot of confusing thoughts regarding Max, I didn't need Sophie adding to them.

But honestly, the main thing keeping me from saying anything was a feeling that had been slowly growing in the back of my mind. It was a feeling that I was being sucked into the middle of a war, squeezed between two powerful groups.

I could see it happening, but I wasn't sure if I knew how to keep myself out of it. I did know I wanted to do whatever I could to keep my two best friends from being dragged into it with me.

~~~~~

After Gina and Sophie finally had all of their questions answered, I went back to my cubicle. I didn't want to be alone tonight, and my thoughts jumped to Reno.

From the look on his face earlier in the day, I wasn't so sure he'd want to see me, at least not right away. But I decided to give it a try anyway.

I took out my phone and called, but he didn't pick up. I didn't want to read too much into it since he often couldn't answer my calls and usually called me back soon after.

"Hey," I said to his voicemail. "Thanks for rescuing me today. Jackie and I were in a tight spot. It'd be nice to talk to you about it. I was thinking maybe we could get together tonight for dinner, or whatever. If not tonight, then tomorrow? Let me know."

I disconnected and stared at the phone for a moment. I started to pack up my things to go home when the theme from the *Love Boat* began playing on my phone. My heart did a little two-step, and I answered.

"Hello," I said.

"Hello yourself. How are you doing?"

"I'm okay. Thanks for the rescue today. When the storage room door opened, you were the last person I expected to see walking in."

"Glad to do it," he said. "I was wondering if you were free tonight. Maybe I could take you out somewhere nice for a quiet dinner? I'm sure you could use some time to unwind."

"Um, sure. I'd love to see you. But would you mind if we kept it to drinks?"

"Are you still having those conflicting thoughts about us?"

That's an understatement.

"I think drinks would work better for me tonight. Plus, I'm really not dressed for anything fancy."

"Alright. No problem. Where?"

"Let's keep it simple. Back to the Casablanca?"

"Great. See you in half an hour?"

"I have a few things to do before I get out of here."

Like completely redo my face.

"Okay," he said. "Let's make it an hour."

~~~~

As I walked down to the lounge, I was definitely feeling some mixed emotions about Max. It was true, he was gorgeous, and I was definitely attracted to him.

But there were the nagging facts that he committed crimes for a living. I was trying to form a lasting relationship with another man, who happened to be a cop.

Why are things always so complicated?

I got to the lounge first and settled at a table on the patio in the corner. It had a lovely view, and it was far enough away from everyone else so we could talk without whispering.

I saw Max come in, as did several other women in the lounge. Even though I'd sternly told myself he was forbidden fruit, my heart still kicked up a notch, and I'd suddenly developed a case of the butterflies. I also had some naughty thoughts about what I'd love to do to this man if I ever got him alone.

Stop that.

Max sat down across from me, and we each ordered a drink. I had a scotch, and it felt great to take that first sip.

"Are you going to tell me what happened today?" I asked. "Jackie and I were trapped in a storage room, surrounded by a dozen bad guys with guns, and then you come strolling in. Don't get me wrong, I was happy to see you, but what happened?"

"From the information you gave us, we put together where the shipment was going. You said you were calling it into the police, so we wanted to be nearby to make sure things went smoothly for them. We had continuous surveillance of the warehouse from a nearby rooftop location. We saw them bring in Jackie about eight o'clock, and we saw you go in about ten. When the truck with the drugs arrived, and neither of you had come back out, we thought we should set up a distraction and help get you away."

"I appreciate that," I said.

"Unfortunately, by then, the police had started to set up a perimeter. There was no way we could've gotten you out of the building without a lot of uncomfortable questions being raised. I had to be content with moving you to a safer place. Apparently, it wasn't as safe as I thought it was. I'm glad you and Jackie were rescued by the police before the bad guys found you."

"It was close, but we're okay, thanks to you and Gabriella. Would you thank her for me? What about the distraction? What'd you do?"

At that question, Max started to laugh. It was the first time I'd heard him really laugh, and it was a great sound.

Plus, when he laughed, his whole face lit up. He could have been a teenager again, laughing at some joke.

"Yes, well, about the distraction. You see, before your news yesterday, the only thing we really knew about Carlos was the car he drove. It was a red Ferrari Spider, a beautiful car costing over a quarter of a million dollars. From what we gathered, it's sort of his trademark, and he really loves it. He parked it on the far side of the warehouse, away from both the loading docks and the front offices. I guess he wanted to make sure it would be out of the way and wouldn't get any scratches. So, we decided to blow it up."

"You blew up his Ferrari?"

"Actually, it was Gabriella's idea, and it's harder to do than you'd think. Even after we shot a few holes in the gas tank, it still wouldn't catch on fire. She finally had to shoot a flare at it. But once it started, it really went up fast."

"I could see why that caused such a stir. We heard everyone in the offices running around but had no idea what had caused the commotion."

"After everyone emptied out of the building to see what'd happened, Gabriella and I went in and got the two of you. When you both were safe, we went out the way we'd gone in. Everyone was still out by the burning Ferrari."

"Did everyone get away okay?"

"Everyone is fine. We just set the whole thing up as a distraction, and nobody got overly close to where Carlos's men were. It turns out I was the only one that took a hit."

"You got shot?" I almost shouted at him, and my voice raised an octave. My heart started pumping as I frantically looked for bandages or a gushing wound.

"I'm okay. It happened as we were leaving the building. I never even saw who shot me. But, after what happened the last time we had our little adventure together, I made sure to wear a bulletproof vest again. I've now been shot twice while wearing one. Funny thing, both times I've been with you. Maybe you're bad luck?"

"Or maybe I'm good luck since nobody decided to shoot you in the head. Ever think about that?"

We sat and talked for another hour. It was great to be with Max, and the more I spoke with him, the more things I found we had in common.

"Before I forget," Max said. "Tony would like to see you."

What? Damn!

He saw the look on my face. "Nothing to worry about. I think he wants to see for himself that you're okay. Plus, I've got to say, you impressed the hell out of him yesterday. I've been with him for years, and I can count on one hand how many times that's happened. You were able to dig up the information on Valentino in only a few days when we'd tried for months and had come up with squat."

"When does he want to see me?"

"Any time over the next few days. He said he didn't want to inconvenience you. I know he'll be in the office tonight for at least another two hours.

"Tonight?"

Crap.

"Alright," I said. "Let him know I'll be over tonight. Will you be coming with me?"

"Not this time. You know the way, and everyone over there knows who you are. You'll do great."

I followed Max down the stairs from the lounge, and I was sort of hoping he'd turn and kiss me again. When he didn't, I was a little disappointed.

I walked him to his car, which was parked on the street half a block down. When he went to get in, I realized he wasn't going to kiss me or even give me a hug.

"No kiss this time?"

He stopped and looked down at me. "Aren't you the one with the conflicted emotions about us?"

"Yes, but it's not as simple as that. Whenever I see you, I seem to lose all reason. Then I remember you're a professional criminal, and I already sort of have a boyfriend. I honestly don't know what to do when it comes to you."

He smiled and shook his head. He then bent down and gave me the lightest and softest possible kiss. It had the effect of igniting every nerve in my body.

Wow! How can he do that?

"You work out your thoughts about us," he said, "and I'll

be glad to give you a better kiss. Actually, I'll give you a hell of a lot more than just a nice kiss."

Yum.

Chapter Fourteen

I drove up Scottsdale Road to the Tropical Paradise. As always, I was nervous about meeting with Tough Tony DiCenzo.

Sophie was right. Spending too much time with him would almost certainly end badly.

Unfortunately, I still had the feeling I was getting drawn deeper into it. I knew I needed to start fighting against it now, while I still had a chance of getting out in one piece.

I again parked in valet. I recognized the bell captain from the night before, and he also seemed to know who I was.

I took the stairs from the lobby up to the second-floor offices. The guards also seemed to know who I was, and one of them opened the door for me.

Since it was getting late in the evening, only a few people worked in their offices or cubicles. It was a rather creepy feeling walking through the mostly deserted area.

I got to Gabriella's desk and saw she was again working. This time she wore a white button-down blouse, and her hair was down.

Rather than buzzing me in right away, she looked at me. I wasn't sure what to make of it at first, and then I noticed her eyes.

Every other time I'd seen Gabriella, her eyes sent a shiver of fear through me. But tonight, her eyes were softer. For the first time, I saw her as a woman sitting at a desk and not as a predator waiting to pounce.

"You did good today," she said. It was the first time I'd ever heard her speak, and it startled me.

From the way she spoke, I could tell English wasn't her first language. She had a heavy Eastern European or perhaps even Russian accent.

"I did good today?" I asked.

"You did not panic or scream. You helped the other girl. You did good today. You did good last time too, with the diamonds. You saved Tony when I was pushed on the floor. He would have been killed if you hadn't acted."

"Thanks, and, um, thank you for rescuing me today. We were in a tight spot."

"It's okay. Tony and Max like you. I like you too."

I remembered Max said he'd gotten shot. I suddenly wanted to know more.

"Today, after you and Max moved us, did you have a shootout with Carlos's men?"

At my question, Gabriella looked incredibly sad, and her bottom lip stuck out in a pout. She looked like a five-year-old who'd been denied candy.

"No," she said, still with the pout. "No men to shoot today. Max got shot in the vest, but we did not see who did it. I wanted to go back and find the man who shot him, but Max said no. But soon, I know he will say yes. Carlos Valentino is a very bad man, but it's okay. I will kill him and his men. I will kill them all, no problem."

As she said the last, she got a big smile on her face. She then moaned with what I could swear was arousal.

And sometimes I think I have issues?

Still moaning and smiling, she pushed the button under her desk. The door unlocked, and I went into Tony's office.

As before, he was sitting behind his desk and had on his black reading glasses. I couldn't help but see him as another businessman. He looked up, and when he saw me, I thought there was a trace of a smile on his face.

"Laura Black. You've had a very busy day today. There's no mistaking that. I'm about to have a twenty-one-year-old Macallan scotch. Will you take one with me?"

"Thanks, that would be great. One ice cube would be perfect."

Tony prepared us each a drink, then motioned me to sit in a comfortable leather chair that was part of a seating group away from his desk. He made himself comfortable in the other chair.

I spent several seconds watching the ice cube slowly dissolve as I breathed in the subtle aromas of the scotch. Tony took a sip of his drink and started talking.

"After what you told Max about the drug shipment and what you told me about Carlos Valentino, it wasn't hard to put the two together. It didn't take us long to narrow the drop-off down to the one warehouse in south Scottsdale that can handle that kind of shipment. We didn't expect to see you anywhere near the place, of course. But we'd set up a surveillance on the warehouse and saw you both go in. When you didn't come out, we figured you could use a hand."

"Thanks for getting us out of there. Looks like we're even

again."

Tony waved his hand in dismissal.

"I went in to get you partially because I owe you, that's true, but mostly because I needed a solid opening shot in the upcoming war. I wanted Carlos to realize what he's gotten himself into. He probably thought he could fuck with me and come away clean. I've taught him he's wrong, no bones about it. Besides, Max seemed a little upset you'd been captured, and Gabriella always likes to be in the middle of things." As he said that, he gave a small chuckle.

"As things turned out," he continued, "the police arrived in time to confiscate his shipment of drugs and to arrest several of his guys. Now, getting a truckload of heroin into Arizona no doubt took several months of planning and cost his organization several million dollars. They, of course, had been counting on making many times that when they distributed the drugs. Having the police confiscate the shipment will put a serious dent in their operations for a while. It was unfortunate that Carlos was able to get away. My guys were on the lookout for him, but we were forced to back off once the police moved in. But I've known from the first this wasn't going to be a quick or easy problem to solve."

"Tony, I hope I didn't make it worse for you. I didn't mean to get in the middle between you and Carlos."

"Not at all. It was the not knowing who the enemy was that kept holding us back. Now that we know who we're dealing with, we can take steps to correct the problem. You have a solid head on your shoulders. I'm glad you're on my team."

"Tony, I hope you understand the life you have isn't for me. I was only there to help get Jackie back, and then things sorta snowballed."

"I understand, Laura Black. You're a nice girl, and the life we lead might be somewhat outside of your comfort zone. But I do find it interesting that this is the second time we've had a conversation similar to this. If there's a third time, I'll start to wonder if you're truly not interested in becoming more involved in our little family."

Yikes!

~~~~~

Reno called me back as I drove home. I could tell he was still annoyed with me, but he sounded sincere when he said he'd been busy all night and hadn't been able to talk until now.

I told him I wanted to get together as soon as he had a night off. He said the first time he knew for sure he was going to be off was on Friday, three nights away. Again, he sounded sincere, so I set up a dinner for Friday night at Frankie's.

~~~~~

On Thursday morning, there was a beautiful funeral held for Roger Wade. Most of Scottsdale's old money and elite came to the service. In all, there were over three hundred people.

Several people spoke about Roger and the exceptional man he had been. Everyone talked about the Wade family and the part they'd played in building Scottsdale into what it is today.

The mayor and most of the city council were there. I saw that both Muffy Sternwood and Tony DiCenzo were among the mourners. I even saw Howard Spencer and Terry Lennox in the back of the crowd, although they both left as soon as the service was over.

Jackie was there and doing well, considering the

circumstances. Although she still seemed somewhat shaken, she was surrounded by her friends and family, and she seemed to draw strength from them. Even though she'd experienced a troubled marriage and she'd been separated from Roger for almost a year and a half, I could see the deep emotions Jackie felt as they laid her husband to rest.

~~~~

After the funeral, I stopped by the office. Lenny had given me several days off, but I hated to be out of the loop for so long.

Of course, my days off were always subject to a new assignment coming in. I told myself I could only chat with Sophie for a few minutes. Otherwise, I knew Lenny would think up something for me to do out of reflex.

When I walked into reception, Sophie and Gina were both there, still talking about the funeral. When she saw me, Sophie perked up.

"I forgot to tell you," she said, "but you have a box."

"I have a box?"

"Yeah, a delivery guy brought it over yesterday afternoon."

"Where is it?"

"It's sittin' on your desk."

"What's in it?"

"Don't know, but it sloshes when you shake it."

Curious, I went back to my cubicle and found a box, a little bigger than a shoebox. It hadn't been sent through one of the major carriers. Instead, it looked like a courier service had driven it over from somewhere local.

I looked at the box for a minute, wondering if perhaps it had come from Carlos. It made me wish I knew more about mail bombs.

I carefully unwrapped the outer paper and slowly removed the lid. Inside was a bunch of bubble wrap and a beautiful wooden box with a card on top. I took out the card and read:

Dear Laura,

I know I told you the other night, but I wanted to thank you again for everything you did for my family and me. I remember the first time we met, you seemed to particularly like this. I hope you enjoy it and think about me when you drink it.

Sincerely,

Margaret Sternwood

I unwrapped the bubble wrap and opened the box. Inside was a bottle of Balvenie Cask-151 scotch. The hand-numbered label said it was bottle fifty-seven of eighty-one.

I remembered when Muffy had first given me a glass of it. She told me it was older than I was and even she thought it was expensive. If Muffy Sternwood thought it was costly, it must really be pricy.

Overcome with curiosity, I went to the computer and looked it up on the internet. I then walked out to where Gina and Sophie were laughing in the reception area.

"What's up, girlfriend?" Sophie asked, slightly concerned.

"Yeah," Gina said. "You look kind of pale. Did you get another death threat?"

"And what was in the box?" Sophie asked. "Not another

severed body part, I hope. Whenever you get a severed body part, I always feel like vomiting in the nearest trash can."

"Muffy Sternwood sent me a bottle of sixty-year-old scotch costing over twenty thousand dollars."

"What?" Sophie asked. "Are you serious? Holy crap!"

"Is that the scotch you were telling us about?" Gina asked. "Liquid sex?"

"I guess Mrs. Sternwood doesn't know what a piece of shit car you drive," Sophie laughed. "If she did, she could have gotten you one of those instead."

"Oh, I don't care about my car," I said. "It was sweet of her to think of me. Let's wait for a special occasion and open it up. You both should know what liquid sex tastes like."

"Works for me," Gina said.

"Me too," Sophie said. "But don't wait too long. The thought of liquid sex is starting to turn me on, you know, a little bit."

~~~~

After making sure it was all right with Jackie, Lenny invited her and her friends to the office Friday evening for a private gathering. By six o'clock on Friday, the office was closed for the week. Sophie and Annie had set up the wet bar and a small buffet in the main conference room. Gina had found some lovely piano Jazz and was playing it over the office sound system.

By six-thirty, the cougars had already started to arrive. By seven o'clock, they were all there: Jackie, Pam, Elle, Sonia, Shannon, Cindy, and Annie.

As always, I was totally impressed seeing them together as a group. Since it was a Friday evening, they were all dressed for a night of trolling for men at the clubs.

They had perfect hair, perfect makeup, perfect shoes, and perfect clothes. As usual, the delicate scent of their mingled perfumes filled the air.

The lone exception was Jackie. She was dressed in a conservative navy-blue pants suit, and her hair was pulled back into a ponytail.

Everything considered she seemed to be taking events in stride. Within a few minutes, the room was filled with talk, music, and laughter.

I wore my diamond pendant for only the second time. Sophie had told Gina about it, of course, but this was the first time she'd actually seen it. After they both had a nice laugh at seeing the real thing, Gina broke out in a big grin, held up her hand, and gave me a high-five.

When Lenny saw it, he stared for a moment but fortunately didn't say anything or ask any questions. After all, how could a simple investigator at a law office possibly have a real diamond that was anywhere close to being that big and sparkly?

You wouldn't believe me if I told you.

After everyone had an hour of eating, drinking, and telling stories about the past two weeks, Lenny called the group together in the ample open space in front of Sophie's desk.

"Everybody, I want to thank you all for coming here. Today is truly a great day. After much delay, today is the day our friend Jacquelyn Wade officially comes into her own. Jackie, if you would, please come up." He then waved Jackie to the front.

To the sound of everyone clapping and cheering, Jackie

walked up to where Lenny was standing. Lenny reached into a folder, which sat on Sophie's desk. He pulled out a creased and battered document with several signatures and notary stamps on it.

"This piece of paper has caused us all a lot of trouble," he said. "This is the document transferring ownership of the Scottsdale Saguaro Sky Resort from Jackie to Spencer-Wade Land Development. I'd like to give Jackie the honor of destroying it."

Everyone in the room clapped and shouted as Lenny held out the document to Jackie. She took it with a trembling hand.

She then looked down at it with an odd look of wonder and anger, probably thinking of the problems and damage it had caused. She closed her eyes and slowly tore the document in half.

There was a loud cheer from everyone in the room, and Jackie collapsed in Sophie's chair. There was a look of relief on her face, and I knew in my heart she was going to be okay.

Lenny popped the corks on several bottles of Crystal champagne. At the same time, Annie and Sophie walked around the room, filling everyone's glass. Lenny then held up his glass for a toast.

"To Jackie Wade. You are now the sole and permanent owner of the Scottsdale Saguaro Sky Resort. This is in addition to the partial ownership of five other Scottsdale resorts and several undeveloped Scottsdale properties. Once the estate clears, this will make you one of the largest land and resort owners in the state of Arizona. Congratulations."

We all clapped and cheered, and then everybody drained their glass. I saw Elle and Pam smiling and crying over the good fortune of their friend.

Seeing Annie standing with the cougars gave me an idea.

I called Sophie and Gina over, and we had a conference.

We came to a quick agreement and elected Gina to be our spokeswoman. We then motioned Annie over.

"Come with us," I said.

We walked over as a group and stood in front of Lenny. He was seated in one of the red leather chairs, still sipping champagne.

"Lenny," Gina said. "Annie will be graduating in two months with an associate's degree in business. We'd like you to take her on as the new admin."

Annie broke out in a huge smile, then looked expectantly at Lenny. He thought about it for a moment.

"Actually, that's not a bad idea," he said. "We still need an extra pair of hands, and she doesn't seem insane like Amber." He looked over at Annie, who was closely following the conversation. "Well, what do you think? I should warn you, I've often been told I can sometimes be, um, difficult."

Sophie barked out a sharp laugh. She realized what she'd done and quickly covered her mouth with embarrassment. Her face had turned bright red.

Lenny glanced over at Sophie, a little annoyed. "Okay," he said to Annie, "I'll be honest. I'm a pain in the ass. But, what do you say? Would you like the job? You can work part-time until you graduate, then switch over to full-time. We'll negotiate your salary, but I think you'll be happy with it."

Annie squealed with happiness and started jumping up and down. She spread her arms and hugged Gina, Sophie, and me. We all took this as a yes.

Everyone had another glass of champagne, and we were all starting to get a little giggly. As we were celebrating, Pam came over and gave me a nudge.

She motioned me to look over at Lenny. He was now standing with his mouth open, staring across the room. When I saw what was going on, I laughed and nudged Gina, who laughed and nudged Sophie.

We looked and saw that Lenny was staring eagerly at Elle. What was funny was the look she was giving him back. She looked like she was hungry.

Champagne glass in hand, Elle slowly walked toward Lenny, like a lioness stalking a wounded gazelle. She swung her long dark hair and licked her lips as she leisurely closed in on her prey.

She reached Lenny and stood close to him. In her heels, she was several inches taller than he was, and Lenny was having a hard time deciding where to look at her.

We saw him nervously start to fidget. I couldn't help but think, "Beauty and the Beast."

"As you know, I usually don't date guys my age," Elle softly said as she lightly brushed her fingertips across Lenny's cheek. "But there's something about you. I like the way you took control and handled the situation for my friend. After this is over, why don't we go out on the town and make a night of it? Can you cook? I have a big kitchen. You can make me breakfast."

"Ah, um, sure," Lenny stammered. His face had turned bright red.

At this, we all held up our champagne glasses in a salute, and everyone was laughing. Lenny was never very good at talking to women in social situations, especially if they were beautiful. But I got the feeling Lenny wasn't going to need to do a lot of talking with Elle tonight.

Jackie walked over to me. She paused for a moment, took off her thick diamond and ruby bracelet, and handed it to me.

"Roger gave this to me when we built our first resort together, and I've worn it ever since. Even after we separated, I've worn it to remind me of the good times we had together. But, after everything that's happened, I think it's time for me to let him go and to say goodbye. I know this doesn't nearly make up for everything you've done for me, but I wish you'd take it. Think of me when you wear it. I think it'll look great with your diamond pendant."

"It's not real!" Sophie and Gina said together.

I took the bracelet from Jackie and then burst into tears. I couldn't stop them, and I didn't even want to try.

It had been a long two weeks, and I was happy everything had worked out so well. It could have easily gone horribly wrong. I gave Jackie a long hug, and I knew I'd made a lifelong friend.

After they all had another glass of champagne, the girls were ready to hit the town. Taking Lenny in tow, they took off through the front door, and we heard them singing and laughing as they walked down the street to one of the nearby clubs.

Gina had stopped drinking after the first glass of champagne and was giving Jackie a ride home. Before she left, Sophie and I hugged her again.

We extracted a promise from her to send out daily status reports on her mood for at least the following week. We then made plans to all go out together as soon as she was up for it.

Sophie had a date arranged with Milo for after the party. They'd planned on meeting up at a club, but she called him and told him to pick her up at the office instead.

From the tone of her voice and the soft pink glow that was coloring her cheeks, I doubted if she and Milo would make it any further tonight than the bedroom in her apartment. After all, Sophie is a woman of many needs. Somehow, I got the feeling Milo wouldn't mind the change in plans.

~~~~

Reno and I had planned on meeting at Frankie Z's for a late dinner. So far, he hadn't called it off, and Lenny hadn't come up with any new assignments for me. I took both as good signs.

After the first glass of champagne, I'd switched to Diet Pepsi in anticipation of actually being able to see Reno. As I drove to the restaurant, the thought of spending time with Reno gave me an incredible case of the butterflies.

I was starting to hope that maybe Reno and I could be together tonight for more than dinner and a quickie in the parking lot. Perhaps we could even have an actual date, like ordinary people. Maybe even a date lasting until Monday morning.

A girl can always dream.

When I walked into the restaurant, Frankie greeted me and walked me into the lounge. As usual, Little Zappy was mixing drinks behind the bar, and he waved when he saw me.

The place was full of people, all laughing and talking at once. Reno had a table in the corner of the lounge, and I sat close to him. After a minute, Dominick came to our table, and we each ordered a scotch.

We slowly sipped our drinks and talked. Every few minutes, Dominick, or one of the other waiters, would bring out a food tray from the kitchen. As they walked past us, we'd catch the wonderful smell of the dinners.

We each ordered our favorites and then had a few minutes to talk before the food arrived. I knew discussing the rescue was probably a bad idea.

I also knew Reno had been upset about finding me in the warehouse, but I still had a few questions nagging at me. Plus, the champagne and the scotch were making it hard for me to keep my mouth shut.

"What happened the other day?" I asked. "How'd you find us?"

At first, he looked at me as if he wasn't going to say anything or maybe even start to get angry. Instead, he hung his head in defeat. After a moment, he looked up, lowered his voice, and started talking.

"We'd been getting indications for weeks that there was a truck coming up from Mexico with a shipment of heroin. By late last week, we'd narrowed down the date to Tuesday. Unfortunately, we didn't know where it was headed. Border patrol let it through on Tuesday morning, but only after they'd put a tracking device underneath the trailer. The truck had passed through Tucson when we got a tip. The drugs were going to an abandoned warehouse on Mary Street in south Scottsdale. The tipper also said the drugs were being transported by a group called the *Muerte Negra* cartel, and it was possible Jacquelyn Wade was being held as a hostage there."

"So, you got a lucky break, having a tipper call it in?"

"Yup, we caught a break. It gave us enough time to set up a plan to go in and make the arrests. Unfortunately, we didn't have a lot of information on the group. They apparently haven't been operating in the area for long. We made some phone calls to the DEA and found out this group is headed in Arizona by a man called Carlos the Butcher."

"That's still a pretty scary name."

"Yes, but other than his name, that's about all the information they had on him or the group. Since you'd already said someone called Carlos the Butcher was holding Jackie Wade as a hostage, we took the tipper's information to be credible. So, in addition to our drug intervention team, we also called in the hostage rescue team. We were looking for Jackie Wade. We weren't looking for you. I had to look twice when I saw you there. I'm still not sure why you're always in the middle of everything."

"I found Jackie, but then we couldn't get back out. Thank the guys for rescuing me."

That was the second time I was rescued that day.

"I'm just glad we were there. Those drug dealers didn't look like nice people."

"How is the murder investigation going? Howard Spencer said Carlos was the one who shot Roger Wade."

"He told the same story to the detectives, plus we found the gun that shot Roger at the warehouse. It appears Jackie had nothing to do with the murder. It looks like Lenny's string of getting people off of murder charges will remain intact."

"That's great. This way, he'll get his fee, and I'll get paid. Seems like everyone wins."

"Well, we confiscated a lot of drugs, and the department will use that for all they can. There's nothing like pictures of a truckload of heroin coming into the city to keep our funding levels high. We arrested several people at the scene, but Carlos the Butcher got away. Apparently, his group has been doing a lot of things under the radar that we've been missing. The captain's already told us we're going to form a team to go after Carlos and his organization. The drug war never stops."

Dominick brought out our dinners. We then spent a long time eating and enjoying each other's company.

As always, I felt totally comfortable being with Reno, and I loved the way I could talk to him about anything. Well, almost anything.

Dominick brought out coffee and gelato for dessert. When we finished, Reno looked at me.

"Your phone hasn't rung all night. I take it you aren't working this weekend?"

"Lenny gave me a few days off. I'm hoping to stretch that into Wednesday or Thursday next week. Still, realistically, if I'm off until Tuesday, it will be great. I've got a ton of shopping to do."

"Good to know."

He reached over and took my phone. He hit the off button and powered it down.

"Hey, what gives?" I asked.

"You won't need it tonight. Actually, I'm thinking you won't need it until Monday morning."

"Oh really? Why's that?"

"I have two days off, you owe me big time, and I'm going to collect. You and I are about to have a weekend you won't soon forget."

"Oh yeah?"

"Oh yeah."

Yes!

As a special bonus,

please enjoy the first chapter of:

Scottsdale Sizzle,

the third book in the

Laura Black Scottsdale Mystery Series.

Scottsdale Sizzle

Chapter One

Ask any tourist. Summers in Scottsdale are hot.

Scottsdale is where hot water comes out of both taps. It's where people use oven mitts to open their mailboxes. Summer temperatures have reached as high as a hundred and twenty-two degrees, and that was back before global warming was even a thing.

At the moment, I was trapped in a stuffy closet in George Anson's upstairs master bedroom. I was hot to the point I was about to pass out.

George was a wealthy businessman and a prominent name in central Arizona. He owned seven or eight auto dealerships in Scottsdale and throughout The Valley of the Sun.

I'd seen dozens of his TV commercials over the years. They were usually funny and always ended the same way: he'd look straight into the camera and say, "I'm Honest George Anson, and you can bet my tattoo on it." He'd then turn to show the big tattoo of an anchor on his arm.

I'd been in the process of installing spy cameras in the bedrooms of his north Scottsdale home when he unexpectedly showed up with a woman. I barely had time to hide in the closet before they walked into the bedroom.

George's wife had assured me he would be at his Sun

City dealership for a day-long meeting, but it looked like she'd been misinformed.

George Anson's wife, Debbie, was a client of Lenny Shapiro, my boss. She'd recently hired Lenny to gather evidence that her husband was cheating.

I'd met Debbie at the law office a few days earlier, and she seemed like a nice person. She didn't know who the other woman was, but Debbie suspected the affair had been going on for some time.

She thought they even sometimes cheated in the family home. Although there was no prenup, Lenny was sure that George, being the community big shot he was, would be glad to provide a generous alimony rather than have his sordid affairs become public knowledge.

Using a key provided by Debbie, I'd let myself into the house a little after noon. By twelve-thirty, I'd installed a tiny battery-powered video camera in each of the two guest bedrooms.

I had just walked into the master bedroom when I heard the sound of the front door opening, followed by male and female voices coming up the stairs. I didn't have time to think. I opened the nearest set of folding doors, sprang into the space, and quickly shut the doors.

Based on the dresses and racks of shoes surrounding me, it was clear that I was in Debbie's closet. Unfortunately, the slits in the door were too narrow to be able to see properly into the room. All I could catch were fuzzy shapes and the movement of bodies.

As I heard the clothes come off, I tried to learn what I could about the woman. She had the strong and confident voice of a woman in her late thirties or early forties. From what little I could make out through the door, she appeared to be a brunette with a relatively thin body.

I wanted to crack open the door to get a better look at her, but I didn't want to risk being seen. Being discovered could be dangerous, and worse, they'd most likely find a new love nest.

George was a big man, and he wasn't stupid. He'd know why I was there, and I didn't want to get into a fight.

Using my stun gun on him was an option, but that was never a sure bet. If I missed, he'd only get more pissed.

There was also the possibility I would have to explain myself to the police in front of George. I knew from experience things like that tended to mess up an assignment and upset my boss.

George and the woman made it to the bed, and from the noises they made, they were fully enjoying each other's company. After listening to the slurping kissing noises and watching the fuzzy shapes move around using the slit in the door, it became apparent the woman had some pent-up desires she needed to release.

The bed continued to squeak for another few minutes, then the woman suddenly cried out, her voice shaking for fifteen or twenty seconds, her breath coming out in quivering gasps. I was hoping this would be the end of it, but it wasn't long before the entire process started over.

She then repeated it again, and again. She was a passionate love machine, and there didn't seem to be any signs of her slowing down.

Okay, I'll admit, listening to the woman moan for the first half hour did kind of stir me up. My mind kept switching back and forth from my boyfriend, Jackson Reno, an undercover cop for the city of Scottsdale, to Max, a dangerous and exciting man who's second-in-command of the largest crime family in Scottsdale.

I knew from personal experience that Reno could make me moan like the woman on the bed. I wasn't sure if Max would make me moan like that or if my moans with him would be even louder and more frantic.

Honestly, I suspected they would be. Plus, I didn't think Max was the kind of man to lay there and make me do all the work.

Stop thinking about Max! You have a boyfriend.

Unfortunately for me, since no one was supposed to be in the house during the day, the air-conditioning had been programmed to turn itself off during the afternoon heat. This is common in Scottsdale, where summer electricity bills can easily run several hundred dollars a month.

If no one is supposed to be home, the air conditioning will run only enough to keep the plants and animals alive. It must have been ninety degrees in the bedroom, where they at least had a big ceiling fan over the bed. It felt closer to a hundred in the closet.

I stood in the cramped and stuffy closet and listened to them for well over an hour. My eyes stung from the sweat that dripped into them, and my legs started to cramp from trying to stay still.

Hot and tired as I was, I had to hand it to the woman. Her stamina was amazing. I couldn't make out if she had a wedding ring on her finger or not, but I assumed she wasn't getting enough attention at home. A woman like that had some obvious needs.

My legs were starting to give out, so I leaned back against a rack of dresses. I desperately wanted to sit down somewhere out of the heat. My hair was limp, and my T-shirt was clinging to me.

I kept rubbing my eyes to get the sweat out, but that only

seemed to make them sting more. Assignment or not, I wasn't going to last much longer before passing out.

Finally, the woman had worked herself into a state of exhaustion. She fell off George and collapsed next to him on the bed. But instead of getting up right away, they lay on the bed, talking in low voices.

Come on, enough already.

Black spots were dancing in front of my eyes, and I knew it wouldn't be long before I blacked out. I cursed my bad luck that there hadn't been time to install a spy camera in the master bedroom before they'd used it for the afternoon.

If I'd been able to get a video of their tryst, I could have quickly wrapped up the assignment. Instead, I was back at square one.

Almost an hour and a half after they had started, I heard George and the woman get up. They went into the master bathroom, and I heard the shower start.

I eased open the door, and I felt relief immediately as a rush of cool air flooded the closet. I stepped out into the bedroom and stretched the kinks out.

Standing under the spinning blades of the ceiling fan felt wonderful, but listening to them taking a shower made me realize how badly I had to go to the bathroom. Now that my core temperature had started to drop, and the more I thought about it, the worse I had to go. I silently regretted the big Diet Pepsi I had drank right before coming into the house.

I knew I should have snuck out while they were in the shower, but I needed to see if I could get a better look at George Anson's mistress. She was twenty feet from me, and this could possibly be my only chance to discover who she was. I went back into the closet, but this time, I left the door open with the slightest crack.

The woman was only in the bathroom for about five minutes before she came out, got dressed, and began making the bed. With George still in the bathroom and the woman distracted, I took a chance and eased open the closet door, just enough to take a peek.

Now that I had a good chance to look at the woman, I saw she was medium-height with a nice figure. She had great taste in clothes and had spent top dollar on her shoes. When she pulled back her long auburn hair to put it into a ponytail, I noticed a Cindy Crawford beauty mark next to her mouth.

Seeing her face, I thought she looked vaguely familiar. This wasn't unusual for me since I tend to meet a lot of people during the course of my day.

It's rare for me to go into a restaurant or bar in Scottsdale and not recognize *somebody*. Not wanting to press my luck, I carefully closed the closet door and waited for them to leave.

It took another twenty minutes of fixing makeup, pulling on clothes, and cleaning the bedroom, but they eventually left. As soon as I heard the front door close, I bolted from the closet and ran into the bathroom.

Once I finished heeding nature's call, I went down to the kitchen and drank three glasses of disgusting Scottsdale city tap water. But I didn't care about the foul taste. I needed to hydrate.

Sometimes I hate my job.

Since I suspected George and his mistress would continue to use the master bedroom as their main love nest, I went up and installed three of my tiny spy cameras throughout the room.

I hid them well and chose angles that would give the most dramatic effects. I then went back downstairs and took off.

Still feeling dehydrated from standing in the hot closet for over two hours, I stopped by the first convenience store I saw to grab a Diet Pepsi. I'd just made it to the door when two boys in their late teens came walking out.

They stopped, and both looked me up and down. I knew my thin T-shirt was plastered against my body, and I must've looked like someone from a wet T-shirt contest.

"Hey babe, looking good," the older of the two said. His friend stared at my T-shirt and snickered. It was like an old episode of *Beavis and Butthead.*

After all the frustrations of the afternoon, I instantly got pissed. "What are you little twerps looking at? Get the hell away from me before I pound the snot out of both of you."

"Whoa, babe," the older one said. "No need for violence, I was only admiring your awesome boobs."

Sometimes I really hate my job.

My name is Laura Black. I'm an investigator for the Scottsdale law firm of Halftown, Oeding, Shapiro, and Hopkins. Over the years, one of the founding partners of the firm retired to Florida, and two of them died.

The remaining partner, Leonard Shapiro, my boss, has transformed the firm into one of the most successful boutique law offices in Scottsdale. He mainly handles high-profile criminal, civil, and family law cases.

Unlike most lawyers, Lenny loves it when his cases are mentioned in the papers. I've often noticed that whenever one of his cases is featured in the news, Lenny raises his rates another notch.

I keep waiting for him to change the name of the firm, but

I don't think he ever will. Even with all the money he makes, I can't see him spending a dime to change the stationery.

I woke up early the next day and lay in bed while I decided what to do for the morning. I only had one assignment at work, and that now involved nothing more than reviewing the videos from the spy cameras I'd placed in George Anson's house. Since there probably wouldn't be anything to see for a day or two, I knew I was basically going to have the day off.

My bad side reasoned that I could lie in bed all morning and maybe binge-watch a half-dozen episodes of *Say Yes to the Dress*. My good side reminded me there were bills to pay, and I should probably go into the office and see if I could wheedle another assignment out of Lenny.

My good side eventually won out, but that's mostly because my bad side likes to eat, and for that, I need a paycheck. I stumbled into the kitchen, put on a pot of coffee, then made my way into the shower. I wasn't in a rush, so I stood there for almost twenty minutes, letting the hot water pour over me.

After the shower, I went into the kitchen and poured coffee into my *Doctor Who* mug. I was a little surprised that Marlowe, my gray and white tabby, wasn't in the kitchen demanding to be fed.

But since it was after eight o'clock, I knew he was most likely over at Grandma Peckham's, mooching a late breakfast from her.

As I got dressed, a sudden feeling of happiness came over me. It was as if I knew I was going to have a good day. Maybe it was only from the caffeine in the coffee, but I hoped it was a premonition of good things to come.

I locked the apartment, went out to the parking lot, and unlocked my car, a cappuccino-colored Accord. I'd bought it new and successfully paid it off, but it was starting to show its age.

This was mainly due to a few modifications to the body that were not included in the original factory specifications. I sometimes think about getting a new car, something classy, or maybe even a convertible. But it still runs great and who has the money for a new one?

As I drove to the office, I couldn't help but smile. I was still in a great mood, and I started to think it had something to do with the summer heat finally starting to kick in.

Unlike the winter tourists who disappear at the first signs of summer, I actually love the heat. I also love the way Scottsdale empties out when it starts to get hot.

Work had been slow the last several weeks as the city wound down for the summer. As the weather warms up and people leave town, there's also a decline in the number of new clients Lenny takes on. As a result, in the summer, I'm almost always broke.

I drove down the alley behind the law office and pulled into my assigned covered parking space. Covered parking is essential in Scottsdale during the summer months. A car sitting in the full summer sun can easily have an interior temperature over a hundred and forty degrees.

I parked between Lenny's red Porsche 911 and Sophie's yellow Volkswagen Bug convertible. I didn't see the black Range Rover, so I knew Gina hadn't made it in yet. I also knew I wouldn't see Annie's sky-blue Fiesta since she was taking the week off for finals.

Using my key, I entered the office through the heavy security door in the back of the building. I walked past my cubicle in the back offices and up to the front reception area.

Sophia Rodriguez was sitting at her desk looking at pictures of some snowy mountains on her computer. Sophie's the paralegal and the receptionist for the law office. In addition, she's also my best friend.

Sophie grew up in southern California and spent her youth as a wild-and-free surfer chick living in Laguna Beach. For rent money, she'd worked as a catalog model and as a singer in a local punk-rock band.

She got married early and then followed her husband out to Arizona. The husband soon became an ex-husband, but Sophie seemed like a permanent resident.

My best friend is tall and thin, with long black hair going halfway down her back. Her smile dazzles, and whenever we go out, she always seems to attract a crowd of guys.

Where I've come to appreciate the summer heat in Scottsdale, Sophie never has. I don't think she ever will.

She loves Arizona's warm winters, gorgeous springs, and extended falls, but Sophie hates Arizona summers with a deep and sincere passion.

I've noticed that in the summer, she spends a lot of time daydreaming she's somewhere else. Usually somewhere cold.

"Do you know there's a ski area in Colorado called *A-Basin* that's still open?" she asked as I walked over to her desk. "There's one still open in Oregon, too. They have a webcam, and you can see people skiing on the snow on Mount Hood. I wonder what it's like to live somewhere where it snows. I bet people love living where it's icy and cold all the time. I imagine they dance with joy whenever it starts to snow. I know I probably would."

"A lot of them seem to come down here for the winter, so maybe they all don't love it."

"Well, I'd take the snow over living in a furnace."

"But, Sophie," I laughed. "Haven't you heard? It's a dry heat."

Sophie gave me a sour look that made me back up a step.

"If I hear that 'dry-heat' shit one more time," she said. "I swear I'm going to vomit. I don't care how dry it is, when you live inside a big pizza oven, it's fricking hot."

"How'd your date go on Saturday?" I asked. "Weren't you supposed to go out again with Michael?"

Michael was a police officer Sophie had met while helping me with an assignment a couple of months before. Due to some scheduling conflicts, the relationship started out slowly, but now it had started to pick up some momentum.

"Well, I was supposed to have a date," Sophie said, "but the jerk canceled. Something about a change of shift or something. I'm starting to feel your pain with the whole dating-a-cop thing. I ended up going out with the Cougars on Saturday. I would have called you to come along, but I knew you had a date with Reno."

We'd become friends with a group of Scottsdale Cougars a few months before. They were wealthy, middle-aged women who liked to hit the high-end clubs and hook up with guys half their age.

They were a fun group to be with, and Sophie, Gina, and I ended up going out with them two or three times a month. When going out with the girls, we were known as their pumas or "Cougars-in-training."

"How was it?" I asked. "Did you meet anyone?"

"Not really. Don't get me wrong, I love going out with the girls, especially now that Jackie's started to come out again. But I'm starting to think being a puma isn't all it's cracked up to be."

"What's not to like?" I asked. "Between the girls and the guys, you go to the best clubs in Scottsdale, and it doesn't cost you a thing."

"Oh, I love the free drinks and being treated so nicely by the bouncers and everything. The part I'm starting not to like is that I'm only a puma and not a full-fledged Cougar. The guys look at me as more of a consolation prize than anything else. I can see it in their eyes. First, they try with Jackie or Elle. If they strike out there, they take a shot at Shannon, or Sonia, or Pammy, or Cindy. If none of the Cougars are in the mood to flirt with them, they come over to me. I guess I must have a look of hungry desperation that turns a guy on."

"I know Annie never minded being the puma of the group," I said. "But I guess it's not for everyone."

Annie is a college student who works part-time at the law office, filing and doing some administrative work. About six months before, I met her while working on an assignment. She'd been friends with the Cougars even before we got to know her.

"I know," Sophie said. "Going to the clubs is fun and all, but I think I'm starting to lose interest in hooking up with the guys. Meeting a guy and heading over to his place is starting to feel less like fun and more like work. I think I may be looking for an actual boyfriend again. Maybe even a long-term thing."

"Does Michael have any potential? You've been out with him six or seven times now. That's a good sign."

"Well, Michael's nice, and I'm not embarrassed to be seen in public with him, but I'm thinking he's more for hooking-up than boyfriend material. He doesn't really seem interested in anything other than drinks, dinner, and then a hop in the sack. But at least he usually buys dinner."

"Well, what about Milo? You dumped him last month when he wanted to start getting serious. Maybe that's what you're looking for?"

"I don't know. Milo and I get along okay, but somehow, a low-level henchman in the mob doesn't seem like a good move for the long term. Now, if I had a crime lieutenant, like you have with Max, I could be a happy girl. That man's hot. Whatever happened with him? Did you ever see him again after Jackie got kidnapped? That was like two months ago. You got really quiet about giving out the details on him."

"Nope. After we got Jackie back, I only met him one night for drinks. That's been it."

"Well, at least you have Reno. He's a fine-looking man, and you don't need to make up stories when someone asks you what he does for a living."

"Um, well," I said, "about Reno."

"What? What happened to Reno? Is there something you aren't telling me?"

"We sort of had another discussion on Saturday."

"Was it a *little* discussion or a *big* discussion?"

"Sort of a medium discussion."

"Was it about the same thing as always?"

"Yup," I admitted. "He doesn't want a girlfriend he needs to worry about. He says he's constantly waiting for a phone call that I got shot, or stabbed, or kidnapped."

"He forgot blown-up," Sophie said. "You were almost

blown-up that one time, remember?"

"He wants me to go back to being a bartender or something boring like that."

"You'd think he'd understand, being a cop and all."

"That's what I thought, but somehow it only makes it worse. Every time something happens to me, someone in the department rushes to tell him about it, then we have another argument."

"Well, you two always get back together whenever you have a 'discussion.' It'll probably work out. When are you seeing him again?"

"We're supposed to meet tomorrow night for dinner at Frankie Z's," I said. "Hopefully, he'll still want to go. Whenever we have a discussion, he's skittish for a few days."

"Have you decided yet what you're going to wear to Danica's wedding? It's a week from Friday, and I still don't know what I'm going to wear. Gina's not stressed about it, of course. She says she'll root around her closet and come up with a dress. But it's driving me crazy."

"I know what you mean. We got the invitations a month ago, and I still have no idea what to wear. But it'll be great to see Danica and Muffy again."

We'd met Danica and her fiancé Alex during an assignment six months before. There'd been the usual amount of mayhem, but things eventually worked out for the best. We also met Alex's grandmother, a wealthy semi-retired land developer named Margaret "Muffy" Sternwood.

I was a little disappointed I wasn't a closer friend with Danica. She seems like a nice person, and we get along well. Unfortunately, she works nights as an exotic dancer at Jeannie's Cabaret, and our paths almost never cross. I was hoping we could rekindle our friendship at the wedding.

"How's Annie doing?" I asked. "Have you heard from her?"

"Nope," Sophie said. "But since it's finals week, she probably has a lot on her mind. Don't forget she graduates on Saturday, and she expects the three of us to be there."

"It'll be great to see her graduate. I'm also looking forward to the reception at the Saguaro Sky. I've only been there a few times, but it's always gorgeous."

"I wonder if Jackie's had time to do anything new with it yet?" Sophie asked.

Jackie Wade's one of the Cougars we'd recently gotten to know. As a result of an assignment a couple of months ago, we helped her take ownership of the upscale Scottsdale Saguaro Sky Golf Resort. The graduation reception on Saturday was going to be our first time there since Jackie had become the boss.

"I don't suppose any new assignments have come in?" I asked. "I'm beyond broke, and the rent's due soon."

As though he heard me through the closed door, Lenny stepped out of his office. He saw me and smiled, and as always, seeing him smile gave me a creepy feeling.

"Laura, I'm glad you're here. Come on in. I've got something for you."

Lenny disappeared back into his office. Through the open door, I heard the clink of ice cubes falling into a glass. I looked over at Sophie.

"What's up with Lenny?"

"A courier brought over the settlement check from the Bowden versus Martinez case about an hour ago. Lenny's been smiling and in a good mood ever since he got it."

"That lawsuit was settled like nine months ago," I mused.

"We're only getting the check now?"

"The wheels of justice."

I walked into Lenny's office. He was sitting behind his desk with a half-full glass of Jim Beam in one hand and one of his high-dollar Cuban cigars in the other.

He saw me and waved me to one of the two wooden chairs in front of his desk. Leaning back in his chair, he took a long drag on his cigar and blew a huge puff of foul-smelling smoke in the air.

He waved his glass in the direction of the wet bar in the corner of the office, offering me a drink. I shook my head since it was still too early for alcohol.

He shrugged as if to say, *suit yourself.* Setting down his glass, he picked up the check sitting on his desk, gently waving it at me.

"This," he said as he gave a small chuckle. "This makes it all worthwhile."

"The final amount was good?"

"Three-point-seven million dollars."

Damn!

"How much are we going to get out of that?"

He took another puff on his cigar. "Well, you see, that's the beauty of the situation. As of this moment, my fee is whatever I want it to be."

I raised my eyebrows, questioning both his ethics and his sanity.

"But, I thought the fee was agreed to ahead of time," I said.

"Naah, you don't understand. That doesn't matter. The agreement was only meant to ease the client's mind. A beautiful work of fiction. I should know. I wrote it up. This is what matters," he said, again waving the check at me. "For an attorney, this is the magic moment. This is why I worked nights and weekends for almost half a year."

I still didn't get it. Lenny saw my confusion and went on.

"You see," he said, speaking slowly as if he was talking to a child. "The judge ordered the respondent, Bowden, to pay three-point-seven million dollars. Now Bowden has paid it. As far as Bowden is concerned, the case is over, and if he never thinks about it again, he'll be all the happier for it."

"But what about our client?" I asked.

"Our client, Martinez, on the other hand, was never guaranteed to get a dime out of the lawsuit," Lenny said, still with a huge grin. "When I go over tomorrow and hand her a check for over a million dollars, she'll be so floored she isn't going to quibble too much if she gets a million and a half, two million, or three. Whatever she gets, it will be more money than she could have ever imagined getting in her entire life. I can keep whatever I want and call it a fee."

"And no one will complain?"

"Oh, sure, some of her relatives will bitch a little that my fee was outrageous, but the contract she signed states that in case of a dispute over my fee, the entire settlement will be held in escrow until the dispute is resolved."

"In other words," I said, "if she objects, she won't see a dime until it goes through the system, which will take a couple of years."

"Exactly," Lenny said. "Besides, after Martinez starts promising to spread the settlement money around to her family, the 'sue the lawyer' talk will die down. It always does."

Maybe I should go to law school?

"You said you have something for me?" I asked.

"A new client, Lester Murdock, will be in town for a few days. He's cleaning up some issues surrounding an inheritance. It'd be good if he had someone who knows the city to show him around and help him out. I was thinking having you do it would be better than hiring out a driver."

Better? You mean cheaper.

"So, you want me to babysit?" I asked, somewhat skeptically.

"Yeah. But don't think of it as babysitting. Think of it as earning a paycheck. There aren't a lot of cheating spouses needing to be caught at the moment. You have one, Gina's working on two, and that's it. But trust me, with what I'm going to bill this guy, it'll be worth babysitting him for a few days. Besides, you always like doing good deeds and helping to save the world. Maybe helping out this guy will count towards that."

"Somehow, I don't think it will," I said. "Am I only supposed to drive him around?"

"That and help him out. His grandfather died a few weeks ago. They read the will yesterday, and our client apparently inherited some very valuable things. He's in town from Chicago to pick them up. His attorney's an old friend of mine. I got a call this morning to see if I knew someone local to drive him around."

I sighed and registered defeat. "Where's he staying?"

"He's in one of the high-dollar suites at the Tropical Paradise. He got in late last night, but he should be up by now. I'll call him and let him know you're coming." He wrote down the room number and handed it to me.

"It figures," I said with a laugh.

"What? Is there something I should know about the

Tropical Paradise?"

"Nope, it just brings back some memories."

The Scottsdale Tropical Paradise is one of the nicer golf resorts in Arizona. It's owned by a group called Scottsdale Land and Resort Management, Inc., which is run by Anthony "Tough Tony" DiCenzo. In addition to building and running golf resorts, he's also head of the largest crime family in Scottsdale.

Because of certain events that occurred during some of my previous assignments for Lenny, I've gotten to know Tough Tony and some of his associates. This includes his second in command, a gorgeous man named Maximilian.

I've had a few adventures with Max, and I know he's interested in me in a way that goes beyond being strictly professional. Tony has his business offices in the Tropical Paradise, and I've been to meetings with him there more than once. Now, I was headed back to the resort.

Hopefully, I wouldn't run into Tony, or Max.

About the Author

Halfway through a successful career in technical writing, marketing, and sales, along with having four beautiful children, author B A Trimmer veered into fiction. Combining a love of the desert, derived from many years of living in Arizona, with an appreciation of the modern romantic detective story, the Scottsdale Series was born.

Comments and questions are always welcome.

E-mail the author at LauraBlackScottsdale@gmail.com

Follow at www.facebook.com/ScottsdaleSeries

Made in the USA
Monee, IL
10 January 2025

76557848R00194